This is a work of fiction. Si
are entirely coincidental.

HOW TO CAPTURE A DUKE

First edition. July 20, 2018.

Copyright © 2018 Bianca Blythe.

Written by Bianca Blythe.

HOW TO CAPTURE A DUKE

ONE RECLUSIVE BLUESTOCKING...

Fiona Amberly is more intrigued by the Roman ruins near her manor house than she is by balls. When her dying Grandmother worries about Fiona's future, Fiona stammers that she's secretly engaged. Soon she finds herself promising that she will introduce her husband-to-be by Christmas.

One dutiful duke...

Percival Carmichael, new Duke of Alfriston, is in a hurry. He's off to propose to London's most eligible debutante. After nearly dying at Waterloo, he's vowed to spend the rest of his life living up to the ton's expectations.

One fallen tree...

When Fiona tries to warn a passing coach about a tree in the road, the driver mistakes her for a highwaywoman. Evidently he's not used to seeing women attired in clothes only suitable for archaeology waving knives. After the driver flees, Fiona decides she may as well borrow the handsome passenger...

HOW TO CAPTURE A DUKE is the first book in Bianca Blythe's *Matchmaking for Wallflowers* series.

The Ladies Ultimate Guide

EXCERPT FROM *Matchmaking for Wallflowers*, The Ladies Ultimate Guide, Autumn 1815

For the woman lacking in advantages in appearance and wit: Get him alone. Men are simple-minded creatures and are prone to succumb to a woman's charms, however meager they might be, when removed from all other distractions.

Chapter One

CRISP JINGLES CHIMED through the cold air, merging with the rhythmic trot of horses, and Fiona Amberly had never been more convinced of her utter abhorrence of Christmas. She poked her head from the archaeological site, brushed a hand smudged with clay through her hair and peered in the direction of the sound.

A coach barreled down the slope, pulled by two pairs of prancing white horses, and her throat dried. Red and green plumes perched from the horses' headgear, an unnecessary nod to the approaching holiday. The sun glowed over the glossy black surface of the coach, flickering over its vibrantly painted wheels and golden crest.

She tightened her fists around the slabs of timber she used to fortify the pit.

Only one person had threatened to visit her.

Madeline.

Fiona hauled herself up and rushed to the road, dragging her dress through more mud. The coach thundered toward her, and she waved both arms above her head. Now was not the time to muse on the ridiculousness of her appearance.

"Halt. Halt."

The coach slowed, and she hastily brushed some dirt from her dress, managing to remove a few specks.

"What is it, Miss Amberly?" The driver was sufficiently trained not to openly gawk, but his gaze still darted to her ragged clothes and the pile of excavation materials.

Never mind that. Red-headed women with freckles were never destined to possess elegance.

"Is Lady Mulbourne inside?"

The driver nodded, and Fiona rushed to the door. The question was foolish: only her cousin would have asked for her coach to be decked out in such finery for a five-mile jaunt.

Madeline poked her head through the carriage window, and Fiona hastily brushed a few more specks of soil from her dress.

"Happy Christmas," Madeline chirped.

"Er . . . yes."

"You have a remarkable ability to never change."

Fiona shifted her feet, and her boots crunched over dried leaves.

"So unconstrained by the pulls of even the most basic fashion rules." Madeline's eyes flickered over her, roaming over every button and pleat with the eagerness of a general scrutinizing a map of enemy territory. "And still in half-mourning, I see."

Fiona stiffened and pulled her hands back. No need for her cousin to comment on the frayed hem of her sleeve as well as her gray dress.

"Would you like a ride? I'm on my way to see Grandmother."

Fiona didn't want a ride. She wanted to work more on the site. Winter was approaching, and if the farmers were right about their grumblings regarding the shade of the sky, the place would be covered in snow soon.

But ever since Fiona had blurted out to Grandmother that she was engaged to the most brilliant man in the world, it was vital that she not allow Grandmother to be left alone with Madeline.

The captain was everything a man should be: handsome and brave, smart and funny, and since the Napoleonic Wars had ended, finally living in England.

At least he would be if he existed.

Fiona groaned. Yes, Christmas was firmly relegated to the short list of things she despised. The holiday surpassed dress fittings, empty dance cards, and mushrooms in horribleness. Only Napoleon, carriage accidents, and somber-faced doctors ranked higher on her list of hated things.

How on earth had the emperor had the indecency to give up the war before Fiona had had the foresight to invent a death worthy of her dear, valiant, charming fiancé?

Fiona glanced at the site. "Let me just rearrange some things."

Madeline nodded, and Fiona hastily covered the pit, casting a lingering look on the Roman finds. The shards of pottery and coins buried within the clay were so near, and she ached to remain and unearth more, to feel the giddiness and delight that rushed through her with every discovery she made with her trowel.

Instead she hurried back to the carriage. A familiar dread tightened her stomach as she climbed the metal steps, but she steeled her jaw and rubbed her hand against her hair, dislodging a lock from her chignon.

"How pleasant to see you," Madeline said in a too-sweet voice, and a prickly warmth dashed up the back of Fiona's neck. "I was hoping you might be able to attend my Christmas Ball this year, given that you have never attended before."

Fiona smiled tightly at her one-time friend as she struggled to repin the lock of hair. She settled onto the bench and flickered her gaze downward. Telling herself not to dwell on the smudges of dirt scattered on her dress failed to lessen her embarrassment.

Disappointing people was a skill she had acquired in childhood, simply due to the apparent misfortune of her hair color. She'd long ago accustomed herself to her striking inability to fulfil the ton's expectations. Her unfashionably curved figure had frustrated her dressmakers during her shortened season and made her conspicuous against the sleek, willowy figures of the other debutantes.

"I suppose it must be terribly trying for you to attend a ball, given that you have so little practice in looking pleasant." Madeline smoothed the golden ringlets that framed her face. Every flourish, formed in the proper manner, with curling tongs rather than nature's haphazardness, was immaculate. "Unless perhaps you can grace us with your presence after all?"

"I'm afraid it's impossible," Fiona said. "Regretfully."

"Oh." Her cousin's lips stretched into a straight line.

"It is unfortunate you had to travel all this way. I would have thought the postal system would have managed to deliver my regrets," Fiona continued.

Madeline pressed her lips together and swung her gaze to the window and the view of heavy dark clouds that floated over the jagged Dales.

The light from the carriage windows slid over her cousin's pale blond hair, framing it like a halo, and cast a glow over the glossy silk ruffles of her dress. Somehow her cousin had managed to travel five miles and appear impeccable, and Fiona could scarcely travel a few feet without finding herself in difficulty.

Holly and mistletoe dangled from the ceiling of the coach, bright bursts against the staid black walls. Such greenery had been but a mild curiosity to Fiona before the accident, but now it signified everything dreadful.

If Christmas did not exist, her cousin would not be across from her, and Fiona most certainly would not have abandoned perhaps her last chance to visit the archaeological site in order to sit in a closed and jostling coach, striving for an excuse to skip the woman's ball.

"Now do tell me," Madeline said, "Whatever were you doing standing in a pit in the earth?"

"I—"

"It's the sort of thing that gives Yorkshire women a bad reputation," Madeline continued, and her nose crinkled. "You really must reconsider your habits. It will be trying enough for you to find a husband without behaving like the local madwoman."

Fiona squared her shoulders. "How kind of you to worry. Really, it's wholly unnecessary. And I'm not in the least need of a husband."

If only Grandmother would believe that.

"You're always in the habit of saying the most curious things," Madeline remarked. "Most fascinating."

Fiona gave her a wobbly smile and considered divulging her secret. She pondered the pottery, the Roman coins and helmets, the vases and mosaics she'd found on the border of the apple orchard.

She longed to share everything. There were so many brilliant objects. It couldn't be sheer coincidence. There had to be a Roman palace buried there.

Cloudbridge Castle lay on the route toward Hadrian's Wall, and it was not entirely absurd to think that the Romans may have built a palace on the way. Perhaps the Romans had had a tendency to wander around in togas, but that didn't mean they hadn't enjoyed fine homes as well. The materials she had found were too ornate for a simple station for soldiers of insignificant rank.

But her cousin wouldn't understand. The last person Fiona had told had been Uncle Seymour. She'd wanted his permission to excavate the apple orchard, and he'd exploded at the prospect of chopping any of the trees to discover if some broken cups and plates might be underneath. Though Uncle Seymour visited infrequently, the estate belonged to him, and once Grandmother died, he would move in.

Fiona drew in a breath. Some things were better not dwelled on. And perhaps Madeline was right. Perhaps she should attend the ball.

"Will the baron be there?" Fiona tilted her head, thinking of the materials she'd found underneath the apple orchard.

Madeline's husband's advice in assessing the objects would be invaluable. The baron was a renowned art critic, and his work on the Elgin Marbles was genius. She was sure his favorable assessment had spurred the new British Museum to acquire them. Unfortunately, he seemed to favor London far more than Yorkshire.

"My husband?" Madeline's voice faltered.

"I would like to speak to him about some findings..."

"Oh." Madeline's long black eyelashes swooped down over her eyes. "Perhaps I might be of some use—"

Fiona shook her head. The less people she told about the apple orchard the better. The ones she had told already thought her mad for believing there was a Roman palace buried underneath there. Her cousin was not the type to lend herself to confidences.

Right now it was more important that Madeline did not learn of Fiona's supposed engagement; her cousin was the largest gossip in Yorkshire. Fiona had no inclination to be a laughingstock, and any hope of the credulity and support the baron might give her theory on the Roman palace would be destroyed if he were to discover she'd invented a fiancé.

Though she'd long abandoned any aspirations to marry, she couldn't bear the thought that all her work, all the carefully collected and recorded artefacts, would lose all significance because their finder was deemed a foolish girl. No one would donate funds so that the rest of the palace might be dug from the ground, and any mosaics, any sculptures, any pottery would remain firmly in the earth to be forgotten.

Fiona's conviction that a Roman palace lay under the apple orchard would be deemed ridiculous, and anyone she told would be reminded in giggling tones that Fiona also had insisted she was betrothed to a wonderful man, when the man had turned out to be entirely imaginary.

The coach pulled in before Cloudbridge Castle, and Fiona exhaled. Gray stones blended into the harsh gray sky above, as the castle thrust its jagged turrets, defenses from a former age, into the sky. In another age her ancestors would have warred against the neighboring aristocrats; now they were supposed to be friends, simply for their shared status.

Her cousin exited the coach and glided toward the butler, padding her lace boots over the cobblestones. Fiona lifted her gray dress and proceeded. The coarse wool prickled her fingers, and she stumbled on a worn cobble.

"Madeline." Grandmother's astonished voice rang out from the open door of the castle, and Fiona quickened her pace.

Murmurings sounded. Fiona couldn't decipher her cousin's doubtlessly refined answer. Madeline's delicate soprano voice never carried, a fact her cousin had exploited once she discovered she could make snide comments about everyone, assured that only her seat companion would be able to hear.

Fiona entered to discover Grandmother leading Madeline toward the Great Hall. So much for any hope of speaking with Grandmother alone. Fiona followed them, and her dress swished against the antiques cramming the narrow hallway.

"I was just telling Fiona that I was so hoping you might grace us with your presence at this year's annual Christmas ball," Madeline said.

Grandmother laughed as they settled into the velvety armchairs that surrounded the table in the Great Hall. "My days of balls are behind me, though Fiona might attend."

"How splendid." Madeline clapped her hands together.

Fiona moved a finger to her collar, brushing against her mother's favorite brooch. "Thank you for inviting me, but I fear I cannot accept the invitation."

"But dearest!" Grandmother exclaimed.

Fiona stood up, coughing. "I fear I'm getting a cold. You must go, Madeline. I would not want to inflict anything so despicable on my dearest cousin."

Madeline's thick eyelashes, far longer and more elegant than Fiona deemed necessary, fluttered downward as she blinked. "I'm sure I do not fear any cold that you might have."

"Then you are a brave woman, baroness." Fiona strove to keep her face solemn.

"But you truly should consider attending!" Her cousin leaned forward, and her eyes sparkled. Her voice took on an affable tone at odds with the smug manner she seemed to favor. "I'm sure we can find you an eligible bachelor with whom to dance. Cousin Cecil is attending."

"Indeed."

"Why, he shows as little interest for dancing as you do! Uncle Seymour and Aunt Lavinia say it is sure to be an ideal match. He has no title, but not everyone can be sufficiently fortunate to marry a man with one." She beamed, perhaps contemplating her own accomplishment at acquiring a baron.

Fiona strove to nod politely. Best not to mention that she suspected it was not within Cousin Cecil's nature to find doing much of anything with a woman appealing.

A maid appeared with tea.

"You must find yourself a husband," Madeline said. "It is the natural course of things, and your sister is no longer here to keep you company. And the ball will be marvelous. They always are."

"How delightful." Grandmother picked up the teapot and poured tea into a cup. "And by then Fiona's—"

Fiona coughed. Not in the most elegant manner, but she was aiming for loudness, not delicacy.

Madeline moved back a fraction, and Grandmother's eyebrows jolted up.

"My dearest, you are doing quite poorly. I don't think I've ever heard you cough quite like that. It was as if—"

"As if you were trying to emulate a carriage." Madeline bit into a sweet.

Grandmother fixed her gaze on the baroness. "I wouldn't have termed it in quite that manner."

"Oh, yes!" Madeline said. "The kind with multiple horses, and driving on poorly maintained roads. Like in Scotland!"

Fiona's chest constricted. At this moment she could only hope her grandmother had thoroughly forgotten everything Fiona had ever told her about Captain Knightley. She heaped a generous amount of sugar into her teacup, snatched a silver spoon, and stirred the tea with vigor.

"I might not be well enough for the Christmas ball." Fiona touched her forehead and ventured another cough.

"My dear!" Grandmother's hand flickered to her chest, and Fiona cursed the lie. Grandmother worried far too much.

"I mean," Fiona stammered, "I am sure I will eventually recover, but—"

"Splendid!" Madeline nodded. "The ball is not until Christmas Day, and you will have four days during which you might make your recovery."

"I am wary of risking the health of the other guests."

"I have the utmost confidence in your health." Madeline accepted the cup Fiona's grandmother offered and raised it to her perfectly formed lips. "It would be odd indeed if everyone in Yorkshire were attempting to sound like carriages."

Fiona gulped her tea. The hot liquid swirled down her throat, and she grabbed the teapot to pour herself more, sloshing tea over the delicate lace tablecloth. Heat prickled the back of her neck, and her hands shook as she sopped up the amber puddle with a napkin.

"And of course," Madeline's clear voice continued, "We were also sorry to miss having you last year, and the year before as well. But then I suppose you might find it uncomfortable, now that you've reached such an advanced age with no husband—"

Grandmother's mouth opened, and she seemed more alert than normal.

"I must go." Fiona leaped up. Perhaps if Fiona hastened, her cousin would follow and then—

"She's already got one!" Grandmother beamed and selected a sweet. "Next year she'll be hosting her own festivities."

Fiona stiffened.

"Excuse me?" Madeline halted, and a knot in Fiona's stomach hardened. *Of all the times for Grandmother to be vocal.* Nothing delighted Madeline more than gossip, and her ties to London were strong.

Fiona's knees wobbled, and she sank back into her chair. If the world were ending, she may as well be comfortable.

"Surely Fiona hasn't found a husband?" Madeline leaned forward.

"She has." Grandmother gave a contented sigh.

Madeline's smile broadened to an almost unladylike extent. "However did you find a husband?"

"Fiancé." Fiona's voice wobbled at the lie. "That's all."

"Mm-hmm!" Madeline turned her gaze to the window and the jagged curves of the Dales, scattered with snow. "Who knew it would be so simple to find a fiancé here?"

The landscape seemed rather devoid of any dwellings, much less one belonging to an appropriate husband-to-be.

"He's . . . er . . . away!" Fiona said.

"I can't make his acquaintance?" Madeline's tone was mournful, even though her eyes seemed to sparkle with something very much resembling mirth. "He's not an officer, is he?"

"That's it!" Fiona exclaimed. "So he's very much gone."

Madeline's perfectly groomed eyebrows arched up. "How astonishing. What's his name?"

"Um . . . We're trying to keep the engagement secret now," Fiona said. "I hope you can be understanding."

"So he lacks a name?" Madeline asked, her voice calm, though her lips extended upward briefly, before she hastened to sip her tea. "I look forward to meeting such an extraordinary person."

Fiona averted her eyes. Her gaze fell on the tea caddy. Dust clung to the mahogany box, and Fiona brushed her finger over the wood. Visitors were not common at Cloudbridge Castle.

"He is said to espouse all the best possible qualities," Grandmother declared.

"Indeed?" Madeline tilted her head, and for one blissful moment the woman seemed uneasy. The baroness's eyes soon narrowed. "To think you met someone here, without any assistance. And how unlikely that he should be in possession of such apparent brilliance."

"Ah, but you forget that Fiona is brilliant herself." Grandmother beamed. "I was so concerned about her future and was relieved to find she was engaged all along."

"Secretly!" Fiona hastened to add. "A secret engagement. In fact, we met in London, during my season."

"Those two weeks?" Madeline's eyebrows soared upward.

"Which was why Fiona was so eager to return home," Grandmother added, but her voice faltered somewhat, and her gaze rested on Fiona too long.

"I see," Madeline said. "Likely even our grandmother has not had the good fortune of meeting this ideal man."

Fiona coughed now, and this time the pain in her chest felt real.

"Well I am sure that now all the soldiers are being returned home, you will have no more need for discretion." Madeline smoothed the folds of her dress. A ruby ring sparkled from her finger against the green fabric. "One week. Grandmother will desire the meeting as well. You wouldn't want her to suspect you invented the man!"

Madeline laughed, and Grandmother joined her after a trace of hesitation that Fiona despised.

Fiona wanted Grandmother to believe what happened three years before hadn't mattered. She couldn't stand Grandmother continuing to worry about her, all the while being visited by doctors with increasing frequency and expense. "He'll be there!"

"Wonderful." Her cousin rose.

"I only hope he'll be able to make his journey over to Yorkshire safely. Perhaps he'll be delayed—"

"The man's survived the worst war mankind has ever seen," Madeline said. "He'll be fine."

"I'm so happy for you." Grandmother's eyes took on a blissful, dreamy expression, one Fiona knew well, but which she had seen too little of ever since the doctors' sober news. It was that expression that kept Fiona from admitting that she'd lied last year in a foolish attempt to keep Grandmother from worrying about her future.

Fiona rubbed a hand against her hair, and another curl dropped from her chignon.

"Unless there's a problem." Madeline smirked. "Sometimes when men don't see their betrothed for long periods of time, they find they do not anticipate the meeting with the requisite eagerness. Perhaps—"

Fiona's lips settled into a firm line. "The captain is devoted and true. He is kind and brave and dashing. He is everything a man should be."

Madeline offered her a wobbly smile. "Marvelous."

Fiona raised her chin and struggled to maintain a composed face. She had no desire to suffer humiliation from the ton, but there was no way in which she would allow the truth of her behavior to reach her grandmother. Even if concocting a fiancé might not be specifically warned against in etiquette books, the consequences of being found out would be no doubt distressing.

"Then I will leave." Madeline swept her emerald green skirts against the furniture, and she exited the room with as much determination as she had entered it. She paused to glance at the ceiling.

Fiona followed her cousin's gaze. Shapely goddesses with white wigs and scant attire stared at her. No doubt they would think Fiona repugnant as they perched from their fluffy ivory clouds, their pale, unfreckled skin raised toward the sun. None of them would invent fiancés.

"Really, you should have this restored. There are many treasures here. Aunt Lavinia says when—" Her cousin halted and her cheeks pinkened. "Never mind. I am happy for you."

"Thank you," Fiona squeaked.

Anyway. It would be easy.

All she had to do was find a fiancé.

In four days. In the middle of nowhere.

When no man had ever expressed an interest in her before.

How hard would it be to find a man by Monday? She didn't need to *marry* the fellow. In fact, he needn't even attend the ball. He just needed to prove his existence, a feat that would suffice in impressing the others. If she only succeeded in introducing somebody to Grandmother, all would be fine.

Or mostly fine.

Chapter Two

MADELINE'S COACH LURCHED forward and jostled over the cobblestones. Her cousin might be flinging herself into a glamorous new life, a continuation of her glamorous former life, but Fiona had more serious things to concern herself with.

She sped through the vacant corridors of Cloudbridge Castle. No flowers were in season to fill the elaborate Chinese vases, and the empty porcelain and jade sat alone on carved sideboards. Fiona pushed open the door to her room.

Painted portraits of her ancestors peered at her from gilded frames hung over long faded wallpaper. Sturdy medieval chests squatted beside slender-legged French chairs, a haphazard assortment of furniture unified only in that the pieces were unclaimed from more important relatives.

Uncle Seymour had taken the longcase clock that had once merrily ticked across from her bed, citing a sentimental connection to her grandfather that Fiona could not share, since she had never known him, and a need to determine the time that Fiona could not grasp, since nothing she did was of any importance anyway.

Fiona strode past her bed, draped with a stiff canopy, toward the view. A stack of Loretta Van Lochen books, a recent indulgence, sat on a table beside her bed. She wished she might lose herself in a story filled with handsome highwaymen and seductive spies now.

She pulled a pamphlet titled *Matchmaking for Wallflowers* from below the stack of romances. Her sister had given it to her last year, and Fiona skimmed the bright pages that showed cheerful women wearing pince-nez grasping the arms of tall Corinthians. It was unlikely there would be anything of use, but she flung the pamphlet into her satchel.

She heaved on her woolen cloak. She yanked her sturdiest boots over her calves and tied the laces with an expertise most women of her class took pride in lacking. Her lady's maid had long resigned herself to taking more time assisting Fiona with her special projects than with the clothes she'd been trained for.

Fiona exited her bedroom and descended the staircase.

She bade a hasty farewell to Grandmother, told her she might spend the night at her sister's estate, and then departed the manor house before Grandmother could bombard her with questions. Perhaps Rosamund might offer her some advice.

She marched toward the stables. The wind slammed against her, and the thick auburn curls that made even the most somber outfits seem ridiculous spilled from her hood. She nodded at the groom. "Please prepare Ned."

"But the weather—"

"I'll be fine."

The groom stiffened. "Very well, m'lady. Shall I accompany you?"

She shook her head. She traveled with a knife, and she had little inclination to force the groom to ride in this weather to preserve her reputation, when riding with a man might also damage it. "I'll ride astride."

The groom nodded, accustomed to her eccentricities. She sighed. She couldn't even present herself as a fine lady to her servants; no wonder she'd failed so miserably as a debutante.

The wind gathered in more force, thrusting its way through the trees, tearing any remaining leaves down. Dull orange carpeted the ground, and the leaves scraped her boots with each new gust.

Fiona shifted her legs, but before she could reconsider, Ned stood before her. The horse's brown coat gleamed, and she stroked his face. The groom assisted her onto the saddle.

Fiona gave a curt nod and urged Ned forward.

Harsh wind brushed against her, and her curls toppled from her hat anew. She pressed her hand against the furry contraption, but the wind continued to bluster, tearing off her hat. Red locks swirled before her eyes, and she raked her hand through her hair, conscious of the groom's eyes still fixed on her. One benefit of having a large estate was that there were few men to scandalize with her reluctance to ride sidesaddle. Even Marie Antoinette had at one time favored riding astride, and she did not have an archaeological site to tend to.

She moved Ned into a trot toward the site. Shots fired sporadically in the distance, accompanying the sound of Ned's steady trot. The peasants wanted Christmas dinner, and it seemed everyone had seen the threatening clouds that hovered over the horizon.

The narrow lane sliced through the forest, and Fiona tightened her grip on the reins, careful not to disturb Ned. The days were too short at this time of year, and though it was not yet dark—she wouldn't have been riding had it been—the light was dimmer and duller than she would have favored.

If Fiona were prone to swearing, she would be cursing like a sailor.

For the first time Fiona wished she were not in Yorkshire. Heavens, she would adore to be in London right now. Were she in the capital, swarming as it was with men, she might just possibly find someone desperate enough to pose as a fiancé. Perhaps she might find success by standing outside gaming halls. Or simply by throwing Grandfather's remaining money up in the air.

Few men resided in this section of Yorkshire, and she wagered she wouldn't even be able to find a stable hand willing to play the strong, silent type. Perhaps if she invented some sort of condition that explained why he couldn't speak . . . *Goodness, it was hopeless.*

If word circulated she'd attempted to convince a servant to pretend to be her fiancé, she would be barred from ever reentering society.

The trees cast shadows over the dirt path, and she glanced upward. In the springtime the branches of the trees touched and created a net of pale green leaves and pastel blossoms. Now gaps existed between the stout branches and revealed the gray sky, and the even darker clouds that sailed over it.

This is an ideal day for an accident.

Fiona shivered and forced the image of a coach careening into a boulder from her mind. But it was hard to be successful in doing that, when all she could envision were wheels collapsing and a steel frame bending and twisting, clutching the less flexible figures of its inhabitants.

She inhaled and urged the horse forward. She avoided coaches. No closed, dark rides for her.

And then she saw it.

A tree, long and thick, had fallen across the road, its position just as precariously placed as in all her dreams. Pine needles covered its branches, but Fiona knew that underneath the pleasant scent hid imminent danger. A sharp curve lay immediately after the tree, the type of curve a coach driver coming from the opposite direction should slow for, but which he might not necessarily do. She didn't want to imagine the horses trying too late to stop.

She turned her head in the direction of the apple orchard. She didn't have time for this. This might be her last chance to do any digging, and she wanted to see Rosamund afterward.

But the impediment was so large, and the potential destruction so severe.

Fiona slowed Ned down and examined the sturdy trunk and the jagged branches. She slid from the horse, tied him to a tree, and then returned to examine the obstruction. The horizon had narrowed to a thin sliver, and she pressed her lips together.

If only she'd brought a shawl that she could have used as a warning.

She exhaled. Maybe she could remove the offending tree, so even the most unobservant driver could safely barrel down the road. She grasped a branch of the tree and attempted to drag it.

The tree did not budge.

She removed her knife. She sawed off some of the smaller branches and shoved them to the side of the road. The trunk was still too heavy for her.

She sighed. She would need to return to Cloudbridge Castle. She would send some of the male servants back to complete the job of clearing the road, hoping that they could get to it in time.

She pressed her lips together and tried not to think about whether any passer-by had spotted the tree that her parents' carriage had collided with and had decided not to move it.

Trotting hooves and jostling wheels interrupted her thoughts. She swung her head toward the sound that was coming from farther down the road.

She scurried forward, accidentally sweeping her skirt and cloak through a puddle. *No matter.* Right now the only thing of any importance was to warn the driver.

A post horn sounded.

She hastened around the corner.

A dark coach pulled by four horses sped along the road, and Fiona hollered at the driver to stop. She picked up her skirts and marched over the lane. The wind blew against her, and her hair spilled from her hat. Mud coated the edges of her cloak. The knife was still clutched in her hand, and she waved it.

Chapter Three

PERCIVAL CARMICHAEL, seventh Duke of Alfriston, was hurled from his seat.

He landed on the wooden floor with a thump, reflecting that some pieces of advice his former governess had been prone to bestowing had an irritating propensity to be correct. The advice that soared most prominently in his mind was her warning not to drink in a moving carriage.

His governess had been referring to apple juice, his preferred beverage at the time of his pre-Harrow education, but he contemplated that the advice still held true when imbibing a wider variety of drinks—in this case, brandy.

His cravat displayed distinct tawny spots now, an addition his valet would be most disapproving of. He also would criticize the alcoholic smell that now infused the velvet cushioned seats, the maple floor, and particularly Percival's attire.

Blast. Yorkshire was every bit as horrid as the ton claimed.

He would have enough scrutiny tomorrow without appearing with a stained cravat.

He pulled himself back onto the seat. Speed was of importance, and the driver knew it. Percival had expressly promised him a significant tip if they reached London before tomorrow evening. The driver should be aware that a significant tip from a man who possessed a vast amount of wealth was nothing trivial.

Percival patted the package and pushed away the uneasy thoughts that consistently forced their way through his mind when he devoted too much attention to his impending engagement.

The driver said something, and the horses restarted their trot. *Thank goodness.* Percival stretched out his leg, and his Wellington struck the opposite seat. He gritted his teeth and closed his eyes. Soon he would be in London, ensconced in a life everyone would envy, until they learned about the accident.

"Halt." An alto voice cut through the sound of whinnying horses. The voice was commanding, different from the high-pitched murmurings and giggles of the debutantes and young widows with whom he tended to consort.

The coach continued on.

"Halt!" The voice called out again, and this time the carriage wheels screeched. The horses snorted and stomped their feet, and the driver uttered an ungentlemanly word.

Percival swept the curtain back.

A tall woman in a cape stood beside the road. She clutched a knife, directing it at the coach. The woman's eyes were narrowed, and red hair swirled in the wind. Mud crusted the bottom of her dress, and pine needles cleaved her cloak. The blade of her weapon glinted underneath the flickering lanterns of the coach, and her expression was solemn.

By Zeus, we're being attacked.

He stuffed the package into a fold of his great coat. This was everything the dowager had worried about, and everything he'd sworn he wouldn't allow to happen.

No one was supposed to know he was here. How in Hades had this person found him?

Blast.

The driver hardly resembled the brave type. Mail coaches lauded their tendency to employ former soldiers, but Graeme must have been a veteran from the war with the colonies, if the color of his whiskers was any indication.

Percival pulled his knife from his boot. So much for conquering Napoleon at Waterloo—now he had to suffer the indignity of being attacked at home. He should have stayed in London. Even the most tiresome balls didn't involve weapons.

It would be a blasted pain if this ended up in the newspapers. Cartoonists were eager enough to chronicle his brother's misdeeds, now that there was less reason to draw unflattering depictions of France's onetime emperor, now safely imprisoned on St. Helena.

The woman hadn't lowered her knife. He hoped she was not gifted at knife throwing.

Something sounded outside, and the woman's red lips parted, her eyes appearing wider than before. "You're pointing a weapon at me?"

"You bet your pretty face I am," the driver said.

She blinked.

"Anybody with you?" The driver's voice was firm, and Percival almost cheered. Maybe he wouldn't even need to be heroic.

FIONA STARED INTO THE barrel of a musket. The experience proved as horrid as she would have imagined. The wind seemed to cease its frantic swirl, the leaves paused from rustling, and all she could focus on was the long blunderbuss fixed directly on her.

Guns were not supposed to be pointed at her. Not now, not ever. Her life was quiet. Weapons were things that were directed at other people, who did reprehensible things. "You've made a mistake."

"I think not." The man's hands were steady.

Every aspect of the driver's appearance seemed ordinary, and the coach itself was a mere mail coach, lacking any embellishment. And yet the driver's bushy eyebrows crinkled together, as if she, not he, were acting inappropriately.

She raised her chin and strove to keep her voice steady. "Please put the weapon down."

He laughed, a deep rumble that grated against her. The frigid temperature verged on unbearable, the icy wind stung her face, and she had no patience to converse with some argumentative driver whose life she was attempting to save.

"There is a tree in the road. If you go much farther, your coach will be crushed."

The driver narrowed his eyes further.

"No doubt you will consider that it is winter and you are over a mile from the nearest estate."

"What is it, Graeme?" A deep voice startled her from her musings. The voice was authoritative and the accent cultured, sweeping her away from the Northern accents, devoid of polish, to which she was accustomed.

Her heart hammered, and she reminded herself that just because a person was in possession of a pleasant voice, did not indicate a person's propensity for regular features, wide shoulders, and all the other traits of handsomeness.

The man peeked out from behind the curtain.

He was only lifting his head from a carriage window, but it may as well have been from the clouds that soared above.

Chestnut curls peeked from the satiny edge of a beaver top hat, one more fashionable than any the local vicar was accustomed to adorning himself with, and the features of his face were composed in a stern expression that resembled the driver's. His nose lay in a straight, unwavering line, and high cheekbones dominated his face, bestowing him a regal look.

Every feature belonged to a paragon of masculinity.

Fiona firmed her stance and dug her boots further into the muddy ground. Dried leaves crunched beneath her feet, and she flickered her gaze to the gray sky.

Dear Lord! No chaperone, no friend, and here she was in the presence of a practical God.

"We've got a problem, sir. This 'ere lady." The driver continued to fix his musket on her, and his voice was mournful. "I am afraid, sir, that we are being besieged by a highwaywoman."

"Excuse me?" Fiona stuttered and her heart sped, though this time, the handsome man lay not entirely responsible for the blame.

The man frowned. "Do something, Graeme."

"I cannot shoot a woman."

The man rolled his eyes. "I would not have you shoot her."

The wind that swept over her seemed to have transformed to ice, and she shivered. No way did she resemble a highwaywoman. They must be mad to even consider it.

"We've got ourselves a female highwayman," the driver said. "Didn't know there was such a thing."

"Women are perfectly capable of many things." She moved her hands to her hips, remembering only now that she still clutched the knife. *Oh.*

"The woman claims there's a tree knocked over in the road!" the driver continued, still gazing at her, as if his mere stare might prevent her from moving.

"I am not lying!" she said. "And your lives are in peril if you continue any farther. So you should—"

"Disembark and wait on the side of the road?" The driver sneered.

"Why, that might be appropriate."

"Or perhaps you would suggest that I separate and leave my charge behind with you?" The driver raised his eyebrows.

"I am doing nothing wrong—"

"Naturally not!" The driver scowled. "You're simply conducting illegal activity."

"Sir—"

"Put that knife away." The handsome man frowned, his voice solemn.

"I wouldn't irritate her," the driver declared. "Women are emotional creatures, sir. Wouldn't want to think about what they can get up to under stress. Not like us logical males, sir."

"That's enlightening to hear upon returning from a useless war created by men," the handsome man said dryly.

"Well, well." A tinge darkened the driver's cheeks. "We should all be thankful Napoleon wasn't a woman."

"Who knows what would have happened then!" The handsome man shook his head, his expression filled with such dismay, that Fiona almost believed he was teasing.

"Dreadful things, sir!" The driver's voice sobered. "Dreadful things for sure."

The two men stared at her, and Fiona shivered under their scrutiny. Her heartbeat galloped. They thought she was a highwaywoman. She'd tried to explain, but they hadn't believed her. And they were pointing a gun at her. One that might go off at any moment.

She needed to seize control.

The driver grinned. "I'm sorry, darling, but you won't be getting any money from us."

"Not that we have any," the handsome man added hastily.

A gun roared.

Fiona didn't flinch—the peasants were still hunting. But the firm expression of the driver wobbled.

"You're not alone!" The driver's voice trembled.

Fiona was most certainly alone, but she could not permit the driver to keep on pointing a gun at her. That was how accidents occurred.

This was her chance.

And she seized it.

Fiona forced her voice to remain steady. "Lay your gun down."

The driver hesitated, and then, another gun shot fired.

Fiona narrowed her eyes. "You are surrounded. This is your final warning."

The driver's hands shook, and he set the gun down. Relief flooded through Fiona, and she grabbed the weapon, directing it at the driver.

The driver sank to the earth, holding his hands above him. "What do you want? Please, show us mercy! We'll give you anything!"

"I—" An insane idea sprang into Fiona's mind, and she took another glimpse at the passenger.

The fabric of his clothes was impeccable, and his hair color was perfect.

Chestnut colored like spun gold. Nothing like the red hair that crowned her figure like a flame. This man's skin resembled buttermilk, with no freckle in sight, and his eyes were a deep blue color, as if she were staring into the heavens of an Italian painting.

He was an Adonis suited for the finest debutante, for a woman with a Grecian name and skin as flawless as his. No doubt such a woman would be able to sing like an angel, in between giving birth to tiny cherubic likenesses of himself, and then would paint the offsprings' likenesses in beautiful, delicate watercolor renderings. Such a woman would never, ever have told her family that she had a fiancé when she had none. Such a woman wouldn't have needed to do so.

He was just the man she required.

"Who are you?" the driver gasped.

This was the time to explain herself. This was the time to explain who she was and apologize for frightening them, even though the notion that she should scare large men like that was absurd.

But if she could only get the handsome man to introduce himself to Grandmother—she wouldn't need to take him to the ball—it would be enough for Grandmother to be assured that she need not worry anymore. Perhaps the handsome man and the driver could help her move the tree. Cloudbridge Castle was a quick jaunt away, and they were going in that direction anyway. If they thought her a highwaywoman anyway, they would listen to her demands. Maybe no one would want to play a fiancé for a bluestocking, but they would listen to a highwaywoman.

Once they were at the castle, well then they would be so grateful she intended them no harm that they would help her. Neither the driver nor the gentleman appeared to be from Yorkshire. She could get away with this.

Something like hope fluttered in her chest. Perhaps, just perhaps, this would be worthwhile.

Fiona thought of mosaic fragments and ancient civilizations and her dear grandmother. She held the gun steady and flung her curls. She channeled every single story from Loretta Van Lochen and raised her voice. "They call me the Scarlet Demon."

Both men's eyes widened, and she attempted her very best snarl.

Chapter Four

SO MUCH FOR A QUICK dash to his new estate and back to grab the jewels. He should have trusted a servant to bring them after all. He hadn't liked the thought of appearing weak before the dowager, but finding himself in this position rather seemed to epitomize weakness.

Blast.

So much for not protesting when the mail coach guard fell ill, in some mad attempt to not draw attention to the value of what he was transporting and to arrive in London on time. His nostrils flared. How on earth had the woman found him?

Double blast.

Everyone knew forests in remote areas were dangerous. Everyone knew the war had made people more and more desperate as the economy had plummeted, and everyone knew local magistrates struggled to control their respective districts, when all their strong young men battled overseas.

She was mad if she thought he would give anything to her. His grandmother's sapphire ring, his great-grandmother's pearls, and a few other pieces the dowager spoke in raptures about, but which he had never quite managed to keep straight, were intended for somebody else.

He pulled his gaze from the woman to the dark trees that loomed behind her. Thick pine trees that smelled like Christmas, and nothing like the nightmare he'd been hurled into, stretched overhead. The dark green needles and sweet-scented pine cones conjured images of yule logs, long days of sledding with a cousin who no longer existed, and mince pies. Slender trees stretched beside the pines. Their leaves were gone, the branches ready for snow to descend on them. They ranged from a cold white to a warmer amber, and he focused his attention on the spaces between their branches. Maybe he might spot another thief and see just how many people were robbing them.

The Scarlet Demon raised her chin. "I've got four other men with me."

"Indeed."

"They're large men," she said. "Very muscular."

"And armed?" Graeme asked her, his eyes wide.

She nodded gravely. "We were able to overtake a wagon filled with army supplies last week."

"Oh?" Graeme's lower lip appeared to be trembling.

Percival fought the urge to bite back a laugh. Clearly a viper-tongued woman was all it took to dissipate Graeme's arrogance.

"Yes." The highwaywoman nodded her head again.

"Is that so?"

"It is indeed."

"And you managed to overtake the British army's wagon?" Graeme stammered.

"Indeed." The woman paused. "You don't want me to call for my men. Any signal from me is a signal for utter destruction. My men are fearful of being identified. If you obey, you can escape with your lives. If not, the men will come forward, and if they're recognized, they'll have to kill you."

"We won't recognize them," Percival said.

She tossed her head. "They won't believe you."

A series of loud shots fired from the forest. Percival stiffened, his chest constricting, and the Scarlet Demon only smiled. "Those are my men now."

"Don't kill us," Graeme pleaded.

"It would be amusing." The Scarlet Demon tapped her long, slender fingers together, and then exhaled. "But I don't want that to happen. You're very fortunate—I have another thing you can help me with."

"We'll do anything!" Graeme cried. "Anything at all."

Percival scanned the forest again. "It's possible she might not actually have a swarm of men hidden—"

The woman swung towards him. "How do you think my hair turned so red?"

"Blood!" Graeme gasped. "I always knew redheads weren't trustworthy."

Percival fought the urge to roll his eyes in the face of the woman's earnestness and Graeme's credulity.

The woman's face tightened, but she simply replied, "Then sir, you are a very wise man indeed."

Graeme's chest jutted out.

"What do you want?" Percival finally asked.

She hadn't referred to him as His Grace yet. If there was a chance she did not know his identity, he wasn't going to tell her. He was thankful he'd kept the fact a secret from Graeme. Who knows what she might do with the information. They could overpower her, but he rather doubted he and Graeme could tackle four strong, muscular men.

Percival swallowed hard. For a moment he'd forgotten that using force to battle anyone was something that belonged in the past. The cold air blew against his face. He shifted his knees. The position was uncomfortable, but he had no desire to exit the coach.

The woman pressed her lips together and then glanced at Graeme. "I need an audience with your charge alone."

Blast. She knew who he was after all.

It was perhaps impossible to hide his position. Fame was inevitable when one possessed classical good looks, vast wealth, an elevated position, and a roguish reputation.

The latter had already changed.

Something flickered over Graeme's face. "Tell you what. I'll let the highwaywoman discuss her exact requests to you in the coach. More private that way."

The Scarlet Demon hesitated. "I would prefer a meeting outside."

Graeme snorted. "Worried about preserving your reputation, darling? I'm sure your crew can rescue you. And believe me, you won't be needing rescuing."

Percival tightened his fists and fought the urge to scowl.

Graeme turned to Percival. "Unless *you're* concerned?"

Percival exhaled sharply. "I am quite capable of being alone with this woman."

Graeme shrugged. "Suit yourself."

Percival hadn't fought Napoleon to be treated like some damsel. He unlocked the carriage door and pulled the blanket over him. He inhaled and waited for her footsteps.

After a few agonizing moments the carriage door swung open. The scent of vanilla, warm and soothing in a way that a highwaywoman should not be, wafted over him. She fixed her dark green eyes on him, narrowing them before he could contemplate the gold rings that sparkled against the emerald shards. He blinked.

He didn't need to look her over again, but he found himself doing so all the same. That hair. Red and flowing and unlike all the structured, conservative hairstyles that donned the chits at balls. Her dirty cloak and dress were nothing like the fur-lined coats and glossy gowns he was accustomed to seeing ladies parade around in. The woman wasn't even wearing a hat. Nothing tasteful about her at all.

Which maybe was why she'd gotten herself into this mess.

She raised her chin. "A gentleman always keeps a door open for a lady."

"You were never a lady," he replied.

Her cheeks flushed, and she stomped by him, her skirts brushing against him in a manner that wasn't, he was sure, strictly necessary in the nearly vacant carriage. She strode to the seat opposite him, weapon in hand. Her boots clinked against the floor, and if someone had told him he was hearing the sound of his heart, he wouldn't have doubted it.

FIONA DIDN'T NEED TO ponder whether her behavior verged on the inappropriate. It was obvious she'd abandoned all propriety.

And the man, this strange gentleman, a man more handsome and dashing than even the most well-loved hero from Loretta Van Lochen's romances, sat in this enclosed space with her.

"Welcome, highwaywoman. Or do you prefer to be called Scarlet Demon?" The man yawned and stretched his arms. The action caused the material of his clothes to tighten, revealing a firm, broad chest. "I must say, I rather like the idea of meeting in the coach. Too many robberies lack organizational prowess."

A plaid blanket draped over the man's legs in perhaps an attempt to appear casual, but his furrowed brow and tight lips denoted a less than lackadaisical sentiment.

What she was doing was wrong, but it would all be over in a few hours. She sucked in a breath of air. "You're not really in a rush."

His eyebrows lifted. "I think I can judge that."

"There's no dying parent you're hastening to see. No wife in labor."

"Would you call off your ruffians if I had one?"

Fiona folded her fingers on her lap. She'd never been in a space this small, this confined with any man, much less a specimen of masculinity, the very sort her art instructors would laud. Fiona's breath quickened, and suddenly she had absolutely no problem with the cold winter air. She forced her gaze from the satisfactory width of the man's chest and lifted her nostrils. "Is that—brandy?"

Her voice shook. It wouldn't do for the man to realize just how much his presence affected her.

"Indeed. Should I compliment you on your sniffing abilities?" Sarcasm riddled through his velvet voice.

"I—" Fiona's mouth dried. She lifted her gaze toward him, meeting his blue eyes. They had a knowing look to them as if accustomed to seeing women's eyes melt. She dropped her eyes to her lap, focusing on her thick cape. The worn fabric was convenient for outdoor pursuits, but the plain material differed from the luxurious appearance that the man opposite, only slightly rumpled from his journey, managed to convey.

"Get to the point, woman. Or are you in awe of being in such a glamorous place?" The handsome man's tone was sultry, and he moved his hand toward Fiona.

"Stay right there!" she cried.

His hand wavered in the air, and she was conscious of the size and breadth of each finger. The man's skin was bronzed, and dark curls encircled his wrists. She wondered whether the dark curls trailed up the rest of his arm, and whether his chest was bare or not.

She swiveled her head toward him, and his hand brushed against hers again. Her heartbeat quickened, as if her whole body yearned for more of him, even though she didn't know anything about him, even though she was pretty sure he wasn't even very nice.

Before she had a chance to berate him for affecting her with his presence to an extent she would be mortified to admit, he was gone. He relaxed against his seat, and a smile played upon his lips. "Please be comfortable."

"Right." She cleared her throat and tried to channel one of Loretta Van Lochen's bravest heroines. "You're a gentleman."

He smirked. "It must be an unusual pleasure for you to be in such splendid company. But I'm afraid I don't have time for much chit-chat. What do you want?"

"You." The word escaped her lips before she had a chance to hold it back.

His eyebrows rose, but the cocky grin she expected never appeared. Instead his shoulders sank a fraction, and his jaw firmed.

"I mean..." Fiona forced a laugh, "Not really you. Of course not."

"That would be insane," the man offered.

"Yes," Fiona hastened to reply.

"What on earth would you do with me?"

For one moment she was tempted to tell him everything. For one moment she wanted to share with someone just what a mess she had managed to get into. For one moment she desired to laugh and maybe cry and hopefully be told she wasn't entirely mad.

But instead she lifted her chin up. "Never mind."

She could tell him who she was later. Right now she needed him to be intimidated of her. Maybe no one would do a favor for Fiona Amberly, the woman too frightened to finish her season, the woman no man had wanted to dance with. But displaying the most fearful highwaywoman from Loretta Van Lochen might be more convincing.

She leaned forward. "I won't hurt you."

"You don't seem the type to maintain noble standards of decency."

The man was perfect, and that seemed reason enough to despise him. His complexly tied cravat, perfectly styled hair, and immaculate cane represented everything she abhorred. Except... Her gaze drifted back to the man's cane. It looked almost like it was actually meant to be used. A silver dome rested on it, but the black rod was imperfectly polished, the length longer than average, and grass clung to the end of the cane, as if—

"What in the Lord's name are you looking at?" the man practically growled.

"I—"

"Leave, highwaywoman." The man's brusque voice interrupted her thoughts. "If you were aiming at seduction, you should have been prettier."

Any spell, any attraction she may have felt vanished at this moment. She bit her lips and strode from the coach.

She couldn't do this. She needed to be back at home, where she belonged, and not in a coach with a strange man.

It didn't matter. He never would have agreed to her plan anyway. She'd just get Ned and ride away. She stepped into the cold air, bracing for the harsh words from the coach driver.

But only silence greeted her.

Chapter Five

THE DOOR SWUNG BACK open, and the woman glared at him. She raised her hand, and that blasted blade glinted again in her hand. "Your man is missing. Where is he?"

His heartbeat quickened, and he resisted the temptation to pat his great coat in which the jewels were hidden.

"Put that down." It was easy to make his voice sound commanding; he'd never had to struggle to make his soldiers obey him.

The woman wavered, then raised her chin.

"He's gone." She tramped toward him, and he stiffened as her skirt swept against the woolen blanket he'd taken to carrying with him. The woman's voice held the same unflinching resolve of the severest army commander. "Rise."

"I—"

"Now." Her emerald eyes hardened.

"I will not be threatened by a woman."

"You only allow yourself to be threatened by men?" She raised her eyebrows and moved the blade toward him. "Out."

"Careful with that." Percival attempted a laugh.

"Out," she repeated.

The knife was large and all too menacing. But moving would mean revealing his secret to her, and that would be—

The blade inched nearer his neck. If this were the past. By Zeus, then he would have just stood up and defended himself, blade or no blade.

His life was no longer the same now, and he was at the mercy of this red-headed woman who brandished a knife with the same enthusiasm that other women took to sewing work.

The wind rattled the carriage, sneaking in through the coach's fissures and cracks, and fluttering the edges of the blanket.

If only his cousin hadn't been killed. If only Percival had veered more to the left on that one day, all those months previous, he wouldn't be in the mess he was now. He hadn't survived the Napoleonic Wars to become a victim to some woman on some God-forsaken road. So he rose.

The process was inelegant. Perhaps one day he might be able to rise in a smooth, sweeping gesture befitting a man of his station. But now he still stumbled, because blast it, he still felt his leg, and still expected it to be there when he needed it.

He gritted his teeth together and braced his hand against the cold wall of the coach. The wooden stump provided balance, and he turned to the highwaywoman.

Her stony gaze softened, and his heart sank. "Not you, too."

"But your leg—"

"Is of no concern of yours."

"I didn't notice—"

"I thought you did."

She shook her head, her eyes wide.

He sighed. "Everyone expects everyone to have two legs."

"I'm so sorry."

"How sympathetic of you. I wouldn't have thought a robber would care much about the leg count of the people she attacks."

"Very amusing." She sighed and lowered her weapon. She leaned forward, and a surge of vanilla wafted toward him. "Where did your driver go? Is he getting the magistrate? Lord, he's getting help!"

Percival's breath quickened, and he forced himself to remain calm. This was just like being at war. He'd battled enemies with success dozens of times. He hadn't risen through the ranks solely on his father's commission. He'd been publicly commended for his efforts, charged with leading other soldiers.

But back then he'd been armed with weapons. Back then all his limbs had been intact.

Percival sighed. "He must be here. Royal mail and all."

Her eyes narrowed, and it occurred to Percival that Graeme just might have concocted a heroic plan all by himself. Perhaps the driver had gone to fetch help. Hope jostled through him, and he managed to shrug, maintaining an expression of neutrality well-honed from hours of card playing in officers' tents.

"Maybe he's relieving himself." Lord knows the man had drank sufficient ale before the journey, and likely during the drive as well, if his constant singing had been any indication.

"He took Ned," the woman declared. "I went to fetch him, and he was gone."

"Graeme's captured one of the ruffians? I wouldn't have thought him capable."

"My horse!"

"Oh." He rubbed his hand through his hair and stumbled from the coach, his wooden stump clicking against the floor. The wind howled through the open door, and he grimaced as he stepped outside. He glanced down at the tiny metal steps. *Blast.*

The sounds of horses stomping their feet and snorting greeted him. It was bad enough to descend these steps when a driver was there to calm and steady the animals.

He gritted his teeth, and by some happiness of fate that had not graced him at Waterloo, managed to reach the frozen ground without toppling downward in an inelegant situation the highwaywoman might take advantage of.

"Graeme!" His voice barreled through the wilderness, but there was no rustle through the trees, and certainly no answer. He studied the road, but there was no sight of his driver. "Lucky man."

"Oh, this is dreadful." Mournfulness shook the woman's voice. "My poor Ned."

"I wouldn't have taken a woman of your sort to care about a horse."

She jutted her chin out. "It would be a mistake to underestimate me."

"Graeme's already succeeded in getting the better of you."

Something flickered in her eyes. Something that he might have termed fear if he weren't dealing with a woman who stole money from travelers for a living.

He shrugged and found himself reassuring her. "Graeme's a driver. He knows how to take care of a horse. Better than the life you could provide for it."

She stiffened.

He glanced at her. "You should have chosen an honorable profession."

"We have to go." She turned to him, and her arms dropped down. She glowed under the wobbly light of the lantern, and she appeared far more regal than a thief had any right to appear.

"I've no desire to be dragged to whatever low-level place you frequent."

Her eyes flashed. "You don't have a choice."

"You can steal from me here!" He removed a satchel. "No need to travel with you to do it. Just . . . er . . . let me take the coach somewhere. I don't fancy my chances of standing here in the cold."

"I don't want your coins."

He raised his eyebrows, and her cheeks flushed.

"I mean I can steal from you later." She glanced toward the road, and her teeth pressed against her bottom lip. "Let's go."

He followed her glance to the empty road and then understood. She probably worried that Graeme would drag the magistrate and all the magistrate's burliest helpers with him in pursuit of her. She was probably overestimating Graeme's heroism, as much as he claimed to admire the army.

But maybe—maybe if he managed to stall. Maybe Graeme might venture into the forest with help after all.

"Your colleagues aren't here," he said.

"They're here. Though maybe you're right. Maybe they went after Graeme." She leaned toward him, and her eyes were round. "If they haven't killed him already."

He stiffened, and she brushed his cravat with her knife. "You drive. I trust your arms are still sufficiently strong to handle reins."

"Of course." And he'd take them right back to the nearest inn.

"I'll sit beside you." She tapped the handle of her knife. "With this."

"You're mad!" he murmured, taking her in.

She laughed and tossed her hair. "Maybe."

Chapter Six

THE COLD WIND BRUSHED against Fiona, and she pulled her hood over her head. Pink and orange streaked the sky, and the trees cast long shadows on the dirt lane. She stepped into the coach, flickered her eye over a stack of suitcases, and grabbed a blanket. She rushed back outside and dangled the bright fabric between two trees that arched over the road. Hopefully it would serve as a beacon to warn any other people of the tree.

She sprinted back to the coach as her locks tumbled and blew around her. She pulled herself up onto the seat, and the handsome man slid away. His eyes rounded, and he flickered a nervous glance at her.

"You can drive a carriage, can't you?"

"Woman, I battled the French. Of course I can." The man grabbed hold of the leather reins, and with a jerk the horses trotted forward.

"You'll need to rotate the coach. The tree—"

"I've heard enough about that tree," the man growled, but he coaxed the horses to turn, maneuvering the reins with deftness. "Your men shouldn't have cut it down."

Fiona remained silent and fixed her gaze on the horses. They were good and solid, sturdier built than the sleek Arabians she rode at Cloudbridge. The carriage wheels crunched over the fallen leaves, and she swiveled her gaze back, half-anticipating the coach driver to re-appear, gun cocked.

They had to leave.

If only the tree hadn't fallen. They couldn't return to the manor house the way she had come. Certainly this man would be of little assistance in moving the tree. Fiona's desire was to flee as far from here as possible. They would need to take the long way to Cloudbridge Castle.

The cheerful forest she remembered from the summer, filled with lush green grass, a multitude of flowers, and trees bearing pleasing shades of leaves, had vanished, and this place, filled with naked white and brown branches jutting from muddied ground, was still foreign to her.

Feet pattered behind her, and she tensed. *Graeme.*

She swung around, but the sound swishing over the ground was only a badger. But she couldn't allow herself to relax yet.

Not now, not until she'd introduced this strange man to Grandmother, so she might send him from her life with as much swiftness as he'd entered it.

Fresh air swept around her, and the carriage jostled over the lane. Something tinkled and chimed beside her, and she frowned when she spotted the offending item.

The man followed her gaze to the bell, and a small smile grew on his stubbled face. "Not an admirer of Christmas?"

"Not anymore."

"Some wassailers with poor pitch? A bad mulled wine experience?" He chuckled, and her shoulders relaxed.

The bells rang out beside her, an up-tempo melody that matched the speed of the coach. The sound was festive, lacking in seriousness. She sighed. Perhaps that was for the best. Perhaps the man would be less likely to attack her that way.

For as much as she strove to mirror the appearance of a true highwaywoman, she would not be using a weapon on him.

She concentrated on the horses and how their sturdy forms tramped steadily. The orange and pink streaks sank, abandoning the sky to darkness and stars that twinkled in familiar clusters she recognized but hadn't seen in a long time.

Though Harrogate lay nearby, its pump-rooms and assembling halls attracting people from much farther distances, Fiona ventured there infrequently. Her parents' last lesson to her had been of the dangers of coach travel, and Fiona was too timid to enjoy the bustle of a large town.

She clutched the knife in her hands and allowed her gaze to wander to the heavens above. The outside world was grander than she remembered.

She mulled over the manner in which the man beside her held the reins. The action was gentler than she had anticipated, not as if he lacked control, but as if the welfare of the horses was actually of concern to him.

Goodness, spending time with a man was an unfamiliar practice. Certainly she had no regular acquaintance with any man who wasn't gray with age, proudly displaying a hoary beard, or employed to serve her family's needs.

But this wasn't one of her pompous uncles. This wasn't the meek, round-faced cleric who frequented Cloudbridge Castle in the guise of checking up on his congregation, only to spend more time finding delight in Cook's sugar concoctions. This person resembled the smartly dressed men she'd seen during her one, shortened season. This was the type of man she'd seen from afar, the type of man who would dance with women like Madeline, but who would never deign to dance with her.

It wasn't the first time she'd ridden with a man. She'd ridden in a carriage in Hyde Park before with a man more interested in racing than in her. She recalled the sharp swerves, the pounding of galloping horses' hooves, and the blur of men and women in expensive clothes unsuited to the muddy park. Many women wore white despite the weather, flaunting the light garments as badges to display they had maids to sufficiently clean the delicate fabrics, despite the stains that might be cast on them by London's infamous rain.

"You're cold." The man's deep voice, velvety and warm like chocolate, interrupted her musings.

She shook herself. "Nonsense."

"Your teeth are chattering. I can hear you." His tone sounded more amused than it should. Didn't he realize she was kidnapping him?

"I'm fine." She glanced up at him, but his gaze was once again focused before him.

The man must be frightened, but his posture was more relaxed now, and he radiated a quiet calm. Her gaze flickered to his foot. It must be hard to have a leg missing. She couldn't imagine the physical agony he must have experienced as the army surgeon sawed off the leg. And here she was dragging him into the unknown.

"You have a destination in mind?" The man tilted his head toward her, his blue eyes probing hers, and she averted her gaze.

"Just continue North."

"To?"

She paused. "I'll guide you."

No need to let him know their destination yet. Some things could be postponed. It would be better if he were to continue to feel uneasy around her. Because once he found out she was just a wealthy woman from the *ton*, there wasn't a chance he would respect her. She would be labeled a foolish chit, and even though her issues meant everything to her, they would be dismissed. She shouldn't be faulted for the narrowness of her world. She'd had no opportunity to join the war, to arrive home sullen and scarred like him.

She tapped her feet against the hot brick. She needed to ensure he did her this favor. At the very least, once they arrived at the castle, he wouldn't be able to leave without her approval. These horses would be exhausted, and she could direct the servants to keep him there. The place was too isolated for him to wander away from it on foot, and he might find it simpler to consent to playing her fiancé for a few minutes.

"How did you injure yourself?"

He stiffened. "Doing something many would see as dutiful—battling Bonaparte's army."

"And the truth?"

The man sighed. "My cousin was doing something more dutiful. He fought an officer on the imposing side. The man was charging at me on a horse, waving a sword. It was my job to stop him. I was nearer, and yet my cousin stepped in front. He was killed, and I was maimed."

"Oh." Fiona's heart stilled, and her throat dried. She understood the pain of death. She wrapped her arms around her chest and murmured, "I'm sorry. Truly."

The trees thinned, and the handsome man's gaze flickered over her. The horses continued their plod over the road. Before them some wassailers appeared. They were clad in simple clothes, and carried torches instead of lanterns to guide them as they went from home to home, singing.

He slowed the coach, and Fiona's heart quickened. She redirected her knife at him. "Don't stop. Or I'll—I'll—"

"You'll stab me?" He raised his eyebrows. "I'll take my chances. You've got witnesses before you."

The horses slowed, and sweat prickled the back of Fiona's neck. A throng of wassailers peered up at them.

"Happy Christmas," a wassailer shouted.

"Happy Christmas to you," the handsome man answered.

She lowered her knife, her mind grappling for something, *anything* to prevent this man from asking them for help.

His gaze flickered to her lap, and he smirked.

"I'm being kidnapped," his voice boomed. "This woman has captured me. I need help."

The wassailers stopped their song, and Fiona's heart lurched. She forced herself to laugh. though the sound felt unnatural in her throat. "Darling, the things you say."

The handsome man frowned. "I'm serious. She's captured me! Help me! Please!"

"Sweetheart." Fiona forced herself to smile and she slid her arm into his. Heat surged through her as her arm nestled into his.

She might be twenty-two, but this was the pinnacle of her contact with any man, and her heart galloped as she stared at the gathering of men and women before her.

The handsome man sucked in his breath sharply.

A round-faced woman chuckled, and others joined her. "That's the most romantic thing I've ever heard. My dear husband, why don't you say those things about me?"

A man beside her gave a sheepish grin.

"No, I'm serious," the handsome man said. "I've been kidnapped."

"By Cupid's bow?" someone called out.

"No, no. By force!"

Laughter filled the air, and the scent of beer and cider wafted over the carriage.

"Perhaps we should sing you a song," the round-faced woman said.

"How did you get that mail coach?" someone shouted.

The handsome man's expression firmed. "Because—"

"Darling, let me drive." Fiona snatched the reins from him and urged the horses past the wassailers.

"You shouldn't have done that," he grumbled.

"I'll add it to the list of things you disapprove of." She fumbled for her knife and handed the reins back to him.

They continued in silence.

Lights shone off the side of the road, directing travelers to the public houses. The man swiveled his head in the direction of an inn.

"Don't even think about it!" Fiona said.

His eyebrows darted up. "A mind like mine can't be dissuaded from thinking, no matter how eager you are to force on it your lack of education."

She stiffened. "I suppose you went to Oxford."

"No." He stared firmly ahead.

"Cambridge?" The smooth sound of his voice and his consistently rounded vowels spoke Oxbridge to her.

His voice that would make him suitable to pose as her fiancé, until she saw fit to invent a suitable death for him. It was the voice of a man whom she automatically distrusted.

He pressed his lips together. "Edinburgh."

"They do classics there, too?"

"I've got no patience for Latin, woman. Seems people already do enough talking when they're just speaking their own language. Don't need to add additional languages."

Fiona snorted. "How educated of you. I suppose you have a degree in ignorance and close-mindedness?"

His lips jutted upward. "Medicine."

Fiona's eyes widened. People didn't study medicine unless they were genuinely interested in it. "But you were an officer."

"My family thought it more worthwhile for me to kill people than heal them."

"I'm sorry."

He shrugged. "I gave up that dream a long time ago."

"Maybe now—" She paused, and her eyes fluttered to his leg.

"I'm rather occupied otherwise now. I . . . er . . . needed to take over my cousin's business after his death."

"You couldn't be a doctor at the same time?"

He grinned. "That would be highly unconventional with my cousin's business."

"Which you're not going to share with me?"

"No." He shook his head, and his lips arched upward again. "Besides, doctors are rather supposed to be models of health. Not missing vital body parts."

"I'm sure you didn't intentionally—"

"Lose a leg? No, any struggle I have with disorganization is not that great." A chuckle escaped from his lips.

Warmth filled Fiona, and she settled back into the carriage chair. For a moment she might even imagine that the man was really her fiancé, and that they weren't hauling a large, awkward coach, but were in a curricle. The scent of pine would fill the air in just the same way, and the rumble of the man's voice beside her would be a comfort to her instead of a reminder she had to be on guard.

If the magistrate found she'd captured a man . . . Fiona didn't want to contemplate the legal consequences. It was enough to imagine how the action would fuel the *ton*'s gossip, humiliate Grandmother, and confirm all of Madeline's worst suspicions of her.

She'd thrown her reputation away. With one impulsive move, she'd hurried this man, who bore scars from the war, into a carriage despite all his protestations. She'd frightened his driver, and once that man managed to secure help, she'd have the wrath of the royal mail to answer to.

Nice ladies didn't capture men. Nice ladies didn't pretend to be ferocious highwaywomen. Even improper ladies didn't do this—at absolute worst they might permit a rogue to bed them, an experience that did not likely have the rogue cowering with fear.

Her fingers scrunched together, tightening further around the edge of the blade. If this ever got out, and if they didn't get off the road soon, some authority was likely to find them. Then she would never be able to marry, never be able to have anything similar to a normal life. Even her sister would be subject to the tittering of gossip-mongers.

And though she'd long told herself she had no intention of ever marrying, the idea that she'd virtually guaranteed herself society's contempt, that she might actually find herself ushered off to a prison cell for a while, caused her heart to shudder.

The man had been brutally injured in the war. He didn't deserve this. No one deserved this. And yet she couldn't do anything except continue to drive forward. She couldn't go to the magistrate and confess. Not when word might reach Grandmother of her actions. And not when being a highwaywoman was a capital crime. Her chest tightened.

"And do you have a name?" she found herself asking.

"Not for you."

"Then I'll call you Percival."

He swung his head over to her, and his mouth gaped open.

"Your forename was on your valise." She faltered under the magnitude of his startled gaze. "Though it speaks of an informality I'm uncomfortable with."

"I think we left formalities behind a long time ago," he mused, but his voice sounded hoarser than before.

Chapter Seven

PERCIVAL CLENCHED HIS fingers around the reins. She knew his name. *By Zeus, maybe she knew about the jewels.* Maybe she knew he'd recently inherited a bloody *dukedom*. Maybe this whole thing was planned in advance, and he was merrily driving himself to some kidnapper's lair, to the sound of jingling Christmas bells, where he'd wait until the dowager duchess might wrangle up appropriate amounts of money to appease the criminals.

He squeezed his fingers against the leather reins. The now-familiar pain surged through him, and he fought the urge to massage the wound.

The carriage wheels clattered, and the lantern swerved ahead, throwing dim light over the narrow lane. On occasion a fox scrambled from the road toward the tall hedges that soared on either side. He wondered what local gentry lived here and if he might guide the coach to a destination that differed from the one of the highwaywoman's choice.

What desperation had driven her to this life?

He needed to make an escape. No one needed to know that the new Duke of Alfriston was so incapable that he'd managed to get himself kidnapped mere months after taking on the dukedom. But Zeus—she knew his name.

He'd already revealed more to this nefarious-minded stranger than he did to most others. He'd never suffered from chattering too much before. Quite the opposite, if his conversations with the women of the *ton* were any indication. But he'd never quite succeeded in feigning an interest in flowers and dresses, and they'd never quite followed his conversations about war.

In previous years he'd seen the slight, but definite wrinkles of their noses when he'd mentioned that he was the wrong Carmichael, and their eager excuses when he'd revealed that an actual duke, his cousin Bernard, was nearby. Percival's brother Arthur was the fun Carmichael, the one who effortlessly earned himself the reputation of rogue, and his cousin had been the sensible one with the title and the vast estate. He had two sisters as well, Louisa and Irene, though thankfully neither had debuted yet. His mother and stepfather indulged their own interest in travel, though they seemed content in Massachusetts.

He sighed. Bernard wasn't here anymore. The man's last breath had been swallowed on the fields of Waterloo, his last action saving his cousin, instead of himself, from the French.

If his older cousin had only married. If only he had not been heroic and sailed to France. If he'd had children, particularly of the masculine variety, Percival would not be under this pressure now, and the dowager would be able to look forward to the good characteristics of her son continuing the line. Percival's youthful desire to become a physician did not endear him to her, and she'd made it plain she thought him untrained and ill-bred for the momentous task of managing the enormous Alfriston estates, sprinkled from Sussex to Yorkshire.

What could he do besides strive to be the best duke he could be? His cousin had died trying to save him. Appeasing the man's mother was the least he could do.

The woman's scent drifted over him, warm strands of vanilla mixed with amber and berries. It seemed more complex, more mature than the perfumes crammed with roses and musk he was accustomed to.

He let his gaze return to her. She hadn't complained once of discomfort. Occasionally her lips contracted as if attempting to prevent a yawn from escaping.

His lips turned upward despite himself.

She would almost amuse him, if he could ignore the fact that she was an outlaw.

His stomach hardened. He shouldn't be seeing good qualities in her. She was a professional. A woman of the very worst sort.

Stopping a coach. Letting the rest of her dastardly band linger in the woods. Yes, she was definitely a professional. He was sure most thieves would want to work up to that point, conscious of the many things that could go wrong.

Likely this woman had already experienced all of them.

By Zeus, perhaps she had even killed people.

He shivered and turned to her. "So do you have a name? Or do you just go by Miss Demon?"

She chuckled, but then shifted her legs. "I'll tell you soon. I promise. Or I won't. It depends—"

"On if you get caught first?"

She nodded.

Did the woman mean to kill him after all? Tell him her name to appease some sort of dying wish, after whatever criminals she consorted with robbed him? He didn't want to speculate on why it would be bad for him to learn her name before the trip, and why it would be fine for him to learn it after.

He scanned the horizon, but no ruffian popped out and no horse galloped toward him, carrying a criminal branding a rifle. His skin prickled, not entirely because of the cold weather.

By summer he would be happy and settled, even if he wasn't a doctor, even if that particular dream hadn't come true. He'd be enjoying all that everlasting love and such. Lady Cordelia—she was it. One didn't need to meet her to know it.

He patted the inside fold of his great coat where he'd hidden the jewels for his future fiancée, and then hastily removed his hand. He glanced at the Scarlet Demon. Her eyes met his, but she remained as before, staring straight in front of her, observing as the coach passed underneath bare branches.

Likely this would all be pretty in the summer, but now snow sat on the branches instead of leaves and flowers, and he'd seen scarcely any animals.

By Zeus, what was he thinking about? Musing about flowers and leaves, like some penniless poet. Though even they had a propensity to wander the countryside, while he was confined to a blasted coach.

"Your great coat. What's in it?" the woman murmured to him.

She had noticed.

"Nothing." He averted his gaze. He told his heart to stop its frantic rhythm of thumps, and he told his breath that it needn't quicken as if he had a cannon trapped in his body.

But he also saw the knife, which was directed far too near him.

He heaved a sigh. "Put that down."

"No."

"It's dangerous." *I don't have time for this.*

"It's *supposed* to be."

"What do you want?"

"What are you hiding?"

"Nothing of your concern." He sucked in a deep breath of air. "It's not money."

"Indeed."

"Anyway, aren't you supposed to be able to get money easily? What with being a thief and everything? You probably have a stack of coins down your boots." He peered down at them. They were worn, but the leather did not seem completely lacking in quality. He shook his head. He'd never met a highwaywoman before, and it was natural for her to not entirely fulfill his expectations.

"You're asking me to steal?"

"No! Though you needn't act so appalled. It is your profession."

"Then why don't you go around shooting people?" She huffed beside him. "Isn't that your profession?"

"If his Majesty's Army wanted me to do so . . ."

"Well I don't steal on whim either." She paused. "Unless the head smuggler asked me to do so. I mean, then I can be exceedingly effective."

"Right."

She lowered her voice, and a trace of a French accent sounded. "You wouldn't want to meet me on an abandoned road."

He sighed. "I already have. And I'm being dragged in the opposite direction of my destination."

Far away from London and the *ton* and the Christmas ball that would mark the start of his new life. He'd made appearances in London since his accident, but now Lady Cordelia, the woman who would have married his cousin, was there. He'd have her by his side, and everything would be different.

He wasn't sure this ride was all that much worse than London would be.

The thought was ridiculous. His new life promised brilliance. That's why he hadn't been spending his time dreaming about it while at war. It wasn't that his new life wasn't something he wanted—it was just that it was better than anything he ever could have imagined.

That was all.

Another carriage approached them with an actual gold crest and brightly painted wheels.

"Oh dear Lord." The red-headed woman ducked her head down.

"You're reaching to religion now?" He tilted his head. "The first thing you could do is release me. I'm sure the Lord would approve."

"Not funny." She gritted her teeth. "Just continue driving. More quickly."

He furrowed his brows and swung his head back toward the departing carriage.

"Don't look!" The woman squealed. "That might draw attention."

"So would a woman pushing her head down. They might suspect—" He grinned, for one second allowing himself to envision just what the other people might be thinking.

"This is a mail coach," she stammered. "They shouldn't see us on a mail coach. That's not the plan."

"Do highwaywomen tend to travel in greater luxury?" He arched his eyebrows up.

The woman drew her head back up at once, staring straight in front of her. She pulled her hood up, and Percival stifled a laugh. "Women rarely ride beside the driver."

"I am not going inside."

He jostled the reins, and the coach darted forward. Soon the luxurious carriage was far behind, though the woman's nervousness had scarcely eased.

"Pull over at that tavern."

"Ah . . . Time for me to eat." Percival patted his stomach.

And run away. But the Scarlet Demon didn't need to know that part of the plan just now. She'd find that out soon enough, hopefully well after he'd expanded the distance between them.

He smiled as he directed the horses toward the half-timbered building. A faded sign said *Old Goblet Lodge.* He just needed to get away before the woman told everyone who he really was. And have dinner. Zeus knew he wouldn't be making any stops after he made his escape.

Her smile tightened. "Just don't flee."

"Better not brandish that knife around there. You might find yourself getting hauled over to the magistrate's."

"I'm sure that's a vision that appeals to you," she said.

He laughed, and they descended the steps of the carriage. He gripped his cane tightly and maneuvered to the cobblestones below.

The Scarlet Demon offered him her hand. He smiled; he would almost miss her.

He forced his gaze away from her, toward the sky. "It's going to snow."

"Nonsense. The stars are out."

"I've spent enough nights looking at the sky. Sleeping outside becomes more appealing when you're in a tent full of snorers."

"How very—individualistic of you."

He nodded, though he didn't mention that it wasn't just snoring he'd longed to escape. The men shouted in their sleep, reliving battle experiences every time they shut their eyes. Perhaps their minds were trying to extract some meaning from their experiences, but it was impossible; there was none.

He pushed open the door to the tavern, the red-headed woman at his side. Her eyes widened as they entered. Groups of men clustered at wooden tables. A few chess boards were scattered around, and in one corner men played darts. Some men were eating. Tankards adorned the tables, brimming with delightful liquids that ranged from gold to amber in color.

He headed to the counter. He would eat, drink, and then flee. The scent of mince pies filled the tavern, and Percival groaned.

"Are you quite alright?" The scarlet-haired woman directed her gaze at him, and he suppressed a laugh.

"I'd feel better if I weren't captured."

Her smile wobbled. "Later."

Yes, later was definitely not anything he wanted happening anytime soon. The floor creaked underneath his steps, and he ducked to avoid the wooden beams. "Some of the patrons look like they've been here for centuries, gossiping about Anne Boleyn."

An elderly man cleared his throat and narrowed his eyes slowly as if the action drew all his exertion. His gaze dropped to Percival's wooden stump. "You look a mite ragged yourself."

"At least I was once handsome." Percival ignored the stern gaze the man fixed on him. He hated when people drew attention to his leg. He put his hand on the small of the woman's waist and raised his voice. "These people lack all sense."

Greenery dangled from the ceiling, and the scent of mulled wine mingled with the ale dispersed about the pub. He tried to relax, but the group of men scowling at him unsettled him.

The Scarlet Demon eyed a group of flamboyantly dressed woman. "Such strange clothes."

"I take it I shouldn't add experience with whoring to your list of crimes."

Her eyes widened, and he grinned. In the light her emerald shards really shone. So much life in them. He could almost forget she'd taken him to this God-forsaken place. Nobody to help him here, that was certain.

A barmaid marched to them. "Ale?"

"And meat," Percival said.

"For me too," the Scarlet Demon said. "And um—potatoes and broccoli."

"I knew you were hungry," Percival said.

"You're paying."

"I wondered when you were going to start robbing me."

She chuckled, and Percival almost laughed with her. He tapped his fingers against the table and considered informing these people he'd been captured. That hadn't worked before, and the thought of the magistrate locking her up somewhere didn't fill him with the pleasure it should have. No, far better to slip out quietly. He wouldn't have a scandal, and she wouldn't be harmed.

She sat across from him, and it felt far too intimate. He'd never eaten with any of his mistresses, and though he'd been placed next to women at London parties and expected to converse with them, he'd always had the advantage of having other people beside him.

The barmaid set towering tankards of ale down, and foam sloshed on the wooden table. He grinned when she put the food down. Definitely no need to leave yet.

He eyed his companion. "So what is it like being a highwaywoman?"

She leaned toward him, and her voice lowered to an almost seductive tone. "Wild."

He shivered and then took a long slurp of the ale. "And how did you get into that career?"

Her red lips extended upward. "Complete chance."

"Oh."

"It could happen to you." The woman tossed her hair, and scarlet curls resettled into a new, alluring pattern. The strands were bright sparks of color in the grim tavern, and Percival forced his gaze away.

No way would he let her see him eyeing them. Any curiosity might be taken for admiration, and he did not admire highwaywomen. His Majesty's Army would not condone it, even if there might be some merit in the curve of her cheeks.

He'd been too long without a woman. War would do that to a man, at least one who'd had no desire to fulfill his urges at a brothel, and who was under strict instructions from the dowager to rectify his rakish reputation before he got betrothed.

Perhaps he was using the dowager as an excuse to avoid making a love-match. Perhaps he was worried his injury would hamper any attempts to find true affection anyway. He shook his head. "Tell me about yourself."

"Me?" The Scarlet Demon's gaze flickered to his torso, and she tucked a lock of auburn hair behind her ear. Her voice seemed more high-pitched than it had before, a breathless tone, no less appealing, that made him scrutinize her.

A pink tint spread over her cheeks, and she dipped her head down. The gesture only made more of her mane of hair topple forward, and for a strange moment Percival pondered what it would feel like to move his fingers through her thick curls.

He'd traveled through France, Spain, Russia, and the Hapsburg Empire, but by Zeus, he'd never met any woman like her.

The Scarlet Demon inhaled, and though that dreadful cloak covered her completely, he would be lying if he said he hadn't noticed the way her chest moved, and considered whether underneath all the wool there was a bosom he could grasp. The woman was rounder than he was used to. The chit had apple cheeks he wanted to stroke, and full lips that the warm tavern must have turned red, because they were the most enticing color.

He tightened his fists together. Clearly he'd simply gone far too long without a woman. That was it. *Naturally.* He concentrated on cutting his food and savoring the rich meat taste.

"What is this?" She poked the thick tan crust, and dark liquid oozed from it.

"Steak and ale pie." He tilted his head. "How have you managed to avoid eating those? The only people I know who haven't eaten them are members of the *ton*."

She shrugged. "We highwaywomen are frightfully refined."

"Clearly." He concentrated on his food. Much less confusing than continuing to make conversation with his captor.

Before long he stumbled to his feet. A few of the men glanced at his wooden leg, and he stiffened. He'd been accustomed to drawing people's glances because of his Carmichael features; now it was his tendency to totter and sway that attracted attention. "I'll pay."

She lurched up, and her chair scraped against the wooden floor. "I'll come with you."

Percival nodded; he'd anticipated her action.

They strode toward the counter, though Percival's steps were rather less elegant than the highwaywoman's. Her gaze swept over the room, and she appeared fascinated by the space and the long bar with the many men sipping ale. He almost wanted to laugh.

He grabbed hold of his purse and dipped out some of his gold coins. He handed her his still heavy bag. "This is yours."

"I—"

In the next moment he knocked two tankards from the table. Then he was off, dragging his bad leg behind him, and gripping his cane as if everything depended on it, as murmurs broke out.

There was no way she was going to start flinging her knife at him now.

He increased his speed, grateful for the clusters of men. She'd have trouble coming after him.

He smiled. He wouldn't need to worry about her anymore. The highwaywoman was in the past. He'd even left her some coins. To distract her. Not because he was worried what would happen to her, now that she was stuck in a strange place by herself.

Not at all.

He rubbed his hand through his hair and pressed the door to the outside. Cold wind slammed against him. The snow that he'd predicted had started to fall. He swore. Why on earth did he have to be so bloody right about everything?

He stepped over the icy cobblestones. Snow clung to his clothes, and the ground grew ever whiter. The groom helped him onto the mail coach, changed with fresh horses, and Percival took the reins quickly before the man might ask him any questions about why he was not wearing a uniform.

He pressed the horses forward, leaving the light of the tavern as he sauntered into the darkness toward freedom. *And Lady Cordelia.* He sighed, trying to summon thoughts of his future bride.

Chapter Eight

HE WAS GONE.

She'd pressed after him, but the thick cluster of men swarming the broken tankards had impeded her path. When she'd reached the door, he'd already vanished with the coach.

Just like that her hope for the future that would satisfy Grandmother's dreams for her was extinguished.

She scrunched her fists together.

"What's wrong, love?" A burly man with a bushy beard not quite masking a rosy face called from a table.

"I—" Fiona swallowed hard.

This establishment was not a place she ever should have found herself in. The throngs of workers and scent of alcohol embodied everything Grandmother's manor house was not, and she stepped away. She bumped into something—someone, she realized, and the man's eyes narrowed.

"Forgive me, sir."

"You're not lost, are you? Want to have a drink? We've got mulled wine." The man turned to someone else. "My wife always likes a bit of mulled wine. The cinnamon and sugar go well with the hot liquid."

Fiona groaned. She was not going to sit in some establishment, listening as thickset men discussed Christmas drinks. "I need your help. The gentleman you saw—well, I need to find him. I fear he ran away."

"Hobbled away," the man corrected, and Fiona frowned.

The man sighed. "Look, love—why ever would he do that?"

His voice boomed, and more heads swiveled in their direction. Fiona shifted her legs, and the wooden beams of the floor croaked beneath her. A fire leaped and swirled in a great stone hearth beside her, the flames merrily devouring the mound of logs and kindling. The twigs snapped and sparked, and the smoke stung Fiona's eyes.

Her chest constricted, and she moved her hand to her neck, fiddling with her mother's brooch. The sharp swerves of the flower-shaped design provided little comfort now.

Fiona sucked in a deep breath of air, conscious of the inquiring gazes fixed on her, and patted her stomach.

"Lord." The man stared at her abdomen. "He's done a runner, has he?"

She nodded, her heart pounding wildly.

"My daughter went out with a man who did a runner, and I've vowed to murder him. Strangle him. Or shoot him with one of those fancy rifles the former soldiers are always going on about." The burly man rubbed his hands together. "I'm going to the bottom of the world to track down the man who ruined my precious daughter. I reckon this one hasn't gotten quite so far away."

"Probably not in New Holland," one man shouted and the others hooted.

"Well—" Fiona faltered. "Could you help me find this one?"

"Sure will." The man leaned toward her conspiringly and whispered, "And I'll kill him for you too."

"That's—that's not necessary," she squeaked.

"After the man deflowered a pretty duck like you?" The man's eyes roamed her body, and she shivered. "Got you pregnant? And then abandoned you before Christmas? I would consider it my Christmas gift to you."

"I—"

"Don't worry. I'll let you think of a gift you can give me." He winked and dropped his gaze to her chest again.

Fiona tightened her cloak around her. "I just want him back. That's all. I don't want you to harm him! He's, he's—"

"Yes, love?" A more grandfatherly type prodded her, and she searched for something she could say that might lessen some of the tension roiling through the room. Her heartbeat hammered against her ribs. The men shouldn't do anything drastic. "He's my husband."

"Oh." The burly man's mouth parted, and he stepped away. "Pardon, Mrs. . . . er . . ."

Her cheeks heated. "Mrs. Percival."

"I'm Bill Potter." The burly man directed a thick thumb toward the grandfatherly man. "And this 'ere is Mr. Nicholas."

"Pleased to meet you." She gave an automatic curtsy, and the men guffawed. Warmth seared the back of her neck, but Mr. Nicholas merely shook his head.

"I've been waiting seventy-four years for someone to treat me like a proper aristocrat. I think we got to help the lady now."

She hesitated. "I'm not sure it's best..."

"Nonsense." Mr. Nicholas shook his head. "Now tell us what happened."

"Her bastardly husband left after she told him she was with child," Mr. Potter interjected.

She inhaled. "You all saw him. The handsome—"

"I don't want you to be describing him in that manner." Mr. Nicholas shook his head gently. "That's where all the problems start, or at least that's what keeps them from ending."

"Just help me." She gave a nervous glance to Mr. Potter. "But please no shooting. Or strangling."

The man nodded solemnly. "Though you shouldn't trust a man flouncing around in all those silks with all those airs."

Mr. Nicholas smiled. "We'll bring him back. Don't you worry."

Fiona sighed. "Thank you."

"Let's get going," Mr. Nicholas said.

The men strode from the tavern, and Fiona scurried after them.

Right now she wasn't Fiona, the woman who had refused to go to London. Right now she was a completely different woman, one who frequented taverns and chatted with the people inside.

She wasn't sure which one felt more like her.

The stars had disappeared, replaced with thick clouds. Snow thundered down, burying the cobblestones.

"Now who would have thought it would start snowing?" Mr. Nicholas peered at the sky.

The other men murmured bewilderment, and Fiona bit her tongue to keep from declaring her husband had it figured out all along. It was no good acting love sick for a man who'd never been and never would be her lover.

"We shan't catch up with him now," one of the younger men said apologetically. "But don't you worry. If it's a home for the baby you need, me mam runs a farm for ladies in particular situations."

"Thank you," Fiona croaked. She fiddled with her cloak, wondering whether she might be fortunate enough to evade being recognized. "But I would appreciate if you could keep my situation a secret."

The men nodded. "That we can do."

"This 'ere lad isn't sure how babies are made anyway," Mr. Potter said.

The men guffawed, prodding each other, and the face of the man in question reddened, matching Grandmother's Christmas decor.

"Please. Gentlemen. Sirs." A few of the men raised their eyebrows, but she carried on. She had to remember that tonight she was one of them. Just a girl who could be any of their daughters. "Please just help me find the man I was with."

"He went South. Toward London," the groom said. "He took off with one of the horses."

"Then South we go."

"It will be hard going in this weather. The wheels aren't suited for it and the next inn is far away."

Fiona stared at the snow storming down and pulled her cloak more tightly around her.

Of course it would all be for naught. *Of course.*

The man didn't want to be found. And even though she'd gotten so close to finding him again, even though she'd enjoyed his company, she would never see him again.

She sighed. There had to be something they could do. Something that could keep this opportunity from sliding away. Something that . . . She tilted her head. "Do you have a sleigh?"

"Oy! We do. We never use it—haven't seen snow like this in years, and it will be melted by the end of the week."

Fiona smiled, and the groom led the way to the sleigh. It was black and glossy with dark black wedges. She smiled. "It's perfect."

"Jump inside, darling!" Mr. Potter bellowed.

The others piled in and the groom hooked four horses to the sleigh. They were big and strong looking, stomping their hooves in the snow and tasting on occasion the snowflakes that toppled downward.

With a jolt the horses moved. Their pace was steady, faster than Fiona expected, and hope grew within her when the sleigh left the road, moving to where the snow was thicker, and headed in the direction of the flickering lights of the next village.

"We haven't had so much excitement since we had a Frenchman hiding in one of the barns!" Mr. Potter declared. "He came all the way from Dover, rounding the coast as if he were some sort of holiday goer."

The men shook their heads, heaving deep sighs.

"Though who knows!" Mr. Potter shrugged. "Maybe that's the French idea of a holiday. What with Bonaparte as a leader and all."

"We'll catch up with him soon, love," Mr. Nicholas said gently. "Don't you worry."

The horses dragged the sleigh swiftly and expediently through the thick snow. The men sang Christmas songs, clapping their hands and stomping their feet.

More wassailers appeared through the midst of snow.

"Oy!" Mr. Potter stood on the sleigh and waved at the wassailers. "Oy!"

The wassailers stopped.

"We're pursuing justice!" Mr. Potter's voice thundered through the wind. "We're going to find a rascal. We've got a lady who's with child and we're off to get her fleeing husband to make sure he stays to care for it."

Fiona cringed and wrapped her arms together.

The wassailers' faces darkened. "We'll help you. No lady should be in trouble on Christmas. This is supposed to be a joyful period. A time for families."

"Aye, aye!" Mr. Potter added emphatic nods to his declaration. "A pretty young woman shouldn't be experiencing Christmas in distress. That just won't do. Not in this 'ere village. We'll bring 'im back. Dead or alive, that's what I always say."

"Alive!" Fiona squeaked. "He mustn't be harmed! I mean—I've no use for him dead."

"There, there, don't you worry," Mr. Nicholas murmured in a tone likely meant to soothe her, but it did nothing to quell Fiona's surety that she'd never needed to worry more.

SNOW FELL WITH INCREASED rapidity, and the horses' pace slowed. The snowflakes blurred together, and a sheet of white replaced the flurry of delicate shapes with pointed edges and intricate patterns.

"Blast." Percival gripped onto the reins. Wind struck his face, and white flecks clung to his attire.

This would not have happened in Sussex. Snow there was a rarity, just as it should be. An inch there would be deemed a disaster.

Percival surveyed the landscape before him. Definitely far more than an inch, and the snow showed no sign of ceasing its downward plummet. He tightened his fists. The coach wouldn't be able to make it through the snow for much longer.

The snow stung his skin, and he pulled his scarf more tightly around him. He'd been through worse in Russia.

Except then he didn't have a throbbing leg to contend with and wasn't stuck on a carriage that might collapse at any moment. Mail coaches were built sturdily, but this weather was battering this one.

At least he had the package. Percival patted the fold in his great coat.

He'd escaped. That was the important thing.

The woman, no matter how effective she'd been at capturing him by herself earlier, didn't have the benefit of her backup ruffians now. He'd left behind some coins, and she'd realize she should just keep the money, even if she did know exactly who he was.

The horses stumbled and stepped into a snow drift. They lurched, panicking, and it was all Percival could do to calm them. He tried to edge them back onto the road, but it was dark, the horses were scared, and his wooden leg wasn't helping matters. The last thing he needed was for the horses to gallop off without him once he inelegantly disembarked.

Lights flickered beside him, moving through the snow, and he swore and tried to urge the horses to the main road. Finally—finally he succeeded, and his heart slowed to a steadier, calmer beat, until—

"Sir!" A man's voice shouted, and a chill descended on Percival. "Halt."

Percival gritted his teeth. This was Yorkshire, and he didn't know a soul. No way in Hades would he stop.

"Sir!" The voice rivaled the sound of a cannon ball's roar, except now no firing muskets or storming cavalry competed with it.

Percival directed his gaze toward the ferocious man.

A group of men on a wide sled and a few on horseback gazed back at him, waving their arms.

A hefty man with a bushy beard rose and pointed a pistol at him. "If you don't halt now, you bloody bastard, we'll come over there and tear your bloody limbs apart!"

A woman shrieked, and a few men wrestled the weapon from the crazed man. Thick-accented curses soared through the wind.

Percival dropped his hands from the reins, and his heart sped. The sleigh moved in his direction.

"You'll go no farther," another man shouted.

"Why in Hades not?"

"None of your blasted arguing," the hefty man roared.

The ache in Percival's leg intensified, and he squirmed. "I've got urgent business in London to attend to."

"You forgot something," another man said.

Percival rubbed his hand through his hair.

"Please do not claim you've forgotten me." A clear, alto voice soared over the deep-voiced grumblings, and Percival blinked when a familiar face peeked from the throng of men.

"You're a witch." Percival's voice was hoarse.

That was the only explanation. Maybe all those people in the middle ages warning about ginger-haired demons had been onto something.

"I had help." The woman rose and gestured to the surrounding men.

"But—"

"You will take her with you," a man from the sled said.

"But—" Percival rubbed his hand over his hat.

"Now."

"I was so devastated when you abandoned me!" The woman's voice sounded mournful.

"Your wife is pregnant!" A white-headed fellow frowned. "You can't abandon her. I don't care how tired you are of your children."

"My children?" Percival gasped.

"She's told us everything. No lies."

"We're—we're not married," Percival stuttered.

"Take her with you now."

"I—"

"Are you planning on abandoning your pregnant wife to the snow?"

"Think of your four babes!" another man shouted.

"I'm just happy my mother is taking care of them now!" The Scarlet Demon tossed her head, her voice still mournful. "How could you have abandoned me? I know it's hard . . ."

The men frowned. "We will not tolerate any man being unkind to his woman. Especially on Christmas."

"Christmas is a time for romance," one person on horseback added.

The white-headed man shook his head. "Just because you used to be a soldier doesn't mean you can put on fancy airs. Seducing women with your uniform. Marrying them. Leaving them when they're pregnant. For shame. You're not at war anymore. We won't tolerate these actions any longer."

"You've made a mistake. A terrible mistake." Percival sucked in a deep breath of air. "And I need to get to London."

"Get into the sleigh beside your wife now."

Percival glanced at the road. Snow swept over it rapidly. Anger seared him. He'd been so close to escaping. He'd even left the woman some money, for some ridiculous reason feeling sorry for her, only to find she'd managed to convince a whole tavern filled with people to capture him again.

He crossed his arms and scowled. "She's not my wife."

The men murmured.

He pointed at the Scarlet Demon. "This woman is a fraud and a liar. She's a highwaywoman who captured me."

Fear flickered over the woman's face, but she then had the indecency to dab her eyes with a handkerchief, as if he were the one lacking in reason. The woman was impossible.

"It's the truth, so help me God." Percival raised his hand to his chest.

A gasp sounded. "You shouldn't do that, lad! You shouldn't lie before our heavenly father."

He gritted his teeth. "This lady is a highwaywoman."

"Darling!" The Scarlet Demon let out an affronted shout.

"She stopped the coach I was in, threatening the driver and me with a knife."

"Where's the driver?" Someone shouted.

"He ran away." Percival flicked his hand. That part was irrelevant. "She demanded I let her take me somewhere."

"Where?"

"I don't know!" Percival shook his head. "But she had me drive the coach north, even though it is vital that I get to London soon."

"Do not believe him." The woman's voice trembled. Though it still had a rich alto sound to it, her manner had changed, as if she were a genteel woman, overwhelmed by the male-dominated surroundings.

She seemed more like a mouse than a fox.

"What say you to this?" one person asked her.

The woman frowned, and Percival didn't fail to notice the worry in her eyes. "I say he needs some rest."

"I don't think we should let you alone with him," the hefty man grumbled.

"But! I'm not the one who kidnapped somebody," Percival shouted. "I'm the one who was dragged miles out of my way. I'm not the person claiming to be someone I'm not. I'm not even married. I don't even have a wife."

"Then who are you?" The white-headed man asked.

He sighed. He hadn't wanted to reveal this, but he couldn't be taken for a criminal by this wild grouping of men. "My name is Percival Carmichael, and I am the Duke of Alfriston."

"That is an extraordinary claim!" The white-headed man frowned.

"No! There's nothing extraordinary about it at all. I'm the one being truthful. All of you are believing a madwoman."

Gasps sounded from the others.

"I am worried about having you alone with him." The hefty man turned to the Scarlet Demon.

The woman's lips wobbled. "He's harmless. He couldn't hurt a fly."

"Oh." The men tilted their heads and stroked their chins, the prospect of believing him apparently impossible.

"The man's perfectly safe. You mustn't harm him. Never even learned how to fire a musket."

"You're insane." Percival frowned. "I lost my leg in the war."

"Farming accident." The woman turned to the others. "One of those dreadful new machines—far too complex for the man. Certainly not a duke."

"I would never have married you," Percival grumbled.

The woman drew in her breath sharply, but then smiled. "Are you saying a demon must have arranged it?"

Percival glanced at the determined faces of the men, so eager to fight injustice, which apparently he embodied. He sighed. "I'll come with you."

"Good." The woman's shoulders slumped though, and her lips fluttered downward.

"It is a crime to abandon your wife in a strange place," the hefty man growled.

"I forgive him," the scarlet-haired woman said.

"You should be in church!" one of the men on horseback said, "Praising the lord that you have such a good wife."

"Come on, darling," the Scarlet Demon said. "Will someone take the man's coach? I'm afraid he must have taken the mail coach by accident."

"We won't report him," the white-headed gentleman said kindly.

Percival cast a mournful look in the direction of London.

Chapter Nine

FIONA EXHALED AS PERCIVAL stumbled toward her through the thickening snow. His gloved hand tightened around his cane, and his wooden leg thumped against the floor of the sleigh. Mr. Nicholas rose and offered Percival his seat beside Fiona, and a man returned the mail coach.

Percival's gaze remained fixed away from her, and something in Fiona's chest constricted as the sleigh sped back over the hills.

They weren't far from Cloudbridge Castle, but Fiona couldn't show up so late with a stranger, even a supposed fiancé, in tow. At least she'd told Grandmother she was visiting her sister.

She glanced at Percival. The man's face was as stony and hardened as a statue, and she averted her eyes. She shouldn't have done it. She shouldn't have gotten him involved, and goodness, she shouldn't have gotten the tavern-goers involved. She wrapped her arms together and pressed her eyes shut, but she couldn't stop the occasional brush of his arm against hers in the jostling sleigh, reminding her of his presence.

Finally, the sleigh pulled up at the *Old Goblet Lodge* and the men toppled outward, hollering something about rewarding themselves with cider and ale.

She cast a glance at Percival's ashen face, and her stomach tightened as if pulled into one of the more complex fishermen's knots. "Forgive me. I—I won't hurt you. You must know that."

Mr. Nicholas snorted, and Fiona frowned.

"Sorry, love. It sounded like you were apologizing to him. After he gone and done a runner on you." His voice sobered, and he shook a finger at Percival. "Young man. You may have lost your leg, but you should be shouting to the heavens in joy that you still have the affection of such an enchanting woman."

Percival's features hardened.

"Mr. Nicholas," Fiona ventured, but the man merely waved his gloved hand at her. Snow continued to topple onto his hair, the thick white flecks giving him a sage-like appearance the man might appreciate, even if she was sure he didn't deserve it.

"You're lucky to have her in your life," Mr. Nicholas continued. "You certainly shouldn't be worried she'll hurt you. Why, this sweet woman is the mother of your children."

Fiona squirmed.

"Let's see if the tavern has a room for you. Bringing another life into the world should be cause for joy," Mr. Nicholas grumbled. "It's a good thing she came after you when she did. That coach wouldn't have made it to the next town, and you would be an ice block."

Percival tensed beside her, and Fiona fought the urge to loop her arm with his and seek to bring him some comfort.

"And where would your lovely wife and children be then?" Mr. Nicholas shook his head. "Ice blocks make even worse husbands than cripples."

Percival flinched.

"You mustn't speak of him in such terms!" Fiona exclaimed.

"Cripple?" Mr. Nicholas raised his eyebrows. "Just saying it how it is. I leave all the gentlemanly nonsense for those men in court with their silk pantaloons and their white wigs."

Mr. Nicholas pushed open the door to the pub, and Fiona and Percival followed him. The men in the carriage seemed well on their way to working through their first celebratory round.

"To the reunited couple," Mr. Potter cheered and thrusted a half-empty tankard in their direction. "We've got you the best room in the tavern."

"That's not necessary." Percival eyed Mr. Potter, as if assessing the likelihood that the man would direct his pistol at him again.

Mr. Potter's eyebrows narrowed. "You want to take this splendid woman to a room that *isn't* the best?"

"I—"

"Because this tavern ain't the place to go for second-rate rooms. You'd be battling the bed bugs enough as it is in the best room. But there's a bloody blizzard out there, and cripples can't be choosers." The man chortled. "Get it? Like beggars, but you're a cripple, see, so—"

"I get it." Percival's voice was flat, and Fiona's chest twisted.

"I think my husband was hoping we could have two rooms," Fiona said finally.

"When you should be busy reuniting? Absolute nonsense." Mr. Potter leaned toward Percival and winked. "You can't worry about getting with child if one's already on its way."

The other men roared, and Mr. Potter downed the rest of his cider before slamming it against the bar.

"Besides. This place is filled. None of us are leaving tonight. So you've gotta share. Better for love-making anyway." Mr. Potter elbowed Percival, and the man stumbled, jabbing his cane into the floor to regain balance.

Percival frowned. "You're right. Naturally, my *marvelous* wife and I will share a room."

Fiona stilled. Women did not share rooms with men. Women like her weren't even supposed to stay in places like this. "Wait. Maybe—"

"Come on, dear," Percival said.

"Don't worry. We'll notice if he tries to escape again, love." Mr. Potter grinned.

"Th-thank you," she stuttered, tucking a strand of hair behind her ear.

"Give her a kiss," one of the men shouted, and Fiona stilled.

"Can't have you upset at each other before bed." Mr. Nicholas's eyes softened. "That's what me wife always said, bless her soul."

"Aye, aye," someone said. "A kiss."

Fiona's eyes rounded, and she was careful to avoid meeting Percival's gaze. "I think we require a bit more privacy for such an action."

"Nah, those rules are just for unmarried people." Mr. Nicholas laughed. "No formality here, right boys?"

"Aye, aye!" The men roared their assent.

"The way I see it," Mr. Potter said, "We reunited you. So we need to make sure you're happy."

"How gallant of you," Percival murmured dryly.

"Now if I was she," Mr. Potter said, "I wouldn't be hanging around with a man without a leg. But that's me. People are different."

"That's big of you," Fiona said.

"Nice, that's what it is." Mr. Potter flashed her a toothy grin.

"Half an hour ago, you were trying to kill me," Percival said.

"Threatening to kill you," Mr. Potter corrected. "It's different."

"Oh, yes," Mr. Nicholas said. "Mr. Potter threatens to kill people all the time. It's his way of making conversation. Practically."

Fiona smiled tightly.

"But maybe your husband here is just not the kissing type," Mr. Potter mused. "Rather a waste of a wife if you ask me."

"I'm not asking you," Fiona said.

Mr. Potter stepped toward her, and his dark eyes flickered. "Perhaps you should. I guess a man without a leg can't be expected to know what to do with a woman."

In the next moment a strong hand gripped her, and she found herself staring straight into Percival's blue eyes. Her heartbeat quickened.

"My wife is completely content," Percival said.

"Y-yes," she squeaked.

Percival pulled her toward him, and Fiona's world shifted. Broad shoulders filled her vision, and her hands itched to touch chestnut hair and high cheekbones.

His gaze was serious, and his hands tightened around her waist. The light played in his hair, revealing honey-colored strands mixed with the chestnut. For a mad moment, Fiona contemplated what it might feel like to slide his wavy locks between her fingers, and if they would feel as silky as they appeared. A dark shadow covered his cheeks and chin, and she pondered whether the texture would feel rough against her cheek, were he indeed to kiss her.

Cheers and clapping sounded in her ears, but they seemed as distant and irrelevant as the sound of owls hooting outside.

The world comprised of two things: Percival and her. And right now that world was changing as Percival's hand stroked her back and his lips moved toward her.

Her heart hammered.

She'd never been kissed before, not even as a debutante. Kisses were things girls with glossier hair and freckle-free complexions whispered about. They didn't apply to Fiona.

Except everything was changing, and warm lips pressed against her, sending a jolt of heat tumbling through every nerve, every inch, every part of her very soul.

For a brief, blissful second his tongue touched hers, and warmth cascaded through her.

And then he stepped away, and everything should have been normal, but she was sure it never could be again.

"I guess he's the kissing type," Mr. Potter muttered forlornly.

"Show us to the room," Percival told the barmaid.

Percival tilted his head at her, and his gaze assessed her. Her heartbeat seemed to compete with the sound of her steps pressing against the creaking floorboards as they followed the barmaid upstairs.

Goodness, if anyone found out. She would be ruined. Utterly ruined. Unmarried women weren't supposed to spend nights with any men, but spending the night with a man she'd just met would produce bafflement in addition to outrage.

And Percival and she had kissed, right there, before nearly two-dozen witnesses, as if she were one of the brightly dressed women who wore copious amounts of rouge and lacked sufficient material to cover their ample bosoms.

Except even those women hadn't been kissing anyone in public.

Fiona's legs trembled as the barmaid unlocked the door, and they positively shook when the barmaid descended the steps again, leaving Percival and her standing before the door.

"You can't stay here," she whispered.

"And have angry villagers after me again? After they've had *more* time to drink? Nonsense." He grabbed hold of her torch and brushed past her. His wooden leg clicked against the thick hardwood panes of the floor. He turned back to her. "Unless your plan is to tell them we're not married after all? And tell them you lied to all of them, forcing them into the cold for absolutely no reason?"

Her shoulders slumped.

"You're acting like some chit from the *ton*." Percival lit a tallow candle, and dim light flickered over his perfect features, twisted into a scowl because of her. "You have no morals. Don't pretend otherwise."

She stiffened.

"Enter," Percival growled.

Boisterous shouts came from downstairs, and the men broke into song. Fiona clenched her jaw and stepped into the room as if she were a brazen harlot.

Dim light flickered over worn furniture, and she started when the door slammed behind her.

"Hello, wife," Percival said, and Fiona knew she should be afraid.

She should not—absolutely should not—be thinking of the man's attractiveness. The idea was ridiculous. Though perhaps not so ridiculous, because there hadn't been a single occasion in her twenty-two years when she'd been alone with a man who wasn't her servant, not to speak of alone in a room intended for sleeping. And this man—dear Lord, this man was what dreams were made of.

A mattress sagged on a small frame, unembellished by even the most austere curtains. He settled into a chair. "I hope you can forgive my lack of gallantry."

"Of course! Take a seat," she chirped, her voice bright in an effort more to reassure herself than him. "I'm glad you were fine. You shouldn't have attempted to drive off like that. That mail coach wasn't going to make it to the next town. You don't know the region."

He raised his eyebrows, but that was fine. He might think her mad, but perhaps then they wouldn't discuss the kiss and perhaps she could forget the way his lips had felt against her own.

"Are you saying you saved me?"

She sucked in a deep breath of air, ignoring the dusty scent that pervaded the room. "It is good you survived."

"So you might steal from me?" His lips spread into something that resembled mirth. His eyes swept over hers. "I know nothing about you."

"I'm not a thief."

Percival rose and strode toward her in quick paces. The man's wooden leg might impede his balance, but it hadn't hampered the man's strength nor the length of his other leg. She was conscious of his size as his six feet, three inches of masculinity barreled toward her.

He strode toward her, narrowing the distance between them in quick efficient movements. Her heart hammered in her chest, and she struggled to remind herself that though the innkeeper had referred to him as her husband, he was not really one. He was nothing to her. And—Lord, from the look on his face, the man despised her.

"Don't come a step closer." The words felt ridiculous on her tongue. Telling him not to come closer was like telling the sun not to shine.

His eyebrows arched up. "You can't pretend to me that you have any virtue."

In the next moment Percival slammed the door and thrust her against it.

He stared into her eyes, and her legs trembled. Images of just what that might entail toppled into her head. He brushed a strand of hair under her ear, and he traced a finger over the line of her cheekbones.

His face neared hers, and his dark eyes, framed with heavy brows, bored into her. The scent of pine needles and cotton wafted over her, mingling with the faint fragrance of ale. The man's broad chest pushed against hers, and her skin prickled at the sudden contact. Her mouth dried, and the space between her legs dampened. She shut her eyes.

"Tell me who you are." His voice was firm and steady.

She inhaled sharply and fumbled for her knife. Her hands moved clumsily, but she managed to grip the hilt. "Please."

His hand swept over her mouth, and he forced her knife from her hand, sending it tumbling to the ground with a loud clatter.

She writhed against him until he loosened his grip. "Do you want me to scream?"

"I—"

"Should I alert all those men downstairs?" She frowned. "Or would you prefer to tie me up and make your escape? I think it would be easy to find you again."

Percival loosened his grip on her. "Forgive me if I'm not clear on the exact etiquette here. It's my first time being kidnapped."

Her heartbeat still raced, and she inhaled.

"You're a thief. And yet you act—" He halted, and a faint blush tinged his cheekbones.

"How do I act?" Her legs had that strange feeling again that they were not really standing on the ground. The world toppled and shifted as if she were floating on a boat, an infrequent experience for her that she took no pleasure in. A glance from him struck her with the power of a wave.

"Like someone I might like." He gave her a harsh laugh. "Forgive me. I just needed a reminder of your motivations."

He glanced at her hand, and her throat dried as she remembered the knife. She returned it hastily.

"I'm not a thief," she repeated, but she knew he didn't believe her.

"What's your name?"

She hesitated. "Fiona."

"We're on a first name basis?"

"That's all I knew about you."

He blinked and then averted his gaze. He settled down, his movements stiff yet determined.

"You're sleeping on the bed?" Her voice faltered and squeaked.

"I have no plan to sleep on the floor."

"But—"

He raised his eyebrows.

"I thought you would be a gentleman," she said, her voice softer.

He frowned. "There's a snowstorm outside and no fire inside. Now is not the time to be gallant."

She fixed her gaze on him.

The man was right, confound it. She didn't dare to speak of propriety to him. He'd just laugh.

He slid underneath the thick blankets.

It was no use protesting. They were spending the night together; everyone would assume it would be more. She slinked in after him, staying at the edge.

"By Zeus, you're trembling like a leaf." He chuckled.

"I—"

"You're not afraid I'm going to harm you?"

"Please d-don't."

He smirked. "I'm engaged to the prettiest woman in London. Practically, at least. You won't need to be in any fear."

The words should have made her relaxed, yet the happiness and relief failed to arrive.

The man was engaged. Of course he wouldn't be interested in a woman like her, even if it was late at night, and even if they shared a room by themselves. Likely his fiancée was everything Fiona was not. Likely his intended was pretty, actually pretty, and not just if one imagined that curves had a certain charm. Likely she had hair that did not stray all over the place, and likely if she were to stop a coach to warn it about an impediment in its path, the driver would not assume her to be a highwaywoman.

Fiona squeezed her eyes shut, and fought to keep her breath steady and not to dwell on the fact that she was alone with the handsomest man she'd ever seen, and he was spending the time utterly uninterested in her.

They'd kissed, but only after a man had implied he wasn't masculine enough to do so. It hadn't meant anything at all to him.

Loretta Van Lochen's women had to fight to keep their virtue, but that was a burden Fiona would not experience.

Chapter Ten

THE WARM SCENT OF VANILLA wafted over him. He nestled closer into soft curves, lulled by the even breathing of—

Someone who wasn't him.

His eyes flickered open. A cascade of auburn curls met his eyes.

Fiona.

The events from last night swirled in his mind, and he gazed at the highwaywoman, the cause of all this dreadfulness, as she slept.

Except—

She wasn't dreadful. Not really.

That kiss had certainly not been dreadful.

Though he'd known that already, had fought the urge to rest his gaze on her too often yesterday.

She was a highwaywoman, one who had introduced herself as The Scarlet Demon, and yet his mind compared her favorably to other women he had met. He hardened at a memory of warm lips against his own.

Blast.

Better not to linger on her much more. He forced his gaze away, though his mind was still filled with the image of the soft curves of a woman's body.

His arms encircled her, pressed against her rounded body. He longed for nothing more than to free it of the constraints of his pantaloons, and to lift the woman's dress and—

His chest constricted as images of him plunging into warm flesh soared through his mind. Long legs would spread, and rounded thighs would part. The urge to groan, to sweep her curved body closer against him, and—

He craved her.

The thought was ridiculous. A fantasy born of having been too long without a woman. Simple proof that he should marry Lady Cordelia, so his life could mold to the demands of the *ton*, and he would be relieved of these strange, unwanted urges.

By Zeus, the woman called herself the Scarlet Demon. She was nothing to be yearned for. And yet—he struggled to resist his desire.

She was so bloody near. She lay in his arms, the picture of innocence. His fingers grazed her chest, and images of luscious mounds surged through him. Would her peaks be tawny or rosy? Would they be thick or slender? And what—Zeus, what would they feel like in his mouth?

The vision nearly shattered him, and he forced a space between their bodies, even though every part of his being seemed to scream at him that his action was foolish. He'd promised that he wouldn't take advantage of her, he'd scoffed at the very notion that he would want to, and yet even then, ever since their kiss and perhaps before, he'd been frustratingly aware of her every movement.

She challenged him. That was it. Simple. Obviously it was perfectly natural that his mind might leap toward the forbidden. He waited for relief to surge over him at the realization, but it never came. Nothing about the woman beside him was simple.

His stomach stiffened. Obviously the dowager was right. How could he attempt to fulfill all the responsibilities of being a duke if his mind was occupied with conjuring up illicit acts?

He pressed his lips together and glided his arm from underneath her head, removing himself from all possibilities of pleasure. The woman swiveled her head toward him for a moment, and he froze.

But she was still asleep. Thankfully.

She'd removed the shabby cloak, and at some point she must have scrubbed her face.

His gaze roamed the planes of her face. Pink tinged the apple cheeks he longed to trace, and long lashes swooped downward. A liberal distribution of freckles scattered around the well-formed composition of her face. Her nose swung up slightly, lending her an almost innocent air, and now that she no longer directed a knife at him, he could see that she must only be in her early twenties. Plump lips, slightly parted, were inches from him, and he longed to narrow the space between them. He longed to swoop his lips against hers, continue where they'd stopped last night.

Instead he yanked his arm away from her.

She woke up.

Green eyes flickered open, and he scrambled away, wobbling as he remembered his wooden leg too late. He rolled from the bed, and his body slammed against hard floorboards.

"Percival!"

The next moment she peered over the bed, and he forced his gaze to rest on her widened eyes and rounded mouth.

Not the sweet dip of her cleavage as she dangled over him.

Not at all.

He would not peek at the tops of her rounded breasts.

No matter how terribly tempting they were.

He refused to.

The woman's grey dress had seemed everything proper, absurd for a highwaywoman, though he supposed the cold and an urge to blend into the night may have influenced her choice of attire.

But there was absolutely nothing proper about the vision before him. His rod ached, and he rolled over. He would not let the woman see how she affected him. Sheets rustled above him.

"You fell off the bed."

"Yes." His heartbeat quickened, and he waited for his hardness to subside.

"Let me help you."

"No need." He uttered an unmanly squeak.

She clambered from the bed, and for a blissful moment slim ankles flashed before him. Fiona bent down, offering him a hand, and he squeezed his eyes shut and forced his mind to contemplate every vile vision he'd seen at war, before he allowed his hand to press against her warmer one.

Heat prickled against the back of his neck, moving toward his cheekbones, and he swiveled away. He clutched hold of one of the thick dark beams that crisscrossed the room, as if the timber protected it from tumbling onto the floor below, and he flung his gaze. Sunshine lit up shabby tables and flimsy lace curtains, and dust fluttered in the long rays.

A faded painting of a buxom milk maiden and her shepherd suitor hung in the room, reminding him that this was meant to be the nicest room in the whole bloody tavern. The milk maiden and shepherd seemed to look adoringly at each other, oblivious to the manner in which long strands of uncut grass clung to their clothes.

"I suppose that's a way to wake up." She let out a throaty laugh, and he swiveled to find the scarlet-haired woman—*Fiona*—peering at him.

Her red hair swept over her shoulders now, crowning her head in a manner more striking than the finest hairstyle of any of the swarm of blonde and brunette debutantes, their locks tamed into a familiar array of shapes. A strand of auburn hair fell over her eyes, and he fought a strange urge to brush the strand away and an instinct to ponder whether the lock might feel silky beneath his touch.

His jaw set. Of course it would feel like hemp, he reminded himself. Only with none of the otherworldly advantages of the sometimes drug. *Of course.*

His unwanted thoughts twisted his stomach, and his heart pulsated with the vigor of one of those Russian pianists, pounding the keys into a thrilling melody.

"How was your night?" Fiona smoothed her dress, unaware of the manner in which her hands caused her curves to be emphasized.

He forced his gaze away. "Uncomfortable. I've always favored a proper bed to blankets on a floor. But shouldn't you know that, dearest wife?"

He chided himself at once for teasing her.

For a moment she stiffened, but her expression soon relaxed. Her eyes twinkled, and she brushed a piece of straw from his coat. "I can be so absent-minded."

A knock rapped on the door.

"Enter." Fiona's voice was clear and strong.

Mr. Potter appeared. "The reunited couple, I see."

"Thank you again for your assistance last night," Fiona chirped.

"Always eager to help a damsel in distress." The man did a short bow, and Percival scowled. Fiona seemed utterly oblivious to the man's interest in her.

"Let's go, darling wife." Percival smiled tightly and fought to ignore the sudden heat that flowed through him, when Fiona slipped her fingers under his arm, as naturally as if they truly were married.

"Let me just tip this man." Fiona removed the bag of coins he'd given her last night and slid one to the man.

Mr. Potter's eyes rounded. "Thank you, missus."

Percival's eyebrows rose a fraction at the woman's liberal distribution of her newfound money.

"Ready to go? Or do you want to stay longer, dear?" Fiona smiled sweetly at him.

He swept his gaze over the faded furniture and sentimental objects. "I will strive to recover from the sadness of leaving this place."

"How very brave of you." Mirth filled her eyes, and her lips spread up.

Percival wished he could put more smiles on her face.

Except that was a ridiculous thought.

Percival's steps were careful as he followed the man down the rickety stairs, and his brow remained furrowed, his mind consumed with unwanted thoughts.

"Is that our sleigh?" Fiona exclaimed. "How marvelous."

Percival followed her gaze. *Zeus on Olympus.*

A bright red sleigh that conjured up thoughts of all things sentimental and romantic sat outside.

The burly chap beamed. "There it is."

"I'll send somebody back with it. We won't be long." She held up her hand and slid into the sleigh. Her hair glistened under the sunlight.

A rosy flush graced her cheeks, and Percival clenched his hands together. No need for her to see them tremble.

Mr. Potter tilted his head. "I figure you need help."

"Nonsense." Percival gritted his teeth and clambered inside, ignoring the sharp pain from his leg. The sleigh was far too small, and he was conscious of the way in which her long skirts brushed against his good leg. His nostrils inhaled that sweet vanilla scent, and he forced his head away rapidly, hoping the warmth rising on his cheeks was not as visible as it felt.

He shouldn't have kissed her last night. He shouldn't have been goaded by the comments of the other men. The thought of reliving that ecstasy invaded his mind, and he should be focused on fleeing her, nothing else.

He sighed. At least he might cause her some discomfit. He pulled her closer to him, enjoying the way in which her green eyes widened and her black lashes swooped up, as if she were truly some innocent chit. "This is not so horrible, dearest."

Mr. Potter waved as they drove off.

"Care to share where we're going?" Percival whispered.

"I live nearby," she said.

"I warrant you're set up in some God-forsaken house."

"Some people might say that." Fiona had the indecency to turn her lips up, as if she didn't recognize his insult.

Percival rubbed his leg. "That blasted floor . . ."

She grabbed the reins from him. "Let me drive."

"No, I—"

"I'll want you nice and refreshed." The woman was matter-of-fact.

"What do you have in store?"

"You'll find out."

He narrowed his eyes. "I demand that you declare your plans."

"That's all?" She smirked, and her green eyes sparkled.

"And release me!" he stammered. "I demand you release me as well."

She laughed. "And leave you on this road? You wouldn't survive very long. You have absolutely no idea where you are."

"I'll have you know that I've traveled throughout the continent!"

"Ah, so has my grandmother."

"Leading troops!" He scowled

Fiona squirmed. She no longer pointed a knife in his direction, and he supposed he could direct the sleigh in whichever direction.

For some reason, he didn't want to, and he despised it. Snowflakes fell more rapidly, a curtain of coldness. They fluttered down in thick, decadent shapes, toppling this way and that, oblivious to the havoc they caused.

"I'm not a thief."

"So you've told me," Percival remarked dryly.

"One year ago I made a mistake." Fiona's voice quivered.

"We've all made mistakes."

"My mistake was telling my grandmother and sister that I was engaged."

"So tell them you're not engaged."

The horses rounded a corner.

And then his mouth dropped open.

A huge castle sat in the valley. Snow covered the sloping roof and turrets, but it was impossible to avoid seeing just how fine the place was. Gargoyles perched underneath the gables, and classically beautiful statues dotted the yard.

Everything was immaculate, and everything differed completely from the abode he'd imagined she'd take him to.

If a criminal lived here, it was not someone who'd made his money robbing travelers. By Zeus, maybe she wanted to steal from the place. Except that seemed unlikely since his leg forced him to be an imperfect accomplice. "What is this place?"

"Cloudbridge Castle." The woman tucked a strand of loose hair over her ear. "I live here."

"As a—maid?"

"Only the unmarried kind."

He tilted his head, and her cheeks pinkened.

"I'm an ordinary spinster."

"Not a criminal."

She shook her head. "I'm not quite as exciting. My name is Miss Fiona Amberly. Perhaps you've heard of my brother-in-law Lord Somerville?"

Percival coughed. "The earl?"

She nodded. "From the Worthing family. His older brother is the Marquess of Highgate."

Percival rubbed his hand in his hair. "So when you said you wanted to kidnap me and bring me somewhere—"

"I wanted to bring you here." The woman spoke matter-of-factly, as if what she was doing was completely obvious and self-explanatory, as if loads of women were in the habit of capturing men and dragging them to their castles.

Percival scratched his head and rather feared that all the intelligence his teachers had praised him for at Harrow and Edinburgh had vanished. Because this—this didn't make sense.

"So this has nothing to do with my position?" Percival spoke slowly.

"Of course it does."

His head swiveled to her.

"You're a gentleman. You'll be very suitable."

He relaxed his shoulders.

"I would be most appreciative if you could tell them that we are betrothed—"

"You want me to pretend to adore you?"

Chapter Eleven

PERCIVAL SCOWLED. "THAT'S the most ridiculous thing I ever heard."

"Please though? Could you pretend you didn't despise me?" Fiona thrust her eyes down, and the pink on her cheeks transformed to a definite red shade. "The story is that we met in London four years ago, two weeks into my season, and you proposed. We decided to keep the engagement secret because you were going to fight Napoleon, and that's the reason I abandoned my season. I called my fiancé Captain Knightley."

He raised his eyebrows. "Like a medieval knight?"

She stiffened. "I suppose."

"Do they expect me to appear on a white horse as well? Just who do you think is good enough to be your impostor fiancé? Are you only after princes? Kings?"

"Please?"

"Find another pretend husband," Percival growled.

He could have escaped, he could have protested, and he'd been too fearful to do so. She wasn't a criminal. She was just a spinster, one too meek to find a husband for herself. And Zeus, she'd barged her way into his most private musings. "I'm not going along with your preposterous plans."

"You won't do it unless I give you a reason?"

"I will never agree!"

She sighed. "I have your jewels."

"Excuse me?"

"The packet... The one you kept touching."

His breath stopped.

"I took them while you were sleeping," Fiona continued.

"So you are a thief."

"I'll give them back to you. *After*."

Percival's hands twisted with the urge to destroy something. Stomping both feet would feel wonderful right about now. He'd met women intent on having him for their fiancés before, but never a woman who wanted him to pretend to be someone else. He wondered whether this was some elaborate scheme for an actual marriage, but the woman seemed completely unaware he was a duke and far more worthy of romantic idealizations than some captain with an absurdly heroic name.

"Please?" Fiona's face took on a mournful expression he abhorred. "It need not be for long. I only want to introduce my Grandmother to you."

"And why didn't you ask me this when you met me?"

"Would you have helped me?"

He sighed. He wouldn't have. He would have laughed and waved her away, leaving her standing on the side of the road. "But pretending to be a highwaywoman—"

"It was an accident." Fiona's thick eyelashes swung down. "The driver assumed I was one, because of my dirty clothes, but really, I was just trying to warn about the tree. I didn't put it there."

"You sure?"

Her voice quieted. "Naturally."

"But I heard gunshots."

"Peasants. Shooting for Christmas dinner."

With effort, Percival swallowed the anger surging through him. He relaxed his shoulders and strove to emulate the nonchalance of a man approaching a country party, and not that of a man discovering some spinster had kidnapped him.

The solution to not having a fiancé was *not* to kidnap an innocent passerby.

Percival crossed his arms. He'd been outwitted. He'd have to face the dowager, have to apologize for arriving late. He'd have to listen to her tell him that her son, the man who would be Duke if he hadn't saved Percival in a moment of insanity, would never have been late like this.

And she would be correct.

Percival exhaled. Loudly. "Is there anything else I should know?"

Fiona shook her head. "The main thing is to keep Grandmother happy. You can speak in moon-like tones about gardening or about setting up some parish somewhere. You needn't mention anything glamorous, and if Lady Mulbourne is here, I'm sure she won't be particularly impressed, but that doesn't matter."

"It seems like just the fact you have a fiancé will be sufficient cause of rejoicing for them," Percival said.

Fiona stiffened.

"And just who is Lady Mulbourne? And what absurd standards does she possess?" Percival normally prided himself on his calm, but normally he wasn't faced with maniac women of means in want of fiancés.

"Oh, she's very important." Fiona nodded. "She's my cousin and she thinks she's in charge of this district, though that's not entirely incorrect. But she's married to a baron. He's of great importance. He's one of the greatest art critics England has ever had. You should read the reflective, thoughtful articles he composes on a range of subjects that would astound you."

Percival scowled. "I see nothing worthy of laudation in a person who devotes himself to the study of inanimate objects."

"Even important objects of cultural significance? Possibly historical significance?"

"There's nothing important about art."

Fiona stiffened. "One favor. A few minutes. Please? And then I'll tell the groom to prepare the coach for you and give you back the jewels. You'll be able to travel to London in far greater style than that mail coach."

"One day later," Percival grumbled.

"Please. If you could be so kind."

Percival raised his eyebrows.

Fiona's face fell. "Forgive me, I was absurd to link 'kind' and 'you' in a single sentence."

"Yes." Percival smiled tightly. "Rather unfortunate for you that I'm not more suitable for your needs. You don't know what kind of uncultured louts lacking gallantry you find in carriages these days. Damned shame."

"Please?"

"I won't be subjected to some strange child's play."

"I'm not a child!" Fiona's voice was outraged.

Good.

"You are worse than a child!" Percival declared. "A child contents herself to demand pretty dresses." He paused to scan her ragged cloak. "You haven't even the sense to ask for the latter."

Percival laughed, or at least attempted to. "So I'd . . . er . . . better get going then. I'll just drive this sleigh back to the inn and get a horse from there to go to London. I don't need your coach."

"But just a few minutes—" A pink tinge lined the woman's cheekbones. "Please."

Her voice quivered, and Percival tightened his fists, as if that gesture alone would be sufficient to tighten his resolve. "You cannot force me. I'll go back to London and—"

"Propose? Won't you need a ring?" Fiona's voice was all innocence.

"I—"

Blast. His shoulders sank. She was right. He needed to do this.

"You bloody bastard," Percival swore, not caring that he was breaching all rules of propriety. "Where the hell is it?"

Fiona blinked. "I hope you don't mean to speak like that in front of my Grandmother."

Percival stiffened and scrunched his fists together. His heart thundered against his chest. He'd begun to care for her; his gaze pulled to hers with too much frequency, as if she were the bloody sun.

But she was not a highwaywoman, not desperate in the traditional sense, not in the least. The manor house enlarged as the horses trotted on, oblivious to the tumult in the sleigh. The façade was more intricate and the statues more sophisticated than even his family's original estate, had dear old Bernard not died and left him a whole dukedom.

She was a wallflower. Even after they'd kissed, after the world had tilted and swirled and it took everything in him to pretend that nothing between them had actually changed after their lips touched, she hadn't confided in him. She'd stayed up in the night instead and stolen his jewels, proving that the dowager was right, and he wasn't a man anymore. He couldn't protect a tiny packet from a chit.

"Look." Fiona swallowed hard. "You pose as my fiancé, and I'll give you your ring and those other jewels back. Just introduce yourself to my grandmother as Captain Knightley and say you've been away at war and that you're looking forward to our impending marriage."

"I hope you haven't arranged that already, too," Percival grumbled.

"Of course not," Fiona exclaimed. "But if she asks, say we'll need to delay our wedding. Maybe you can make another excuse?" She tilted her head. "I suppose you don't think it's likely that Bonaparte will make his escape from St. Helena?"

Percival narrowed his eyes. "No."

She sighed, and he tapped his fingers against the edge of the sleigh. Finally, he smiled. He was practiced at smiling after all. He excelled at turning his lips up when greeting pompous people, and on feigning a pleasant demeanor even when his leg ached from standing. When one smiled long enough, eventually one was even prone to believing the veracity of one's joyous demeanor. "Very well."

Fiona exhaled in obvious relief. The sleigh neared the manor house. She glanced to him, her forehead crinkling. Clearly the woman was more discerning than he'd given her credit for. "Most people would be complimenting the stone facade and the fountains now."

Fiona pulled the horses before the entrance, and Percival staggered from the sleigh and offered his hand to her. In the old days he might have given her a bow, but at the moment he felt sufficiently courteous. His other arm rested firmly on the side of the sleigh. "Let me escort you, my betrothed."

She hurried from the sleigh, decidedly not grasping his hand. "I'm not asking you to be my fiancé for any personal reasons."

Of course she wouldn't really want him. His leg was ruined. He forced his mind from lingering on searing lips, a gentle touch, and soft, luscious curves.

He abhorred her. Utterly and completely.

He followed her gaze to the manor house. A stout, stone fish with well-defined carved scales and speckled with spots of green discoloration squatted in the center of an icy sheet. His head—Percival didn't want to ascribe such an unattractive appearance to a female fish—was directed upward to the grey, cloudy sky. One could almost imagine water spurting from the thick lips of the statue's mouth.

"It is perhaps more stunning in the summer," Fiona said.

"It's divine." *A house like that was sure to be filled with people.*

Chapter Twelve

SERVANTS PEEKED FROM the windows with their heads tilted and their eyebrows raised, and Fiona's heart sped. Sweat prickled the back of her neck, and though she'd kidnapped him for just this moment, fear spread through her.

Percival stumbled beside her, and a strange gleam shone in his eyes, seeming to grow stronger with each step toward Cloudbridge Castle.

Goodness. What in heaven's name had she done?

"Don't attempt anything," she murmured through gritted teeth.

He answered her with a laugh, a low relaxed rumble the man was probably accustomed to emitting in smoky clubs filled with copious supplies of brandy.

Drat.

She needed to speak to Grandmother before this man entered. She hurried forward. Or as fast as one could dash while still attempting to maintain a portion of one's dignity, conscious of various curtains being drawn back in the house. The maids were cleaning, and clearly her late appearance was of greater interest than poking about sooty fireplaces.

She hitched her dress up an inch and proceeded faster. Her cloak billowed in the wind, and strands of hair were flung against her face. Her boots crunched against the sheets of snow that sparkled from the dim sunlight. The servants had attempted to shovel some of the lane, but it was a large job, and she skidded and swerved over icy patches.

Until she fell.

The world veered downward, and her nose squashed against the snowy surface. She pushed her hands against the snow and forced herself up, striving to maintain some semblance of dignity as the wind whirled about her coat and dress.

"I trust you're uninjured?" Percival shot her a cocky grin. His steady pace, even hampered by his injury, placed him at the entrance to the manor house.

The man grasped the cast-iron door knocker and pounded on the bright red door that never quite matched the mourning Grandmother had thrown herself into.

He was not going to speak with the servants before her.

Who knew what story he would tell them.

Like the right one. The pit in her stomach hollowed, and she was only a few paces behind him when the door opened.

Not to a servant.

Grandmother.

Her knees quivered, and it was only focusing on the door that kept her moving forward, because certainly Fiona's natural inclination was to topple forward and pray for the earth to swallow her.

Grandmother peeked her grey head out, and Fiona knew without a doubt that she had seen everything. Fiona was with a man, all alone. Fiona had traveled with him by herself. If she were the type of woman who believed in being ruined, Fiona would have been devastated, though right now she only desired Grandmother to believe her story.

"You must be Captain Knightley." Grandmother extended her hand toward him.

Percival paused.

"You can take her hand, my dear!" Fiona forced a laugh. "He's a bit shy, Grandmother. I should have said."

"I—" Percival swung his head around and glared at her.

"Oh, that's quite alright." Grandmother tilted her head. "My Fiona is very shy too. As you no doubt know well."

A vein throbbed from Percival's temple. "I would not have used that term to describe her."

"My dear, you must come in. It won't do to have you shiver in the English winter, as nonexistent as some people claim it to be."

Percival brushed past Fiona's grandmother. "England isn't supposed to have a winter. It's supposed to be blustery and sometimes damp. That's all."

"My dear Captain Knightley." Grandmother smiled fondly at the man. "How much shock it must be for you now to return to your home country after so many years of fighting."

"You mustn't call me that. I'm just a man who—"

"Adores my niece." Grandmother's smile widened. "You are much too humble, my dear. I can call you that, can't I? I feel you are like family to me. I have heard so much about you."

"I have not heard anything about you—"

"—that has not been pleasant." Fiona hastened to the man's side and then halted. It felt too natural to stand beside him, and she had a strange urge to stand even closer to him, as if her body missed his. She frowned. The sleigh had been too tight.

Percival opened his mouth. "I am afraid that this woman captured me!"

Fiona froze. She steeled herself for Grandmother's reaction, and Percival gave her a smug look, not befitting a man whose jewels she had stolen.

"She held me up at gunpoint and demanded I be her fiancé."

Grandmother tilted her head and smiled. "True love is rather like that. I do envy you both."

"She captured me! Completely against my will!"

Grandmother laughed, though Fiona did not join her.

"One doesn't know when love will strike." Grandmother leaned closer. "But when it strikes hard, when it is so strong, it bodes well for your future. Too many people settle for simple, mutual non-hatred. Even hatred can be more of an indication of true passion."

"But—" Percival's face reddened, not as if the extra color could decrease from the man's handsomeness. He glanced at the butler, and Fiona hastened to slip her hand underneath his arm. *Blast convention.*

"My fiancé finds amusement in jesting about the force of our passion. I'm sure he was about to demand you call the magistrate and notify the local gentry." Fiona tilted her head up at Percival's ever more bemused countenance.

"You take the words out of my mouth," Percival said stiffly.

"My darling." Fiona allowed herself to rest her face against Percival's chest. The woolen fabric of his great coat scratched against her cheek, but her cursed heartbeat still quickened.

Percival tensed against her, but thank goodness, the man didn't push her away. She ignored the sudden warmth that soared through her with inexplicable force.

Though that was absurd. It was Grandmother's scrutiny that brought on her excitement. Nothing else.

Obviously.

Evans' countenance appeared less stern than normal, and she remembered that the butler was himself married to the housekeeper in a match so well-suited that it had produced seven children, despite the discouragement of household staff to create families.

"Where's your sister?" Grandmother inquired.

"She's . . . er . . . still at her estate." She stretched her lips into a wide smile, even though there wasn't anything pleasant about this moment. She resolved to send Rosamund a note at once and inhaled. "Forgive me, I know that it was improper to ride without a chaperone—"

Grandmother waved her hand, and Fiona noticed that her appearance was slightly more frazzled than customary. Her makeup was unevenly applied, as if her grandmother had seen fit to do some touch-ups herself.

"The mail coach was waylaid." Percival scowled.

"I'm sorry!" Fiona squeaked to Grandmother, conscious of Percival's arched eyebrow and his steely eyes fixed on her.

"You mustn't worry, my darling. I'm so happy to see you. And to meet your captain." Grandmother laughed and peered closer to Percival. "Your appearance is quite extraordinary. Most aristocratic. Has anyone told you that you look just like the old Duke of Alfriston? He was quite a handsome fellow in his time. Dead now. And his son after him. So tragic."

Percival stiffened, and Fiona tilted her head. She hadn't wanted to know anything about Percival, but suddenly she regretted it.

"The straightness of your nose and that shade of blue in your eyes... And your chin, such a perfect shape. It is quite extraordinary to find all those features in one person, so much younger than the duke. Perhaps he is one of your ancestors."

Percival opened his mouth, and Fiona stammered. "Most curious. Unfortunately, my darling fiancé will need to leave very soon. But you can see that we are engaged and happy."

She avoided directing her gaze anywhere in the direction of Percival.

"Yes." Percival nodded with such vigor that people might have termed the gesture frantic. "I would not want to encroach upon your hospitality."

"Impossible." Grandmother shook her head. "Your cousin's Christmas Ball is in two days, and my niece must have an escort."

"But!" Fiona's voice trembled, and she shot a glance at the butler who seemed amused by the unaccustomed appearance of a stranger.

"The dear captain will be able to escort me to events for the rest of our lives."

"Starting today!" Grandmother nodded firmly and turned to Percival, who was definitely scowling now. "You would not believe how much my poor granddaughter missed you. Locking herself up all day long in her work room."

"Oh?" Percival's cool, impersonal question caused the back of Fiona's neck to prickle.

"I will not let you venture out in this dreadful weather. I forbid it."

Percival sighed. "But I am afraid the weather will become more dreadful—"

"En route." Grandmother shook her head. "Just when you don't want it to become worse. That's why I favor staying inside. Unless you are willing to risk your good health when you have just arrived from the devastation of battle." She flickered her gaze to his wooden leg, "In order to abandon my granddaughter—"

"Of course he wasn't!" Fiona cut in, forcing a laugh, and ignored the manner in which Percival's jaw tensed, and his scowl deepened. "My fiancé has a dreadful sense of humor."

"Clearly he makes up for it in other respects," Evans said slowly, his gaze scanning Percival.

"Indeed, Evans. Please have the maids prepare the Green Room." Grandmother seemed to be amused. "Let us have tea now."

They strode to the drawing room, and Percival settled stiffly into an armchair. He crossed both arms around him and glared at the furniture of the room with a vigor unsuited to a fiancé.

Fiona's throat dried. "I'm afraid my darling captain is exhausted."

"The Green Room is in the old men's quarter, even though we seldom have male guests now. Some of my brother's old hunting trophies are there. Men have expressed fondness for that." Grandmother paused, and a lascivious grin Fiona rarely saw spread over her face.

"Fiona's room is located on the first door on the right of the women's corridor."

"Grandmother!" Fiona straightened her back, and refused to make eye contact with Percival, though she was conscious of the melodic, low-pitched sound of his laugh. "Captain Knightley will not require any directions."

"Forgive me!" Grandmother said, and Fiona inhaled, even though she could not bring herself to glance at the gentleman. "I forgot that you were a captain. You are probably talented at finding your own way about things. Fiona was telling me that you'd led troops into Russia."

"And the maps there are very difficult to read," Percival said gravely. "They even use a different alphabet."

Grandmother nodded. "You hear that, Fiona? He is impressive."

"I'm sure the captain was able to make use of translated maps!"

"My beautiful fiancée is correct." The captain smiled, and Fiona's heart fluttered despite herself. "Though I confess that I do speak Russian."

"So you could have used one of their maps," Grandmother breathed. "Well done. And how on earth did you learn it?"

"The captain does not need to outline his entire life experience."

"Of course not. It is seldom one comes across a person with such extensive knowledge of the world, and I am confident it would take longer than I have to live to hear all of it."

Percival dotted Fiona a confused glance, and her shoulders shrank together. She hadn't told Percival about her grandmother's illness, hadn't mentioned the ever steadier stream of doctors, and the bowls of blood for the servants to wash, after they'd drained her grandmother yet again, to yet again no avail.

Grandmother seemed more alert than Fiona had seen her for years, and though the fact made Fiona happy, she felt sad that it was all for a lie. Grandmother had reassured her that she needn't worry about leaving the season without a husband, but once Fiona had brought a man back who promised to be a husband, she seemed overjoyed.

Percival cleared his throat. "I am of course happy to oblige you on anything that might bring you pleasure."

Grandmother smiled, and Percival glanced at Fiona.

"Within reason of course." He tapped his finger against the arm of the armchair, tracing the bold blue and white striped pattern.

She wasn't sure which words the man would say next. He seemed to have an uncanny ability to know just what to say to charm her grandmother. The horrible thing was she had a dreadful suspicion that he was charming her as well.

And that couldn't happen.

Because the man before her might be flesh and blood, but his presence was invented more from her desperate imagination than anything else.

Fiona's nose crinkled. "My dear captain, don't you have another battle to get to?"

"I am on Christmas leave, my darling," the man said. "And we've conquered our worst enemy."

Fiona sipped some tea. The water was too hot, and the liquid burned her throat as she forced it down. "But didn't you mention to me that you were getting sick? Sudden, unexplainable nausea?"

"No," Percival said simply. He turned to Grandmother. "What beautiful paintings you have."

Grandmother's cheeks pinkened, and soon she and the imposter captain had entered into a discussion on art, and the overwhelming sadness that the war had closed off much of the continent, so people had had to make do with visiting Cornwall instead of the Mediterranean, which had historic landmarks in addition to a pleasing natural light.

"One day the captain and you will visit Italy together," Grandmother declared.

Fiona swallowed down more hot tea. The two spoke so naturally, as if—as if the man were her real fiancé, and as if he were really interested in everything about her. Right now her grandmother was regaling him with stories of holidays with Fiona and her sister, Rosamund, to the south coast.

"I wish I could have joined," the man said.

Fiona sputtered and coughed. He played the role of her fiancé too well.

"Oh my poor girl!" Grandmother looked at her as if Fiona, and not her grandmother, were at death's door. "Perhaps it is good if you rest."

Percival rose and nodded. "If I may retire as well..."

"Of course." Grandmother smiled.

"You are an extraordinarily understanding woman," the captain said.

"You flatter me," Grandmother said. "Though I am sure that any good qualities I might have are already known to you, reflected by my brilliant granddaughter."

The captain smiled at her, and Fiona's cheeks flamed.

"Your fiancé is quite charming, my dear."

Fiona nodded, and her throat dried. "I am pleased you should find him so."

PERCIVAL WAS NOT AMUSED.

He was many things: furious, angry, frustrated... but no, decidedly not amused.

His annoyance had started once he'd met the blasted woman, and it had not halted after, though it had grown to anger many times.

It didn't matter that the butler had led him into a decent sort of room, with olive green velvet curtains and maple furniture. It didn't matter that a fire was leaping and swirling in the medieval stone fireplace, as if Fiona's grandmother had ordered a servant to light it at the first sighting of him struggling through the blasted snow.

The two women were probably conspiring together.

He needed to get to London. The dowager was depending on him. He turned to the butler, who was obsequiously pulling out all the spare blankets. "Look here, Evans."

"Sir." The man paused, holding onto a fuzzy red woolen blanket that looked damned tempting.

"I need to get to London. At once."

The butler smiled politely.

"Please prepare a horse for me." Percival glowered at the man.

"Her ladyship was clear that your presence is requested elsewhere." Evans continued placing the blankets on the bed.

"This is all a great mistake. I was captured. I never intended for this to happen."

Evans tilted his head. "There is no allowing for when Cupid's arrow strikes."

"Then Cupid was wielding a knife!" Percival muttered.

"Sir?" Evan's lifted his grey eyebrows.

Percival shook his head. "Nothing. Cupid has not struck me."

"And yet you're about to be married." Evans tilted his head, and Percival groaned. He slid into an armchair.

He tilted his head. He should correct the man. He wasn't a sir. He was—well, he was Your Grace. Which had more of a ring to it, one he wasn't yet fully accustomed to hearing.

And at this rate one that he would completely forget about.

He scrunched his eyebrows together. But even though he did rather want to emphasize his title and intimidate the man into arranging a horse for him, he didn't really want it to be known that the

Duke of Alfriston had managed to get himself captured by some chit claiming to be a highwaywoman.

That was definitely gossip fodder. But blast it, he needed to get to London. He swung his head in the direction of the outdoors.

The sky had grown grayer, and though he had a wild moment of hope that the heavens might open up with some very English rain, washing every last flake of snow away, it was really far more likely—far more his luck—that it would snow more.

His shoulders sank. His luck had left him long ago. He was stuck here. "I don't suppose I can send a message?"

"Why of course."

"Of course?" Percival tilted his head at the butler. His esteem of the man had ratcheted up abruptly, and he now considered how he'd ever managed to not see the man's definite intelligence and decency.

"Naturally if you require to get in touch with somebody, we could of course arrange to send a message—"

"Good God, Evans, you're a miracle worker!" Percival grinned wide. "Has anyone told you you're bloody amazing?"

"Her ladyship has been effusive on various occasions, and Fiona's kindness is of course well known among the staff—"

Percival waved his hand dismissively. "I don't need you to number her accomplishments."

"Ah, I see!" Evans gave him a knowing glance. "You clearly are already familiar with her outstanding qualities."

"Er . . . yes." Percival tried to smile at the man. Something seemed to twinge inside him, and he shoved the thought away. It would be good to be rid of this place, and with Evan's help in sending a trusty note, that should be soon. "Anyway, I should find some paper."

Evans nodded. "I'll fetch some. Fiona always has plenty."

"Ah, I wager she's a letter writer."

Everything appeared much rosier. Even the bed started to look tempting, despite or perhaps because of the piles of blankets.

Evans tilted his head. "I suppose she sent letters to you when she was in town."

"Ah, yes." He shuddered.

Evans narrowed his eyes at him, and he forced himself to smile. Mustn't make the man suspicious.

He had a plan now.

He tapped his fingers against the cherry desk. Evans disappeared down the hallway, but he soon reappeared with some paper.

Percival raised his eyebrows when he spotted that Evans' black jacket was speckled with dirt. He didn't want to ponder what sort of mess Fiona's work room must be in. The less he knew about the mysteries of Cloudbridge Castle, the better.

He flexed his fingers and wrote a quick note to the dowager. Writing the words down was every bit as embarrassing as he'd anticipated. He told her there was no need for her to exert her full force, but he would very much appreciate it if a carriage could be sent for him. People shouldn't be allowed to kidnap others. In fact, he was pretty sure they weren't allowed to do so, and by Christmas-time he hoped to be celebrating with his new family and perhaps even his new betrothed.

Soon all of this would be a distant memory.

Chapter Thirteen

THE WILD RUSH OF TRIUMPH she'd expected didn't appear. Grandmother was happy, and that was wonderful, but it was only more indication that Fiona had failed before in making her happy.

She sighed. How she felt didn't matter. It only mattered how her Grandmother felt, which was, fortunately, better.

After retiring for a bath and nap, the latter of which she devoted more to worrying than sleeping, Fiona was contemplating whether she might do some archaeology after all, when a knock sounded on the door.

Percival.

She rushed to answer it, barreling over the cold wooden beams as she threw on her nicest robe and smoothed her hair frantically. She cursed that Grandmother had revealed the location of her room to Percival, but when she swung the door open, it was only Maggie, one of the maids.

Warmth prickled the back of her neck and furled over her face.

"Miss Fiona..." Maggie bent her stout body in a brief curtsy, evidently flummoxed to find Fiona personally opening the door. Her bird-eye gaze flickered over Fiona's no-doubt flushed cheeks, and Fiona was conscious of her quickened breath.

Maggie had been a maid in the house for as long as Fiona remembered, and running in her room was not a general pastime for Fiona.

"I'm not sure if today is the best to help with the archaeology," Fiona said.

Maggie shook her head. "Mrs. Amberly told me I should help you with dressing."

"Oh." Fiona widened her eyes.

"She also said it was fine with her if you wore one of your dresses from the other side of the wardrobe."

Fiona must have appeared puzzled, for Maggie shifted her legs and fixed her gaze on the wardrobe, not meeting her eyes. "The side with the colors. I think she thought that you might be more adventuresome on account of your captain."

"Oh." Fiona settled onto her bed as Maggie slid the wardrobe door open, pulling out colorful dresses Fiona had not worn since her parents' deaths. "I'm not sure..."

"It's been several years," Maggie said gently, and Fiona nodded.

She was right.

Four years ago her parents had died when rushing home for Christmas, to celebrate Fiona's favorite holiday.

Perhaps the coach always would have crashed into that boulder, but it was all too easy to imagine her father's forceful voice in encouraging the driver to hasten, even though it was dark, even though the coach only had a hanging lantern to depend on.

She swallowed hard. When she'd briefly had her season, she'd worn the frilly, vibrant dresses the occasion required, retreating back to half-mourning only later.

The grey dresses, sometimes tinged with lavender, had seemed comforting. If she retreated from the world of fashion, she could not be subjected to the whispers and gossip of others when her bow failed to be the correct width and her hat clashed with her hair.

"I'm not sure." She bit her lip.

Maggie pulled out various dresses, laying them over the bed. Blue and green gowns draped over the plain sheets like jewels. "Mrs. Amberly said that you might be reluctant, but that I was to insist."

"I see." She brushed her hand over glossy fabric. "I suppose I could..."

"Good," Maggie said matter-of-factly, sweeping up the dress Fiona had touched. "You can wear this."

Fiona's gaze flickered to silky green ribbons and puffed sleeves.

"You'll look wonderful," Maggie said encouragingly. "And green is very suitable for Christmas. Mrs. Amberly also said Sir Seymour and Lady Lavinia are coming for dinner with their son."

"Cecil!" Fiona's heart thundered, and she tore her hand through her still damp hair.

Maggie nodded, her eyes narrowed. "She said it was good your fiancé will be able to meet some of your family. She was under the impression that he might not be here for long."

"I see," Fiona said, though in truth, meeting her extended family was unpleasant enough without having a man reluctantly playing her fiancé to contend with.

She acceded to Maggie's attentions, as the servant struggled to summon up how best to arrange Fiona's hair.

"Now your sister used to prefer to sweep her hair up, but with your lovely locks, I think it might be nice to display your hair more."

Fiona scrunched her eyebrows together. Her locks weren't lovely.

Maggie pursed her lips, twisting and pinning her hair.

"Can I see?"

"When you're dressed." The maid picked up the vibrant dress and assisted Fiona into it, fussing over the clasps and folds, and then painting Fiona's face.

Finally, Maggie beamed. "All set."

Firm hands guided Fiona to the gilded mirror, and she prepared herself for the worst. She would look absurd. A crow forced to adorn itself with the feathers of a peacock. Outrageous.

And yet—

She didn't appear outlandish. There was nothing ludicrous about her appearance. In fact, it even appeared . . . appealing.

The emerald fabric of the dress enhanced the green of her eyes and complemented her auburn hair. Her normal grey clothes had cast a sickly pallor over her face, and her freckled skin had seemed garish against her somber outfit. But now her freckles only magnified her brilliant coloring. She lifted a hand to her hair, brushing her finger against a carefully arranged curl.

"I didn't think I could look like this."

"You never tried," Maggie said. "You look lovely."

Fiona dropped her gaze to her dress. The glossy fabric gleamed in the mirror, and curves that she had thought made her body appear bulky looked elegant.

"Thank you." Fiona smiled at the mirror, still awe-struck by her appearance.

"Now go see your young, handsome captain."

Fiona hurried downstairs.

No good risking leaving Percival wandering the castle. When she reached the drawing room, Percival was reclining in an armchair.

Goodness, he was handsome. He was everything anybody had ever dreamed of. He'd looked nicer than she cared to dwell on before, but now that he was not swathed in a great coat, nor displaying his stained cravat and clothes, the man was magnificent. Evans had evidently laid out clothes for him, and he was attired in silk and velvet. The clothes might be out of fashion, just like her dress, but that didn't stop the gold in the buttons from accentuating the gold in his hair, and it didn't stop the blue of the jacket from setting off the blue of his eyes.

His gaze flickered over her, and for a moment a satisfactory feeling rushed through her, though the man's eyes soon clouded, and he fixed a haughty smile she distrusted.

"I trust the accommodations are tolerable?" Her words were stiff and overly formal, more suitable to a conversation with her uncle than to a man she'd spent the past twenty-four hours with.

He inclined his head in a polite gesture. "Indeed."

The smirk did not disappear from his face, as if he knew something she did not.

Fiona fixed a fierce stare in his direction, though her furious glaring could not remove the manner in which the attractive planes of his face had arranged themselves into a smug expression. "What are you thinking?"

Percival's shoulders rose and dropped in a nonchalant fashion. His lips smirked, as if he found her distress amusing. The candlelight shimmered over him, sheathing him in a golden light. "Just enjoying the castle."

"Good," Fiona said uncertainly.

She'd expected the man to tell her he wanted to leave again, but he seemed content to lounge in the armchair.

Well. That was good, wasn't it?

Fiona swung her gaze, but no one was in the hallway. Grandmother was not a very vigilant chaperone.

"My . . . er . . . family is coming for dinner tonight."

"Your parents?" His words were casual, and she stiffened.

Her heart raced, and she dropped into the armchair opposite.

The smug expression on his face vanished immediately, replaced by something resembling worry. Percival's eyes were wide, and he leaned forward. "What's wrong?"

"They're dead," she said.

"Oh." He leaned back, and his expression sobered. "I'm sorry."

She forced herself to laugh. "You didn't know. It happened a while back."

"Both of them?"

She shifted her legs, tucking them under her chair, and smoothed her dress. The dark green fabric seemed fanciful, the forest color matching the greenery excessively. The satin ribbons gleamed, the bows were too festive, the cut too daring.

She missed her predictable grey gowns that honored her parents.

"Forgive me." Percival's velvety voice was deep and reassuring.

She lifted her gaze.

The man's blue eyes had darkened, and she squirmed under the intensity of his expression.

Her eyelashes fluttered down. It had happened so long ago, and it should have stopped being painful, but it wasn't. Her parents had died, and it was all her fault. Their coach had been driving too quickly, bounding into a boulder that shouldn't have been there, but which the driver would have seen if he hadn't been hastening.

She'd loved Christmas, and her parents had known it. Even though not everyone celebrated the holiday, she'd loved the scent of yule logs, loved the music of the wassailers, even when their voices were imperfect, and she'd loved the mistletoe and holly dangling from every archway in the castle.

"It was a coach crash," she said. "It happens all the time. A boulder was in the road, and that's all it took."

She felt his eyes resting on her and looked up.

"You said a tree was blocking the road yesterday." Percival's face was paler than before, not that it hampered the man's handsomeness.

"Yes."

"You really did just stop the coach to warn us," Percival said.

Fiona nodded. "I was surprised when your driver pointed a musket at me."

"I see." Percival shifted his lanky leg and rubbed his hand along the other one.

The thin material of his pantaloons gleamed under the flames from the red candles that sparkled from rod-iron chandeliers and sconces. The light accentuated his powerful thighs, until the material became loose at one of his knees, and a wooden leg poked from the bottom of his pantaloons.

"I shouldn't have pretended to be a highwaywoman," Fiona said, keeping her voice low. "I panicked when I saw the coach-driver's musket, and when the shots from the peasants fired, I took advantage of the situation. I wanted the driver's help in moving the tree. I thought I could explain everything to you in the coach, but when he disappeared, I panicked."

"I'm sorry." Percival's eyes softened, but then he cleared his throat. "Who's coming to dinner?"

"My Aunt Lavinia and Uncle Seymour. He's a baronet and acts like he owns the home. I suppose once Grandmother dies, he will."

"She's very sick?"

"Yes." Fiona said, unsettled by the tenderness in Percival's voice, and the manner in which his blue eyes rounded, as if he were concerned.

Sometimes it was all too easy to believe he really was her fiancé. Underneath all the man's bluster, he was sweet and gentle. She'd been willing to assign every bad quality of the *ton* to him. His concern for her was real. He understood her. And goodness, perhaps she understood him.

Just because a man possessed aristocratic features did not mean he didn't care about others. Percival had suffered. He'd lost his cousin and his leg. He could easily be wallowing at whatever apartment or estate he lived at, but instead he was independent. He traveled by himself, while Fiona, who had the advantage of excellent health, was too timid.

He was vivacious, easily charming Grandmother. Though Fiona found his symmetrical, sturdy features more fascinating than she cared to admit, it was the man's other qualities that most enchanted her.

A pang of sadness thrummed through her, and she shifted in her seat, as if the action might diminish the realization that Percival would never be her fiancé, and if this action was discovered, no man would ever be.

She straightened her shoulders, and strove to smile, no matter how foreign the gesture felt on her face. "Tell me about your fiancée."

Percival pulled his leg back, and his demeanor grew more formal. "She has a high reputation."

"Marvelous," Fiona chirped, sending him another wide smile that she didn't feel in the slightest. "How brilliant for you."

"Er . . . yes."

"And I imagine her hair is not red and curly."

"It is blonde and straight." Percival tilted his head, and she averted her eyes from his gaze.

"Like silk!" Fiona clapped her hands. "That's the best kind."

"So people say."

"They're right."

She tried to reflect on something else besides the copious charms of Mrs. Percival-to-be.

"I haven't actually met her," Percival said.

Fiona's eyelashes swooped up.

Carriage wheels scraped against the snow outside, and Fiona groaned. This was too soon. Far too soon.

Fiona's heartbeat quickened. She jumped to her feet and smoothed her dress frantically.

"You look beautiful," Percival said.

"Oh." She dropped her hand and stared at him. A faint tinge pinkened his cheekbones, as if he'd shared rather more than he'd intended, but he did not break his gaze from hers. His jaw was steady, and he nodded. "Green suits you."

"Thank you." Her voice wobbled, and her chest felt far too tight.

Percival gripped his cane and rose to his feet. "Now tell me, what should I do if they recognize me?"

"Why would they recognize you?"

He looked at her strangely. "They're members of the *ton*."

"But so are ten thousand other people. And you're from Sussex, and they live in Yorkshire. And you've been fighting in the Napoleonic Wars." She laughed. "Uncle Seymour has definitely not been doing that."

"Fiona..." A vein on Percival's temple throbbed. "I am a duke."

"Really?"

"I told you." Percival threw his arms up in an exasperated gesture. "I told you last night. I'm the Duke of Alfriston."

"But—" Fiona swallowed hard. "I didn't believe you. I thought that was just something you said to avoid being captured."

"I told you the truth."

"Oh." Fiona wound her arms together, holding them in front of her stomach. The hollow pit feeling spread.

Purposeful steps sounded outside the door.

She whirled around. "Do you know him?"

"I—"

"Do you?"

Percival's gaze softened. "No, I don't."

Fiona gave a curt nod and then scurried toward the entrance. She picked up her skirt a fraction of an inch as she sped to the entrance, slowing only when she reached the bottom.

The front door was open. Cold air swept into the room, and dead leaves fluttered into the hallway. Percival followed her into the room. He strode toward her until her dress brushed against him.

Her heartbeat raced. His broad shoulders provided a support she had not known she needed, and she longed to lean into him. The touch of his lips against hers was still not forgotten.

She smiled at Grandmother when she appeared in the room and wished that the contented smile Grandmother cast at Percival and her could be a reason that shouldn't be relegated to fantasy.

Uncle Seymour entered the room. Snow clung to his boots, and melting ice splattered onto the floor.

Fiona bobbed down in a deep curtsy. The man was her uncle, but it always seemed particularly trying to show the man the respect his age and supposed worldliness would expect.

"Fiona. You appear just the same. Is that an old dress?"

She smiled. Clearly the man hadn't remembered she'd been in half-mourning these past years. "You look well."

"Ah, yes. That's because I look after myself. Keeping up with the latest fashion and everything. The *ton* in London rather demand one take an interest in those things." Uncle Seymour offered Fiona a polite smile. "But you wouldn't know about that, would you my dear?"

The smile on Fiona's face faltered, and she shivered. A warm hand and a scent she was already becoming way too fond of pressed against her. Fiona slammed her lips together. The temptation to lean back into sturdy muscles, to pull firm arms around her, startled her.

For a moment Fiona imagined that Percival was traveling about the Dales with her, the temperature no longer freezing, with vibrant blossoms and butterflies to accompany them.

The sound of Uncle Seymour clearing his throat hastened her back from the idyllic, absolutely impossible image of her and Percival enjoying life together.

"Who is this?" Uncle Seymour raised his eyebrows even higher than they'd been previously, and his eyes narrowed more than Fiona was accustomed to.

"That, my dear brother," Grandmother announced, "Is Fiona's fiancé, Captain Knightley."

Percival strode forward. Even in the out-of-fashion dinner attire Evans had found for him, the man was magnificent. He bowed. "I'm ever so delighted to meet you, my lord."

"Oh!" Uncle Seymour straightened. His hand flew to his cravat knot, and he shifted his feet, gazing anxiously in the direction of the open door. "My dear wife! Fiona has a *fiancé*!"

Chapter Fourteen

AUNT LAVINIA AND COUSIN Cecil sauntered into the castle and came to an abrupt halt as they took in Fiona and the narrow distance between Percival and her.

"My dear girl." Aunt Lavinia blinked, and her thin hand clutched her heart. She seemed dazed as one of the servants assisted her with removing her cloak. The ruffles on her dress and jewels seemed to overwhelm her bony figure, and her gaze remained fixed on Fiona.

Fiona curtsied.

She'd dreamed about a moment like this, and the expressions on her relatives faces clearly showed they thought they might be living in a dream.

Uncle Seymour and Aunt Lavinia had hinted at a marriage with Cecil frequently, despite the fact that Cecil had never shown any interest in her.

Cecil clutched a bouquet and lowered the bright flowers over his short, rotund body, a testament to his cook's good skills. "I . . . er . . . brought these for you." He glanced at his mother, whose eyes remained wide. He swung his arm to Grandmother. "I meant . . . er . . . you."

"That gentleman is Fiona's fiancé," Grandmother said happily. She pushed her nose into the flowers. "Divine."

Cecil gave her an awkward bow.

"I'm so happy you managed to pull yourself from London," Grandmother said.

Cecil's smile faltered, as if he did not share her happiness.

Fiona stifled an urge to laugh. She had nothing against her cousin, but Madeline had confided in her once that Cecil had a habit of frequenting the most adventurous brothels, the kind known to cater to sodomites.

Fiona hadn't asked her cousin just how she'd garnered this information, but it had rather quelled any impulse to link her life with Cecil's in anything more than the occasional family gathering.

After the requisite small talk, each painful word lessened only by the continued startled glances her aunt, uncle and cousin flickered at Percival, the dinner bell gonged.

They entered the dining room, and a now-familiar heat surged through Fiona when Percival offered his arm to Fiona, gathering force when she pressed her hand against the crook of the man's arm. They strode to the dining room and settled into their seats.

The room was silent, except for the sound of the footman pouring soup into gold-rimmed china bowls. The thick white soup sloshed inside the bowls, visible from Fiona's chair, and a clink sounded when he placed the bowls on the silver platter.

Candle lights flickered from cast-iron sconces, flinging long shadows over the room. Garlands draped from the ceilings, tied with red and gold ribbons. They hung over the swords some ancestor had thought it good to display on the wood-paneled wall. Tonight it was particularly easy to imagine the destruction and terror these weapons must have called when used by some war-minded knight.

Uncle Seymour glanced at the dark beams that crossed over the ceiling. "What this house needs is some redecorating. Less of this medieval nonsense."

Fiona stiffened. She adored this room and all the history within. The house would go to Uncle Seymour when Grandmother died, but that hardly meant he needed to openly discuss the changes. "I find much about the past of interest."

"My niece is prone to lauding the delights of rolling around in dirt." Uncle Seymour directed his gaze toward Percival, chortling.

The footman placed the soup before them.

Fiona's hands tightened over the lace tablecloth, feeling Percival's gaze rest over her. "Archaeology is not rolling around in dirt."

"Why don't you leave the things in the ground be?" Uncle Seymour clutched a spoon in hand and then dipped it into the soup. "Seems rather ghoulish to pore over the once-used pottery of dead people."

Percival cleared his throat, managing to make the simple sound menacing.

Aunt Lavinia fluttered her hands and nodded to Grandmother. "This is delicious. You have a talented cook."

"I have a talented granddaughter as well," Fiona's grandmother said, raising her chin. "I find her idea that there's a Roman palace buried under the apple orchard fascinating."

"Because it's insane." Uncle Seymour took a hearty slurp of wine.

"There's a rumor there's one near Chichester as well." Percival tore a piece of bread and slathered it in butter.

Fiona's eyebrows darted up, and Percival smiled. Warmth bounded through her chest, and she forced herself to avert her eyes.

"Hmph!" Uncle Seymour muttered. "Still doesn't change her macabre tendencies."

Fiona squared her shoulders. "I feel, Uncle Seymour, that there is value in learning about the world and about the past."

"I feel there's value in drinking red wine." Uncle Seymour shrugged and addressed a footman. "Please, fill the glass up."

The servant dashed over to Uncle Seymour's side, appearing rattled that Uncle Seymour had had to ask.

"I mean how does one get interested in a thing like that?" Aunt Lavinia smiled, even though there was nothing delightful about the manner of her lips' ascent. "There is much in this world to explore. One need not go searching four feet underground."

"Sometimes more," Fiona murmured, and her uncle tilted his head at her.

"I find it most enlightening," Grandmother said.

"I had enough of learning at Eton." Uncle Seymour slurped down the rest of his soup.

A footman removed Uncle Seymour's bowl and proceeded around the table.

Percival cleared his throat. "Tell us more about your plans for the apple orchard."

"I'm glad she hasn't bored you with the plans already," Uncle Seymour said. "But then, why bore one person, when you can bore many?"

The footman placed the fish course before them.

Grandmother tilted her head. "But I do not mind."

Uncle Seymour smiled. "Because you are a gentle woman, too forgiving of your niece's most abhorrent inclinations."

"Please!" Percival sat up. "I will not permit you to refer to my fiancée in that despicable manner."

Uncle Seymour narrowed his eyes at Percival, who met his with the same amount of enthusiasm.

Fiona's lips parted. The vision of Percival defending her was everything she'd told herself not to imagine or hope for. Men like him weren't supposed to come to her rescue. They were supposed to defend dainty damsels, so slender that a whisk of wind or even a careless word might harm them. They weren't supposed to defend sturdy-looking women like herself whose own impulsivity brought them harm.

Fiona read books. She knew how things worked.

But Percival still fixed Uncle Seymour with a firm expression until finally Uncle Seymour pushed his plate away. "Young lovers. Impossible to reason with."

Fiona smiled, even though she knew that calling Percival and herself anything resembling lovers was misguided. A jolt of anger swept through Fiona, and her fingers clutched her napkin, tightening it into a hard ball. She'd allowed her uncle to spend too many evenings over too much wine criticizing her. Archaeology was a recent complaint; she'd kept it secret for years.

The man knew nothing about it—nothing at all—and she would not allow him to lean back in his chair, smile at her smugly, and utter scarcely veiled insults in the small space he didn't devote to masticating and wine.

She threw her napkin on the table, ignoring the way everyone's eyebrows jumped. "Your contempt is almost comical, dear uncle."

"Indeed?" Uncle Seymour clutched his goblet with the same vigor one of their ancestors' may have clutched a battle axe.

"The estate is sitting on potentially invaluable history."

"It's a grand estate," Uncle Seymour said dryly, "of course history is attached to it."

"But not every grand estate has history that could change the way we think about the Romans."

"They've been dead for centuries."

"No."

"No?" Uncle Seymour raised an eyebrow, and a condescending smile appeared on his face.

"I mean—" Fiona's tongue thickened, and the temperature of the room seemed to soar. Her heart pounded in her chest, the tempo harder and more rapid than any she was accustomed with.

This was when she was supposed to apologize. This was when every rule of convention and etiquette books told her she should excuse herself and ask for forgiveness for her foolishness.

The man was her uncle, and that fact alone should necessitate her respect. He was older, and should be wiser, and he was a baronet. He possessed wealth, where Fiona possessed none. And one day, Uncle Seymour would be moving into Cloudbridge Castle, and Fiona would be spending every day and every evening with him, unless he decided it more fitting to send her off to be a governess somewhere, if she didn't move in with her younger sister.

And yet Fiona could not hold her tongue and did not even think her inability bad. "Surely you've heard of the plans for a British Museum?"

"I heard it was bloody controversial," Uncle Seymour said.

"And yet we're going to have one, for the public is indeed deeply interested in the ancient Greek sculpture that once were part of a great Parthenon."

"Perhaps . . ."

"Surely you must know that Lord Mulbourne would be completely enthusiastic. He's a respected art critic. Why, he would find the finding extraordinarily valuable!"

"Have you discussed this with him?" Uncle Seymour asked.

"No . . ." Fiona sighed. "But I'm sure he would agree that not digging up the land would be a crime. There's so much of value that could be underneath it. Items that would explain how a whole culture lived over here. We owe so much to the Romans. I'm not asking you to tear up the house. Only for permission to remove some trees that could be replanted somewhere else."

"I'm not sure I've ever heard you say so much," Cecil said. "That's fascinating."

"Here, here." Percival grinned and clinked glasses with Grandmother.

Aunt Lavinia shifted in her chair, and Uncle Seymour sent Fiona a thundering glance that might once have affected her, but didn't now.

Uncle Seymour exhaled. "Perhaps you're right and even members of the *ton* might find some amusement in learning about these people's antics, but I still cannot believe that digging around in the dirt is a respectable pastime for a lady. The only person I know who has done anything similar is Napoleon in Egypt. And my dear niece, I'm sure you understand how difficult it is to support something that that tiny Corsican ruffian might have appreciated."

She stared at him. He'd been disapproving, she'd always expected that, but he hadn't utterly dismissed her. He'd listened.

She relaxed her shoulders. "Thomas Jefferson also has done archaeological work."

"Colonist." Aunt Lavinia shrugged.

"Former colonist," Percival corrected.

"That's not in the man's favor." Uncle Seymour shook his whole head with such vigor that his carefully coiffed hair became frazzled.

The man's valet would soon be added to the list of people disappointed in Fiona.

She sighed. "But you will consider the project?"

"Absolutely not. I will not condone any such venture. Digging up the apple orchard, indeed."

"But there might be treasures—"

Uncle Seymour shook his head. "The past is the past, Fiona. Better to look toward the future. Just like our country is doing. We're the greatest country in the world, with the fastest growing innovations. It's a great time to be British, my dear. No need to think about the past. Certainly not about some long-dead Italians."

Fiona's shoulders slumped. It would have been so wonderful, so amazing if Uncle Seymour had truly seen fit to agree to the project.

The clang and clatter of knives and forks being scraped over the plates pulled her away from her musings. She bit into the fish. Each flake was dry, despite Cook's liberal use of buttery sauce to embellish it.

"Did you see the Elysian marbles?" Cecil asked.

Fiona shook her head. They'd been brought over to London with much fanfare, but Fiona hadn't received an invitation to see them.

"Good thing then," Aunt Lavinia said. "Garish barbaric pieces of stone."

"Beautiful carvings of stone," Percival said.

Uncle Seymour shrugged. "Don't see what all the fuss was about. It was a crime that some of the critics reviewed it so highly. An absolute crime."

"Some of the Greeks said that it was a crime that they were hauled from the country," Percival said.

"Typical thing for the Greeks to say. Still whining now, even though we've just saved Europe from ruin." Uncle Seymour shook his head. "The country has limited its accomplishments to ordinary things for the past two thousand years."

Fiona glanced at Percival, who retained a polite smile, though his face was becoming distinctly more flushed.

Uncle Seymour shook his head firmly and then directed his gaze to Percival. "It's a wonder that you're going to marry this woman."

Percival set his fork down and narrowed his eyes. "I trust you will not insult my fiancée further."

"Well, I—er," Uncle Seymour stumbled over his words, unaccustomed to having to defend himself.

Fiona smiled. And then her heart became heavy.

This amazing man was here, declaring to all her family his place as her fiancé, and none of it was true. Not in the least.

For as charming as he might be, defending her to her relatives, he was no more hers than a vision was. Less hers in fact, for a vision she could call upon from time to time in her mind. When Percival left, it would be forever, and she'd need to spend the rest of her life explaining to her family how she'd let a magnificent man like him amble away, without admitting that she'd never been able to have him in the first place.

The necessity of the project soared. The apple orchard belonged to Uncle Seymour, and the man did not want it dug up, even though he'd never expressed a passionate partiality for apples before.

Once Grandmother died, Uncle Seymour and his wife would move in. She'd been imagining she would be allowed to spend her life occupied with the recording of the objects she discovered in the apple orchard. She'd allowed herself to daydream that she might research the Romans in Britain, in her wilder dreams even contributing papers on the subject, just like a man might do.

But Uncle Seymour's opinion had been firm. Her only hope of swaying him now was Lord Mulbourne, and Madeline was not inclined to be agreeable to anything concerning her. If only the baron did not occupy himself so much in London.

The man was an expert in art, unlike his wife, who seemed to consider herself only an expert in fashion, though she was also unusually gifted in putting other people down, an impressive trait in the gossipy world of the *ton*.

"Come now, eat up!" Uncle Seymour said.

Fiona gazed down at her plate. At some point the footman must have changed it. Dark meat slathered in gravy perched in the center of the plate.

"Aren't Rosamund and her new husband supposed to take you to Harrogate tomorrow?" Grandmother sipped her drink and changed the subject.

"Oh, I despise Harrogate," Fiona said.

"Pity," Grandmother said. "She and her husband are planning to arrive here shortly after dawn."

"It's on the way. They can go without me." Fiona shrugged. She wouldn't give Percival an opportunity to escape. The man seemed far too intrigued by the conversation.

The room was silent. Finally, Percival cleared his throat. "Now tell me, who is Rosamund?"

Fiona's heart sped, and her mind raced for an excuse for her supposed fiancé's question.

"Her sister." Uncle Seymour set his knife down and fixed steely eyes on Percival. "How curious you do not know the name of her only sibling."

Fiona forced a laugh. "Our romance was very quick, and he's never met her."

"Ah, yes. *That* Rosamund. I've heard many tales of them. Playing with dolls. Having tea parties outside. And going to Harrogate." A smile flickered across Percival's face as he said the last word, and his eyes gleamed.

Dread filled Fiona.

"I had no idea you were acquainted with such a wide array of females bearing that name." Uncle Seymour nodded, but his eyes remained narrowed, and his gaze returned to them throughout the evening.

Chapter Fifteen

SUNLIGHT STREAMED THROUGH the stained glass windows, casting colored shadows on the floor, and Percival shut the door to his bedroom and made his way down the corridor. His eyes were groggy, and he pulled his frock coat tightly around him.

He turned his head in the direction of Fiona's room, but the door remained resolutely shut. She must still be sleeping, and he would be able to catch Fiona's sister and new husband alone and convince them to take him along with them to Harrogate.

The floor beams creaked underneath his unsteady steps, but no red-headed woman rushed out to meet him.

I've outwitted her. The realization brought no sense of triumph with it. He'd actually miss this place. *I'll miss her.*

He quickened his pace. He would be able to catch a hack in Harrogate and make his way to a mail or stage coach from there. Soon he would be in London. He wouldn't have the jewels with him, but those had always been an excuse. Lady Cordelia didn't need them when he proposed, and he would have a servant send for them, just as he should have done in the beginning. He doubted Fiona would refuse to give them at that point.

Footsteps padded behind him, and he grinned. *Fiona was there.* He braced his cane onto the floor and turned his head, but the only person in the hallway was a chamber maid. She gave him a tentative smile, and he nodded at her. His throat dried.

He was really leaving. He hadn't needed to wait for his relatives to rescue him discretely after all. Somehow, he'd imagined that Fiona would make some attempt to keep him here. He'd grown accustomed to her spirited motions.

He grasped hold of the banister and made his way down the stairs, grateful at least that no one was there to see his clumsy motions. He'd never much had a use for banisters before, and now they seemed like the finest invention in the world.

The entryway was empty, and he heaved open the door to the outside, to freedom.

"Let me help you with that." A man who exuded Corinthian charm grasped hold of the handle and grinned more than most people were capable of at any time, much less early in the morning. "You must be my new brother."

Percival blinked.

"Lord Somerville," the man said, smiling.

Rosamund's husband.

The earl was clothed in a great coat and beaver-skin top hat. Behind him was a black sleigh pulled by white horses. The horses wore red plumes in their headgear, stomping occasionally on the fresh snow, though appearing on the whole quite relaxed at the prospect of journeying atop it.

"We're still going to Harrogate?" Percival asked. "Miss Amberly expressed reluctance, but I was hoping I might still join—"

"Naturally! We're relatives now. Well, practically." The earl beamed. "My brothers live near here. It will be grand to have another man join us for cards."

"Marvelous," Percival said, though the word exaggerated his emotional state. For some reason, the thought of leaving failed to fill him with joy. He wouldn't be lighting any Roman candles.

"But don't worry about Miss Amberly," the earl said. "The women are on their way."

Percival blinked. "Your wife?"

"And Miss Amberly. She insisted on joining. Said you would be sure to want to go. Mrs. Amberly said you would be sleeping, but it seems Miss Amberly was right after all. True love has its power, doesn't it?" Somerville chuckled.

Percival rubbed his hand through his hair. "I seem to recall that Miss Amberly despised Harrogate."

"Yes, yes. She professes a dislike for shopping. I suppose she couldn't be parted from you after all. It's nice to see her so in love. The way she talks about you." Somerville beamed.

"Er... Yes." Percival peered at the entrance to the manor house.

"Makes me feel like I'm not the only romantic in the world," Somerville mused. "They'll be out any moment now. No need to worry."

Percival shifted, sinking into the fresh snow.

The sound of jingles came from the distance. A set of horses pulled another sleigh. This one was painted a cheerful red. The horses' heads were proudly raised. The sleigh was large with two rows, and a driver occupied one of them.

"I took the liberty of getting the groom to prepare the sleigh here." Somerville laughed. "One day you'll be arranging all of this."

"Right."

He'd only just met Somerville, but the weight of the lie pressed on him. Somerville believed he was meeting his new brother-in-law, and in reality he was simply meeting a stranger whom he might one day encounter in London. Somerville didn't even know Percival's name.

The earl eyed him. "Let's get you into the sleigh, Captain. I'm awfully sorry about what happened to you at Waterloo. It must be a dreadful shame. Such a bother. So near the end too."

"I'm making do."

Somerville's words came from a good place, but Percival was tired of making conversation about his injury, and listening to people alternatively bemoan his poor fortune or laud the fact that he'd made it out alive at all, depending on their propensity toward optimism or pessimism.

But perhaps the problem was with himself, for he seemed equally critical of people who mentioned his leg and of people who avoided mention out of politeness.

The Napoleonic Wars had brought many soldiers back in various states of wholeness, and Percival was far more fortunate than most of those returning.

He made his way to the sleigh, tottering over the snow-covered cobblestones. His hand tightened around his cane, and he allowed the earl to help him inside. A thick woolen blanket lay on the seat, representing everything cozy. The driver nodded to him, and he blinked under the bright, blue sky and the bright rays of sun.

Before long the door to the castle opened. The countess appeared first, and then Fiona. Fiona's face was tight, but when she spotted him, her shoulders relaxed and she smiled.

The countess laughed. "Is that your fiancé?"

Fiona nodded.

The woman's eyes sparkled, and she glided toward him.

"My sister, please let me present my fiancé, Captain Knightley." Fiona's face pinkened a charming color, and she thrust her eyelashes downward. "Darling, this is Lady Somerville."

"I must admit part of me questioned your existence," the countess said. "And yet you are here in the flesh."

"Mostly," he replied.

The countess's eyebrows flew up, and he pointed to his wooden leg.

She laughed and turned to Fiona. "I like him."

Fiona gave her a wobbly smile.

"And really, you mustn't worry about your lack of a leg. I'm sure it's more common than one might think." The countess smiled brightly. "We are departing for London tomorrow. Somerville needs to meet with his brothers—they're such rakes, and I know it does them good to see him."

"Indeed."

"Quite," the countess chattered. "They'll meet at the Duchess of Belmonte's ball. The Duke of Alfriston will even be there."

Percival stiffened and he avoided the countess's gaze.

"Why, he's even missing a leg just like you!" The countess clapped her hands.

"But you haven't met?" Percival asked finally.

"No, no. All a bit mysterious really. He wasn't supposed to be a duke at all. But then his cousin died—that beastly Bonaparte, and now he's rich."

"Imagine," Percival said faintly.

"Life is most mysterious." The countess smiled. "My poor sister was most worried this morning when she did not see you. It was most charming to see. I thought nothing fazed her."

Fiona frowned. "Perhaps we should go."

"Let's leave the lovebirds, darling," the earl said, and Rosamund joined him.

Percival exhaled, as the countess glided over the snow, oblivious that she'd just spoken of him.

Fiona climbed into the sleigh and settled into the seat beside him.

"But what of your hatred for shopping?"

She tilted her head. "You didn't really imagine I would abandon you?"

He snorted, and warmth spread through his chest. "It would be unlike you."

"I aim for not surprising you," Fiona said, and he laughed.

"You're the most surprising woman I ever met," Percival said.

Fiona's eyes widened, and she fiddled with the blanket. Pink tinged her cheekbones.

The sleigh moved swiftly, the horses not impeded with the heavy weight of a carriage. He shifted in his seat.

"Your leg?" Fiona asked at once.

"It's fine."

"Good."

They were silent for a few more minutes. The bells on the horses jingled, and the blanket was a seasonal mixture of red and green, but Fiona did not protest.

"I brought the jewels and money," she said.

"What?" Percival swung his head over to her.

She nodded. "I thought you might want to make your escape in Harrogate. You should be able to catch a hack easily enough that will take you to a mail or stage coach."

"Oh?" Percival tried to compose his features into an innocent expression, but from Fiona's resigned smile, he hadn't achieved much success.

"You needn't pretend otherwise. You were terribly eager to go shopping in Harrogate."

"Perhaps I have a fondness for visiting new tailors."

Fiona's shoulders slumped, and a dull weight pressed against Percival's chest. "You're correct. I did plan to take advantage of Harrogate's connection to London."

"Thank you for everything. You were so kind last night. And I've—I've been horrible to you. Dragging you so far away. I'm so sorry." Fiona passed him the package.

He grasped hold of the thin satin material, and pressed against the stones, feeling the familiar shapes. He'd traveled so far to fetch them, had lost them, and now had regained them.

They weren't his. They should have belonged to his cousin, and soon would belong to Lady Cordelia, the woman whom the dowager never failed to praise.

He frowned. "What's going to happen after I leave?"

"Nothing."

"But your sister, your brother-in-law, your grandmother..."

"I'll let them believe in the engagement, and then at some point—" her voice wobbled, and he wondered if she meant after her grandmother's death, "I will invent a lie, and they'll think it's broken off."

"But—why are you doing this? You must know it will be more difficult for you to find a husband after you've been betrothed before."

Engaged women were chaperoned more lightly, and women who were formerly engaged were regarded as spoiled.

"I won't ever marry," Fiona said.

"But society demands it."

"Society demands many things. One needn't follow it slavishly."

"Right." Percival scrunched his fingers together and thought of Lady Cordelia, his destiny, despite the fact he'd never met her, despite the fact that until a few months before, she'd been his cousin's destiny.

"I would love to travel," Fiona said. "I would love to learn more about the people who lived here before."

"And a family? Children?"

Fiona pressed her lips together. "It's not to be. Not everything is."

He tilted his head to her. "Just why did you leave your season early?"

Fiona sighed, and her fingers tapped a nervous pattern over the blanket. She glanced up at him, and her eyelashes flickered over her emerald eyes.

Something in his gaze must have seemed reassuring, for she sighed and gave a short laugh. "I looked forward to it. Before it happened. Before I knew better. I looked forward to wearing pretty dresses and to having men dance with me. Everyone said debuting would be the nicest part of my whole life."

"And what happened?"

"Nothing." She shrugged and wrapped her arms together. "The pretty dresses I wore weren't considered pretty by the other girls. I suppose I went to the wrong dressmaker. I suppose Grandmother didn't know any better and I thought they were pretty."

"I'm sure you were beautiful," Percival said.

Fiona's eyes widened, and she averted her eyes. He had a sudden urge to pull her toward him.

"I felt foolish amidst the gossip. I didn't know the dances well, and the men soon knew better than to ask me to dance. I suppose I was the typical wallflower, except I never bonded with anyone else either. I had considered Madeline a friend, but she was only too happy to gossip about me."

"So you left."

Fiona nodded. "Grandmother was uncomfortable in London as well. She was older than all the marriage-minded mamas and hadn't been in London in ages. It was easy to convince her to leave. And though everyone told me that I was ruining my chances, I never really believed them."

"I suppose you haven't had any suitors here?"

Fiona faltered and then shook her head.

This time the urge to pull her toward him overwhelmed him. He moved his hand underneath the blanket, and away from any cursory glances from the others.

Fiona stiffened, but her fingers opened to his. He pressed his hands against hers and entwined their fingers.

The snow sparkled against the bright blue sky and the still brighter sun. In the distance children played, their gleeful shouts echoing through the valley.

Soon the sleigh would arrive in Harrogate, and they would never see each other again.

Percival pressed his fingers more tightly around hers, telling himself that it didn't matter how well suited Fiona and himself might be.

She bit her lip. "I had all these ideals, and I'd decided that I had no time for the *ton* and all the vapid, gossipy women. But I sometimes wonder if I was just as vapid, just as prejudiced, because I certainly didn't take the time to actually know any of them. And when I see how happy Rosamund is, I feel so foolish for not having tried harder."

The sleigh vaulted toward Harrogate. Percival pressed his top hat on his head. The crisp wind swirled beside them, toppling the cloak from Fiona's head. Her hair lay exposed, and for a moment, Percival simply stared at her auburn curls. The rich color contrasted with the snowy-white landscape behind her, and her locks twisted and turned in the air.

Her curled locks shouldn't fascinate him. *She* shouldn't fascinate him. Her voice should not sound like the one of his dreams, and when he closed his eyes, her face should not echo back at him.

"Everyone said a husband was vital," Fiona continued, "but I had no desire to be tied to a man like Uncle Seymour. I thought I was doing something noble by not yielding to the pressures of the *ton*, but really I was just being foolish. Perhaps I was afraid I wouldn't be able to find someone and didn't want to play a game I was always destined to lose."

"Not all men are like your uncle."

She turned to him, and her eyes roamed his face. "No."

"I suppose it was fortunate that I had my war injury. It made me easier to capture."

"Oh, I would have been successful either way. I planned to capture you once I called myself the Scarlet Demon."

"Indeed." Percival's voice was frosty, a quality he'd practiced at school, surrounded by the other children of aristocrats, all with morals that tended to be low on the ethical spectrum. He crossed his arms and cursed himself for removing her fingers from his own.

She raised her chin. "If this is about your foot, Percival, you know I don't care about it."

"Excuse me!"

She sighed. "I mean, of course, I care that you got hurt. Of course that's dreadful. And of course I wish you did not have to be in so much pain, and that you did not need a cane, and all of that. But no, I did not choose to capture you because you lacked a foot."

His mouth tightened.

"Anyway," she said. "Once we're in Harrogate, you can make an excuse and leave. Or not make an excuse, though I'd still rather that the true cause doesn't reach Grandmother..."

"I won't." His voice softened. "I find it admirable that you are so close to her and I've little desire to break that trust."

Her smile wobbled. "I'm sure I deserve for that trust to be broken."

"You never set out to be a highwaywoman."

"I took advantage of the situation."

"Perhaps not a completely bad quality."

She flickered her eyelashes down, and Percival averted his eyes. Stone houses dotted the landscape, and in the distance the Ripon Cathedral pierced the horizon.

The fact was agonizingly clear. With Fiona everything was different—truer. The women with whom he'd shared his bed had seemed interchangeable, saying words that had seemed calculated to please him and not reveal anything about their own personalities.

They remained the beautiful blonde debutante or the experienced widow, and he remained the army officer, the cousin of a noble family, and now the duke. They expected him to act poorly, to not call on them, and to leap into bed with them, and he was ashamed that he had lived up to their lack of expectations.

"There are coaches near the Minster," Fiona murmured as the sleigh stopped. "I'll tell the others that you were called away."

"Even though they've seen no messenger?" Percival slid from the sleigh and waited for Fiona to disembark.

Fiona's face tightened, but she nodded. "I will make an excuse. We won't be able to take the sleigh into the town center; the snow will not be thick enough for that. But you should be able to find a hack." She paused and then pointed. "There's one."

He followed her finger. There indeed was a hack. The driver tilted his head. "Cheap rides."

"See—"

Percival sighed.

Freedom.

"Thank you for everything you've already done." Fiona's voice trembled.

Percival nodded. "You were the greatest highwaywoman a man could ask for."

Her face pinkened, and she laughed softly. Her eyes were still sad when he turned to the hack driver. He trudged through the snow, his steps slow and labored. He clutched his cane tightly as it made deep incisions in the snow. When he reached the hack and all its promises of freedom, his heart should have thudded with relief, but instead his chest tightened. He swung his gaze back to Fiona.

She was behind the others as they looked at fabric through a shop window. Her face was rigid, her spine was straight, and his heart hurt.

Blast.

He turned and headed back toward her, making his way through the slushy snow and struggling to maintain his balance.

"But sir," the hack driver called behind him, but he waved his hand.

He strode toward her, and his tongue thickened as he neared her. She wasn't expecting him.

Not that he could leave her.

"Fiona."

She spun around, and relief flooded her face. "But—"

"Let's go back," Percival said.

"But—"

"We'll make your grandmother happy. If I'm to be your fiancé, let me at least be a good one. Let's go to the ball tomorrow. I want to be remembered fondly."

"That would be . . . wonderful." Fiona smiled at him. "But you're in a rush to go to London."

Percival shrugged.

The dowager would be upset at his continued absence. He would send another note to her. His cheeks warmed at the memory of the passionate note he'd sent earlier, calling Fiona a kidnapper. He would send a note to ease any worries she might have. He needn't be a slave to society's desires. Not today. Not tomorrow.

Chapter Sixteen

THE FIRE COOLED, AND the flames that leaped and swirled in the medieval fireplace before Percival's bed vanished, replaced by long strips of garnet and orange that crunched the dark logs.

His mind shifted to the day previous. The sleigh ride from Harrogate had transformed into sipping chocolate in the Great Hall, chatting with her and her grandmother. Chocolate transformed into listening to wassailers, and another sleigh ride late at night, brightened by the moon and the glimmer of frosted leaves and branches.

Something sounded on the balcony.

A bird. Or maybe some nocturnal squirrel, unfazed by the vast piles of snow.

Fiona.

His heart leaped at the thought, despite its ridiculousness. A woman might pretend to be a highwaywoman, but that did not mean she scratched on the window of a man's room.

And yet he still clambered off the bed, even though rising remained a difficult procedure. He still wrapped a robe over himself and he still headed outside, the sound of the clicking of his wooden foot loud in the morning quiet.

He unlocked the door and stepped onto the stone balcony.

Naturally she wasn't there.

The thought had been foolish, and he told himself he was relieved. His life was planned, and now was not the time for romance.

The sun journeyed up the horizon, casting long pink and orange rays over the snow-covered landscape. The sharp slopes glistened bright tangerine colors.

Everything sparkled, at variance with the dour, rain-clogged Dales he'd anticipated, where the sky and ground would share that same, muddied color.

Crisp air swept over his hair. Snowflakes continued their descents, but they tumbled slowly, twirling under the growing light, their distinctive shapes fluttering before they settled onto the piles of snow, merging forever.

Tonight was the ball, and after he would go to London. He would meet his perfect bride, adorn her with the perfect jewels with their perfect history. They would have their perfect children and lead their perfect lives.

They'd spend the season in London, summer at one of their country estates, and when they had the urge to be exciting, they might descend upon Europe, now the war was over.

He bit his lip, uncertain if Lady Cordelia favored travel. His knowledge of her was limited to her passion for needle work, though he'd never comprehended the delight for stabbing a piece of cloth repeatedly to form a rigid representation of a flower.

No matter. The sun clambered up the peaks of the Dales, and he padded farther onto the balcony. Soon uniform white buildings would form his view, their facade only varying with the choice of statue to embellish the home. Apollo or Aphrodite, Zeus or Hera, these were soon to be the large questions.

Some of the servants exited the castle, clothed in dark coats and wielding large shovels. They tackled the snow, bowing their heads down as they lifted up the white powder and flung it to the side. Eventually dark cobblestones poked through the snow, their presence confirming that there would be no cause to delay his return to London.

It was foolish to be anything else than grateful he'd return home soon. He shivered, but he couldn't solely blame the cold.

A woman like Fiona would never be comfortable on his arm. She'd not even lasted a season when she'd been a debutante.

A door creaked open, and he froze.

"Sorry—" Fiona's voice stammered an apology, and he swiveled around.

She was in her nightdress, a long flowing gown that should have afforded no view of her person, but which managed to reveal her every curve.

Or perhaps his thoughts found it natural to dwell on every lustful aspect of her.

It was easy to linger on the delightful manner in which her ivory skin melded against the satin gleam of her gown. It was easy to ponder the charming caramel-colored freckles which dotted her tiny, upturned nose, and it was easy to be drawn in by the shards of emeralds that posed as her eyes.

Her body curved appealingly, and his fingers itched to trace the line from her waist to her hips, from the curve of her neck to the slope of her bosom.

And her hair. *By Zeus, her hair.*

The rich auburn strands would feel rougher than the straight, silky locks of the *ton* he was accustomed to. The only joy there was found in undoing their chignons, though the process usually involved copious amounts of pins.

His fingers tightened, and he averted his eyes.

"Sorry!" Fiona repeated, as if she had no idea how the throaty tone of her voice affected him. "I thought no one was here. I like to watch the sun rise."

"Then we share an enjoyment of the same pastime." Percival cursed the sudden hoarseness of his voice.

She pulled her robe more tightly around her, but it only managed to more clearly reveal the curves of her body.

Percival forced his gaze away. He tried to focus on pink rays that outlined the now-white hills that had occupied his attention so thoroughly before, but the looping slopes of the Dales that men traveled far to see was no competition to the enticing curves of the woman beside him.

I'm spoken for.

A small part of him told him he wasn't spoken for yet, he wasn't actually committed, he'd simply told the dowager he would agree with what she deemed best.

She'd lost her son. He couldn't crush her further.

"I'll return inside." Fiona swiveled, and her auburn locks fluttered in the wind. Large snowflakes had fallen on her hair, sparkling and shimmering as if she were ensconced in a snow globe.

"Wait." Percival stretched out a hand to her, and then hastily dropped it, because by Zeus, it wasn't appropriate to even speak to her like this, much less act like the thought of her leaving pained him.

After all, he was counting the hours to his departure. This had been the most inconvenient incident of the year. And that included six months of battling the French. No way would he stand here in the blasted cold and ponder her beauty.

That would be ridiculous. He shifted on the snowy surface of the balcony. The thought of not spending every moment of the rest of their short time together seemed even more absurd.

He sucked in a breath of air. "I would like to see your archaeological finds."

Fiona blinked. "Are you sure? No one else—"

"I'm not no one else."

Fiona's long eyelashes swooped down, and her cheeks pinkened.

Percival cursed his intensity, and he laughed in an attempt to lighten the mood. "After all, I'm your fiancé."

Fiona's lips turned up as he expected, but no joy sparkled in her emerald eyes. His heart hammered. When he said things like that, it was all too easy to contemplate what it would be like if his words were real.

She wasn't really his fiancée, and after tonight, she would no longer even be an acquaintance. He would divide his time between London and the ducal residence in Sussex. His heart clenched.

"Besides, archaeology interests me. You interest me." Heat pricked the back of his neck, as if he weren't able to cope with the presence of his robe and her presence at the same time. He'd said too much, but he refused to withdraw the words.

The slow smile that spread over her face halted, and her jaw tightened. She placed her hands on her waist. "You should stop that."

"Excuse me?"

She strode near him, not seeming to care that the bottom of her robe trailed in the snow. "You must do a better job of displaying your faults. Because right now you seem perfect, and Lord, I'm going to miss you."

"Fiona—"

It wasn't the first time he'd used her given name in his thoughts, but it was the first time he'd said it to her. Her eyes widened, and she whirled around and returned to her bedroom.

He followed her, dragging his wooden leg on the unevenly packed snow, before she might close the door.

He might be losing all sense—very likely he was—but the thought of never having another moment alone with her seemed horrific.

Much more horrific than it should have been.

His heart hammered, and he poked his head through the door. He scanned the room, taking in her still unmade bed and the long, dark canopies that hung from the bed posts. Not that there was anything drab about the bed—the place seemed filled with significance.

He forced his mind from dwelling on the fact that even the smallest pillow was likely imbued with Fiona's scent, and he definitely refused to ponder what sort of uses a bed might fulfil. He was still in a robe himself, and the long nightshirt underneath scarcely made him decent. Not if his mind was going to ponder—that.

He didn't need to think about a womanly body pressed against soft sheets. He gritted his teeth. "May I enter?"

Fiona paused. "Yes."

He wavered, teetering on the threshold of duty and desire, responsibility and bliss, all that was honorable and all that was Fiona and delightful.

It was almost as if . . . He shook his head.

Love was something confined to fairy tales for little girls. Love was something that grew slowly, if at all, after a lifetime of attending the same balls and sitting across from one another at the same dining room table. Love was something he might experience with Lady Cordelia in a few years if he were lucky, but most likely not. And that wasn't supposed to matter. That's why everyone kept separate bedrooms, that's why brothels thrived.

But it was clear: he adored Fiona Amberly. He was in love with her, blast it. And it didn't seem to matter in the slightest that the fact was bloody inconvenient.

He'd been happy when the dowager suggested he marry Lady Cordelia and that his future would be settled. Perhaps he'd been more sensitive about his leg than he'd let on. The prospect of courting women, seeing which ones didn't mind he couldn't dance with them, and seeing which ones didn't use his interest to catapult proposals for better, two-legged men, failed to appeal.

At one time he'd loved London, embraced the order of its grand buildings and the chaotic frenzy near St. Paul's and Covent Garden. He'd always considered the countryside dull and grumbled at the prospect of spending any time there. Its advantages had seemed limited to the possibilities of pall mall and lawn chess, both games he had little interest in, and its disadvantages had seemed endless.

And yet now—now nothing seemed duller than the prospect of another season, with trained debutantes sneaking glances at him, assessing whether his vast estates and tolerable good looks were worth his present state of less than wholeness.

No, he hadn't wanted to go through that before he'd met Fiona. That's why he'd rushed into assenting to the dowager's pleas.

But now he'd met Fiona, and life was more vivid. She'd cared so much for her grandmother that she'd gone to enormous extents to reassure her. She cherished history and the past. She wasn't the only person he'd met interested in the Romans, but she was the very first who expressed such passion.

Love-sick sonnets suddenly made sense. He had a wild urge to throw her on the bed and to ask her to be his wife. It seemed ridiculous he would declare himself her fiancé in public and not in private.

The world had changed these past few days. Fiona had dragged him from his steadfast life, and he couldn't be more thankful. It was all he could do now to not recite the poetry his tutors had forced him to memorize. It was all he could do to not fall at her feet. His heart thrummed in his chest.

Fiona flashed him a wobbly smile. "Unless perhaps you've reconsidered. That would be fine. Most people find archaeology tiresome."

He squared his shoulders and stepped into the room. "I haven't reconsidered."

Something flickered in her eyes, but she soon swerved around and headed toward a small door in the room.

"This way," she chirped, and he smiled.

Her hands trembled somewhat, and he fought the desire to wrap them in his and reassure her. He brushed some of the snow and ice off and followed her.

She picked up a torch, sucked in a breath of air and flung the door open.

Dim light from her torch flickered over the small room. She lit another lantern, engulfing the room in a warm, cozy light.

He blinked. Pottery sat on thick shelves beside coins and helmets. A mosaic of a woman lay on a large desk beside thick tomes of Roman history in Britain. Gold letters glimmered from the large leather books.

She followed his gaze. "They're my vice."

He smiled. "I'm sure they don't count as one."

Other ladies of the *ton* were prone to drinking, smearing slabs of lead paste on their faces so their skin would not betray their enthusiasm for gin. If Fiona's guilty pleasure lay in reading, he could only praise her.

He scanned the room and gazed at the rows of impeccably cleaned and labeled finds. "This is—amazing."

"You think?" Fiona's cheeks pinkened, and he nodded.

"You really found these on the estate?"

"Yes, near the apple orchard. I suppose the castle has been around for centuries, and even if the current building stems from the middle ages, the site was inhabited well before then."

"And I suppose the estate always belonged to people of importance, so it is understandable why the finds would be here."

She stared at him. "Exactly. Though I would say that every person is of importance; but yes, families with wealth have always lived here."

"Fascinating."

"Please—sit." She pointed at a chair and settled onto a more uncomfortable looking bench.

He sat. His gaze flickered to Fiona, and he imagined her working here, consumed by her dedication to her finds. Her brow would be furrowed and her nose would crinkle in that adorable way.

"I've only excavated a portion of the apple orchard. I didn't want to dig up the trees. One of the older servants told me about some Roman coins someone had discovered there once, and it made me curious whether there was more underneath." Fiona shrugged, as if her actions were the most natural thing in the world, even though he'd never met another person who'd done anything similar.

"What made you want to discover the finds?"

"I was curious." She shrugged. "Perhaps it's reassuring in a way to know that millions of people have come before me, and that others have been living in this area for generations. And there's—there's something magical about touching these objects that no one else has handled for centuries. I like imagining the people they belonged to. And I don't want their lives to be forgotten. They created this rich, vibrant, beautiful world."

He nodded and flicked his gaze back to the art and pottery on the shelves. He pondered whether their lives would be considered interesting by the people who would come centuries after them, or whether any items they had would remain in the ground, with no one spurred to examine them more closely.

"There were multiple military defenses in the area. The Romans were in York, and they also had fortresses on Hadrian's Wall. Everyone said any people there were just soldiers, but they had their families, with their dreams." Her eyes shone as she spoke, sparkling as if they were visiting another land, inhabited by people in togas who looked different, but perhaps weren't really all that dissimilar.

His mind wandered to the *ton*, and to the men and women eager to assert their favorable characteristics by contrasting them with others. They spoke negatively of the people who grabbed the wrong fork at dinner or tilted their soup bowls in the improper direction, but there was more to life than conforming to a pre-established ideal.

Fiona was everything he always should have dreamed of, but never had.

"You're amazing," he blurted, and he slammed his teeth onto his tongue before he could also proclaim his love for her.

The woman seemed sufficiently overwhelmed by his previous statement. Her eyelashes swooped up, and her mouth parted.

She gave a nervous laugh and bent her head, so her luscious red curls hung over one of her eyes. A rosy flush grew on her cheeks, and she shook her head.

"I mean it." Heat prickled the back of his neck, but he continued on. Some things needed to be said, no matter how much they caused his heart to gallop, as if wild horses had taken charge of it. He stumbled from his chair and strode toward her.

Her eyes were wide. They sparkled and shimmered like emeralds, and he settled onto the bench beside her. Only a narrow width separated them, and the space between their faces lessened. He took her hands in his. A flurry of warmth jolted through him at the contact, and he smiled. Everything about her was wonderful. "Fiona Amberly, you are the most wonderful woman I've ever met."

"I—"

He smiled. She had no idea how marvelous she was. He stroked her hands and then leaned toward her. Soft lips touched his, and a sweet sigh escaped.

Chapter Seventeen

SHE WAS BEING KISSED.

It was ridiculous. Men didn't go around kissing Fiona. And not handsome men like Percival. Their eyes weren't supposed to cloud over in something that mirrored desire, and they weren't supposed to gaze at her in reverence.

Firm lips caressed hers, exploring the shape of her lips with his own. Just as she was getting used to the tender game of sucking and caressing, even as she debated whether she had the courage to stop this blissful sensation, Percival's tongue stroked her own in a manner so intimate that warmth catapulted through her body, tightening at her most intimate portion.

They'd kissed before, but that had been at the tavern, before a group of strangers. This was real. No one was questioning Percival's masculinity. If he was kissing her, it was because he wanted to. Her heartbeat raced, and she felt like one of the audacious heroines in the Loretta van Lochen novels. She smiled. The fact was not unpleasant.

Percival drew her nearer to him. No, things were decidedly pleasant. More pleasant than anything she'd ever experienced, and her eyes flickered shut.

She swore she could feel every muscle in his body. She certainly felt his warmth spread over her, even through his robe. Wide shoulders that extended past hers gave her a sense of stability she'd never known she craved, but which she was unwilling to let go.

His morning stubble brushed against her cheeks. The rough texture reminded her that this was not a dream—not some wild fantasy she shouldn't be having, but completely real. Her breath quickened, and she tightened her grip around him. Percival moaned, a low, deep sound that stirred every portion of her body. Her blood sizzled.

Her whole life centered around the ecstatic sensation of Percival's lips, Percival's touch, Percival's scent. There was nothing more. This was it. This was life. This was what brought havoc and scandal to some of the *ton*, this is why even the most matronly members had expressed surprise when she had said she had no desire to marry.

They all knew about this. They all adored it.

"Fiona—" Percival's deep voice was hoarse, and his long fingers gripped her gown. The adjourning door was still open, and it was still winter, but she swore she'd never been so warm in her life.

"One moment." She staggered to her feet, and he blinked back up at her.

She took unsteady steps toward the door and stared at the opening. It would be easy to escape from it, easy to make Percival leave, but instead she kicked it shut.

They were alone. Her heart crescendoed, and Percival yanked her back to him. Her long dress swished against the chair, and he pulled her into his arms. She was sitting on a man's lap. She, Fiona Amberly, had abandoned all propriety.

"Is this fine?" He brushed his hands over her back. His scent filled the small space, and she closed her eyes, allowing the smell of pine needles and cotton to waft over her. He stroked her cheek bone, finding fascination in her face that she did not believe possible, and his hands moved toward her hair. "I've dreamed about submerging myself in these locks."

He peered at her. His eyes were wide, their gaze soft, and she stared at the flecks of gold that danced with the deep blue color. He pulled her against his chest, wrapping his burly arms around her. She pressed her body against his, her heart relaxing its frantic pace as it became soothed by the man's presence. Warmth emanated from him.

Perhaps she'd never been in such a position before, and perhaps being alone with a man like this was everything her former governesses would have warned her against, but right now all she could concentrate on was the delicious manner in which he held her.

His hand cupped her jaw, and his thumb rubbed against her cheek. His eyes didn't waver from her face, and his lips parted in something that resembled awe. "I wanted to do this yesterday."

His voice was hoarse, and she blinked back at him. Words vanished, and all she concentrated on was the sweetness of his presence. She'd never expected to find herself on a man's lap. Grandmother was down the hall, and the servants were working, oblivious to the fact everything in her life had changed.

His head tilted, and she barely had time to gasp before they were once again kissing.

"You're astonishing." The words flew from him, and Fiona waited for him to withdraw them. She waited for his cheeks to tinge pink, and she waited for him to avert his eyes. She waited for him to inhale his breath, and she waited for him to quickly add a "but."

Yet no rebuttal, no modification ever came. Instead he continued to fix his gaze on her, and when a small giggle escaped her, because Lord, what else could she do in the face of so much seriousness, his lips rose.

"I mean it!" he said.

"But—" She paused. He was supposed to give the rebuttal, not her.

He smiled again and stroked her hair. "No more speaking."

Happiness spread through her, starting slowly, but then leaping on to an ever quicker pace, until she was practically grinning at him. She must look a fright, but he only returned her grin, mirth shining through his deep blue eyes.

"You could have anyone."

"You have a good impression of my masculine charms." Percival leaned toward her, and his hot breath brushed against the lobe of her ear.

She tried to smile back. His eyes were soft, almost in wonder, and she exhaled. Maybe she could believe him. Maybe this was indeed all real.

Though didn't a man compliment a woman in any seduction? Wasn't that what made it a seduction? Reality would come this evening, after the ball, when he returned to London. To marry the woman he was supposed to be with.

Guilt ratcheted through her, and she clung to his arms. She told herself that this was fine. He hadn't met the woman yet, they weren't formally engaged, and goodness, he was a man, and wasn't this just what they did?

She should be forcing him out, telling the servants, or just leaving herself. And yet—perhaps this would be her only experience with a man? Perhaps this was it?

He stroked her cheek, and her eyes flickered shut. She couldn't leave.

"You're beautiful," he murmured, and her heartbeat ratcheted up.

His hands glided against her, stroking her firmly. She looped her arm around him. Her fingers explored his hair, and then she moved downward to the solid planes of his muscular back. Like her, he'd only worn a robe, and the thin material left little to her imagination.

Except—she wanted more. The silky robe and undershirt—all of those seemed like an excessive barrier, even though she knew the thought was ludicrous.

His fingers brushed against the buttons of her nightgown, and the space between her legs tightened further. She rolled her body against him, trying to alleviate the pressure, and he groaned.

"That gown better come off," he growled, undoing the buttons and pulling the material up.

"I—"

For a moment the idea seemed dreadful, for he stopped kissing her, and her body was cold when he busied herself with her gown, instead of pressing her as close to him as possible.

He swooped the material over her head. She was naked. Before him.

She shifted, self-conscious.

But his eyes flared, and he stroked her cheek with reverence. His hand trailed down her body, skimming over the curve of her chest, moving to her nipples. He pulled her toward him and kissed her again, this time more forcefully, as if he wanted to meld his tongue with hers. He pulled her back, staring at her, and an open smile spread over his face.

"I'm happy. I'm so happy." His husky voice caused pleasure to shoot through her body again.

He pressed his lips against her neck, and his wet tongue circled and sucked on her skin. His hands moved to her bosom. He rubbed her nipples into tight peaks, and she rocked harder against him.

"You're wearing too much," she murmured, and he shot her a cocky grin.

"Thought you would never ask." He moved to undo his robe, but then his gaze fell on his lap, and he seemed to hesitate.

Her heart swelled. It was the leg. He was worried about it. She gave him her best smile and touched the material. "May I see it?"

"It's not much to look at," he said, and he gave a little laugh that caused another pang to beat against her heart.

"Every part of you is wonderful," she said solemnly, and raised his nightshirt. She didn't want him to feel like he had to hide any part of him. Not now. Not after this.

She'd seen the wooden leg before. The bottom was as thick as the man's other foot, similar to a shoe, allowing him to balance. She traced her fingers over the carved curves. A round joint lay an inch above the bottom of his foot, in the space between his heel and toes, and she wobbled the lower part of the foot. It creaked slightly, and she giggled.

He pulled her upward. "I'd rather you focused on the parts of me I can actually feel."

She laughed, and they kissed again. His hands rubbed her back, and he pulled her toward him, pressing his warm, wet lips to her neck, forming his own trail of kisses. Ecstasy swished through her, and he followed the slopes of her curved waist and thighs with his strong hands.

"Percival." She moaned his name. She'd never experienced this before, but now the thought of stopping, of not feeling him here beside her, was unimaginable. He brushed his hands nearer her mound, and her body tightened, as long, elegant fingers swept toward her. He delved his fingers into her silky, most private curls, and she writhed beneath him.

She wanted—more. She wanted—him. Her body quivered at his every touch, at every flash of his brilliant blue eyes, which stared at her in awe.

"My darling," he murmured, pressing his lips against her chest with increased rapidity and desperation.

He swooped his finger along her bosom, and she trembled. He moved his lips to her crests, immersing them in the hot splendor of his mouth. Every part of her body seemed to exult in the force of his tongue on her.

And then—his hands traveled lower, and oh goodness, they were venturing into a place no one had ever journeyed to.

His fingers delved into her flesh, brushing over her tightest, innermost peak.

"I—" She gasped underneath the blissful force of his attention. He ran his fingers over her core, quickening his pace as if to send her far away, into new realms. She squirmed and writhed. And then the tempo of her breaths increased, pleasure crescendoed through her. Nothing could ever be the same.

His lips spread into a cocky grin, and he kissed her cheeks and mouth. His manhood pressed into her, and she reached for it tentatively. She caressed the velvety sheen of his thickness. He put his hand over hers and guided her. She brushed her fingers against tight, round ballocks, experimentally exploring the man's body. Then she moved back up his rod, sweeping her fingers along Percival's sturdy length. She circled the top, and beads of salty liquid dripped from him.

"Don't stop."

She smiled and then moved her fingers back down his length.

This time she increased her pace, remembering her own blissful sensations earlier, and he groaned.

"Just like that," he murmured. "Just like that."

She continued her speed, swooping her fingers up and down his rigid length. He tightened his grip on her other hand, and his gasps soared through the tiny room. Creamy liquid gushed forth from his rod, and he shuddered. His eyes flickered shut, his cheeks darkened, and his chest rose and fell. A masculine scent filled the room, and he pulled her toward him. She lay against his chest, still rising, still falling. Strong arms caressed her, and for this moment, she felt wonderful.

"I want so much to happen between us," he said.

The tips of her lips moved upward, but her heart heavied. After the ball, he would depart for London to his true life. She swept him closer to her, but that action could not stop his inevitable departure, and soon she would only be left with memories.

Chapter Eighteen

THE COACH HALTED, AND music from the festivities streamed through the windows. Percival crept down the steps. His breath quickened as he turned to Fiona, and he gave her a short bow before extending his hand to her. "My darling."

There was nothing feigned about his words, and his heart swelled when Fiona's cheeks pinkened. She slipped an ivory-gloved hand into his, and he beamed.

By Zeus, his heart shouldn't pound with such force at the mere touch of her satin-ensconced skin. But heaven help him, that flicker drew up a hoist of delightful images. If he had his way, he would be ordering the driver straight back to Cloudbridge Castle.

From the anxious look Fiona directed at the manor house, he wasn't the only person who didn't want to be here, despite the fact this was clearly the place to be. Glossy coaches parked before the manor house, and sounds of people filled the crisp air.

"Maybe we shouldn't go after all," Fiona said.

"Nonsense. We made it this far." Percival smiled down at her, enjoying the sensation of her gloved fingers pressing against his arm. "And you need to speak with this marvelous baron of yours."

Tomorrow he would go to London. He'd speak to the dowager and explain he couldn't marry Lady Cordelia after all, and that he would not propose to her.

Perhaps he'd only known Fiona a few days, but he'd spent more time in her company than with any other woman. She understood him more than any friend, and her body was far more enticing. He had half a mind to stroll around the garden with her, his wooden leg be damned, and propose to her before all the gossips in this God-forsaken county she fretted about.

Perhaps the dowager would not be happy and perhaps she would even comment on his lack of dutifulness. Percival might not make the choices her son would have made, but he'd try his very best to be a brilliant duke and manage his estate well. He'd always make sure the dowager's needs were taken care of, and that would have to suffice.

Yes, after a quick jaunt to London, he could start the rest of his life, the one he'd always heard the great poets laud, but never thought actually existed.

"You're smiling." Fiona slipped her hand into the nook of his arm.

He nodded. "I'm thinking of something pleasant."

She chuckled. "I gathered that. Care to share?"

He shook his head, his lips still spread up. "It's a surprise."

Romance might be a new thing to him, but he was certain a woman didn't want to hear he was in love with her on a crowded path. Those sorts of moments should be confined to places with candlelight, roses, and a great deal of privacy. Those sorts of moments were to be treasured forever.

They strode up the path. The place was every bit as grand as Fiona had said it would be. Roman Gods and elaborate stone vases perched on the facade of the Georgian manor house. A long, man-made lake stretched before the building, and even though ice filled the lake instead of water, and any birds and ducks that used to frequent it had long departed for more sensible destinations, the manor house still retained an impressive allure.

They sauntered into the house, and Percival grinned. Fiona was on his arm, and life was wonderful.

Everyone changed into their slippers, and they strolled past rows of boots of mainly differing sizes of Hessians, into the ballroom.

Mistletoe and holly hung from the ceiling. Red ribbons were tied around each candlestick, and oranges and pine cones mingled together in silver bowls. Fiona had told him the ball would be elaborate, but he hadn't expected this.

Everything was impressive and perfect. A footman offered him a drink, and Percival took a deep sip of negus, smiling as the hot liquid, filled with spices and citrus, swirled down his throat, warming him as effectively as if he'd swallowed fire.

Eight hour candles cast golden light from the comfort of gilded candelabras. A fire blazed in the huge marble fireplace situated in the center of the room.

Musicians played up-tempo music in a corner, their heads tilted as their violin sticks jostled up and down in furious beats that created marvelous music. A large section of the ballroom was devoted to dancing, and men and women formed intricate patterns. He stared at the rapidly changing kaleidoscope of silk and velvet.

Men wore black suits, and women wore pastel-colored gowns. Jewels sparkled from the women's necks and chests, as if they had chosen diamonds and rubies to mask their cleavage. Silver punch bowls, embellished with flowers and leaves, dotted the room, leaving no one in need of an excuse for merriment.

Fiona smiled. "I told you it was elaborate."

"How on earth did the baroness manage to emulate the best of London?"

"I'm sure her life's work is emulating the best of London." She tipped her head to the ceiling. "Or the continent. She had a famous Italian painter come all the way from Venice to decorate the ceiling."

Gods and goddesses perched on fluffy white clouds, staring down at them.

Percival shook his head. Likely they wouldn't approve of the fact that he was feigning to be somebody else's fiancé.

The ballroom was thick with people. Silk-gowned women danced beside black-suited dandies and Corinthians. Women of all ages cast their gazes in his direction, likely assessing his marital status and potential as a suitor, if not for themselves then for their daughters. Their pleasant gazes wavered when they spotted his wooden leg peeking from his trousers.

He'd thought he was going to some local ball—but this, Lord, what if someone recognized him?

Fiona's posture was stiffer than normal, and her lips were pursed into an unyielding line. She glanced around the room. But from the manner in which her hands tightened around her reticule, creasing her long white gloves, she probably wasn't merely in awe of the crown moldings. "I'd forgotten how much I despised this."

He nodded, even though there didn't seem much wrong with a ballroom filled with helpful-looking footmen holding silver platters of drinks and appetizers, long tables topped with even more food and drink, and up-tempo music.

"I hope Grandmother's fine." Fiona bit her lip. "She didn't look that well when we left."

Percival didn't want to agree with her.

His grandparents had all passed away, and he hadn't even had the benefit of any close relationships with them. He supposed that unfavorable comparisons to his cousin didn't really count for a close bond, however instructional his grandparents had intended their unsought advice to be. His brother Arthur had escaped much of their condemnation, perhaps because they'd grown feebler, but more likely because there was never much chance he'd be tasked with the dukedom. And Arthur had of course always been ridiculously charming, as had Percival's younger sisters.

He wouldn't allow her to be unhappy. "The servants will call you if there's any need to return," Percival assured her. "She has a whole swarm of people looking over her. She seemed more excited about the ball than you. Come, you need to get some stories to bring her."

He leaned toward her, and for a moment he almost pecked her cheek, before he had the good sense to halt himself. That action would be inappropriate for an actual fiancée, much less a pretend one. He may have vowed to himself that Fiona would always have a place in his life, but that moment hadn't been formalized yet.

"THERE HE IS—LORD MULBOURNE!" Fiona swiveled her head toward Percival. "He's made an appearance. I almost believed he wouldn't be here. I must—"

Percival smiled. "Go ahead. Dazzle him. I know you can. Your ideas are marvelous."

Fiona spread her lips into a wide smile. "Th-thank you."

The phrase did not suffice in crediting him with everything he had done, but it would have to do for now. The words hardly conveyed the burst of emotion that blazed through her when she thought of him. The man toppled all her pre-conceptions of the *ton.* He'd defended her to her uncle. He'd even stayed longer with her, refusing to journey to London from Harrogate. He'd cared about Grandmother. He even . . . he even seemed to care about her.

He wasn't simple handsome. The man was magnificent: intelligent and far kinder than he desired to display. She forced away the strange flutterings that beat against her chest with frequency whenever she dwelled on him.

The ball was everything she hated, everything that had impelled her retreat from society, and yet it hardly seemed to be the hellish spot she'd imagined it to be.

Some women whispered, and though they might be gossiping about her and her unlikely attendance, they might not be.

"Excuse me . . ." A woman halted her. The woman's eyes peeked from an ornate oriental fan. "Your clothes—"

"Yes?" Fiona paused, bracing herself for some insult, though she doubted that even the harshest one would affect her very much.

"It's lovely." The woman smiled.

"Lovely?" She repeated the word.

"You look quite beautiful. You must give me the name of your dressmaker."

"Oh." Warmth spread through Fiona. It didn't matter whether the woman thought her beautiful or not, but pleasure still coursed through her nerves. "Thank you. You look lovely as well."

She peered over the crowd. Madeline's husband, the baron, stood in the corner of the ballroom. No one else had approached him, and the man seemed content to fix his gaze on the various dancers as they leaped and jostled through the patterned dances, the women's gowns swishing and the men's brightly colored waistcoats shimmering.

"Lord Mulbourne!" She called out, and he turned to her.

"Miss Amberly." His eyebrows lifted somewhat, and Fiona sighed. Everyone was right. She could have been more social. It wasn't good for the husband of her former best friend, the husband of her very own cousin, to express shock at their meeting. "It's a pleasure to see you."

"You too."

"You're looking well."

She smiled. "I'm feeling well."

"Ah . . . The merits of youth."

She nodded, but for the first time it occurred to her that this man, the one whom Madeline had boasted so much about, was perhaps not perfect. Perhaps he was not the ideal match Madeline prided herself in making, and perhaps Madeline had made her own sacrifices to follow the rules of the *ton*. Lord Mulbourne was rather on the wrong side of thirty-five, and grey speckled his thin hair, the pale flecks emphasized by the man's ivory cravat.

"Are you looking for my wife?" He smiled politely.

"No!" Fiona stammered, and then took a breath, forcing her voice to remain calm. "I mean—I wanted to speak to you, though I must speak to Madeline at some point, for I must thank her for this delightful party."

"She mentioned it was a struggle to get you to accept her invitation."

Fiona offered him a sheepish smile and peered around. Though there were some clear couples at the ball, there were also groups of unmarried women sitting on the outskirts. Perhaps they were wallflowers, but despite the term and its decided bluntness and absence of flattery, the women seemed to be enjoying themselves, chattering and sipping mulled wine. "Then I was a fool."

"Is that what you came to tell me?" Amusement filled Lord Mulbourne's voice.

"No—" Fiona smiled. "I wanted to speak with you about something quite different."

He raised his eyebrows, and Fiona forced her voice to not shake. "I rather believe I've discovered a Roman palace buried beneath an apple orchard at Cloudbridge Castle."

Lord Mulbourne tilted his head. "That is rather an incredible statement. Or perhaps not so incredible." He swung his gaze around the room. "Where is my dear wife now?"

Fiona shook her head. "I've come to speak with you. Not her."

"I see." Lord Mulbourne nodded, but his smile wobbled somewhat, and the easy rapport between them seemed to have all but disappeared. "I'm afraid you don't quite understand—"

"I do," Fiona hastened to add. "I understand perfectly. I've read everything you've written about Classical Civilizations."

"You have?" Lord Mulbourne's face seemed a trifle paler than before, and he craned his neck again to peer out over the crowds. His hand flickered up. "There she is."

"And your work is brilliant," Fiona added. "Absolutely brilliant. So very insightful."

Lord Mulbourne relaxed his shoulders somewhat as he gazed at his wife. "I'm pleased."

"As you know, much talk is devoted to digging up Roman sculptures and bringing them over here. Now that Napoleon is gone, it's of course once again easy to get to Italy."

The baron flashed her a tight smile.

"And that's wonderful," Fiona continued, "But I'm convinced there are treasures within Britain as well."

He raised his eyebrows.

"You must have an opinion on it," Fiona leaned forward, and her heart hammered. "What do you think? Your good word would mean everything in giving me permission from Uncle Seymour to dig up the apple orchard."

"I—" Lord Mulbourne stammered and stepped away.

For one moment Fiona thought he'd abandoned her. She peered into the crowd, and for a wild moment she even thought she recognized Graeme, the mail coach driver, but the thought was absurd. Drivers didn't attend balls such as this one.

Lord Mulbourne returned soon, dragging Madeline behind him.

"Miss Amberly was telling me that she believed a Roman palace might be buried underneath her estate. And she wanted to know my opinion on the possibility of it."

"Indeed." Madeline sipped her drink.

"I know the subject has some controversy," Fiona said. "Lord Mulbourne's article on the Roman soldiers' influence on Britain was fascinating."

Madeline's face rosied in obvious pride of her husband's accomplishments; perhaps Fiona's negative judgement of her had been inappropriate.

"But then you will believe," Madeline said, "My husband's opinion that the Romans left no art of any significance here, and that we must go to the Mediterranean to find the true treasures of the Roman Civilization."

Lord Mulbourne cleared his throat. "Yes, yes. Just what I was going to say. You always do manage to take the words straight out of my mouth, my dear."

Madeline's lips flickered up, as if they were sharing a marital secret.

Fiona smiled. It must be nice to know someone so well. She flickered her gaze across the room to Percival, and warmth spread through her. As she spoke to Lord Mulbourne about her findings, she reflected that she'd never found anyone as wonderful as Percival.

This morning's activities had been more than she'd ever imagined, and though she should feel a flurry of unrest that the man was leaving, he'd hinted that there would be more between them.

Life was magnificent.

Chapter Nineteen

"I'VE COME TO RESCUE you, Your Grace!" A deep voice boomed in Percival's ear, and he spun around, tightening his hand on his cane.

Blue eyes peered at Percival from dark hair that curled in locks resembling his own. The man's complexion was more bronzed, the cheekbones more chiseled, and Zeus help him, the man even had stubble, even though whiskers were firmly relegated to the most provincial people, and even though this Christmas ball demanded a certain degree of refinement.

Only one person in his life was so frustrating.

Arthur.

Percival tightened his fingers around the goblet of mulled wine he'd taken for Fiona. The warm metal stung his hand, and the compilation of cinnamon and sugar that wafted upward suddenly seemed sickening as he stared at his younger brother. "What on earth are you doing here?"

"Being heroic." A smile spread over Arthur's face, the sort of smug grin that had earned him his reputation as a rogue.

"But—"

"I found him!" Arthur's voice, unfailingly strong, bellowed over the sound of the violins. "My brother is safe."

"Wonderful, m'lord," another voice boomed from another corner of the room.

Percival swung around. He widened his eyes at the sight of a man in a red uniform with gold epaulets.

"Did you call the army?" he whispered to his brother. Dread soared through him.

"And the magistrate." Arthur's smile widened. "Some people might ignore local law enforcement, but I always say, the locals know the situation on the ground best."

"I—"

"Find the Scarlet Demon," Arthur shouted. "Stop the music! We're looking for a female, red-headed criminal. She may be dangerous."

"Oh, my!" The surrounding women shrieked, clutching their pearls.

"You better go on the floor," Arthur said. "The floor is safest. She's been known to carry a knife!"

Men and women threw themselves on the ground with a vigor he hadn't seen since the war.

"Arthur!" Percival shouted. "You mustn't!"

"Mustn't what?"

"You don't know what you're doing." Percival glanced at the glossy fabrics crushed against the marble tile. He raised his voice. "False alarm! It's fine. No trouble!"

"Percival!" Arthur swung his head to him. "I'm saving you."

"I don't need to be saved."

"Ah... You already incapacitated her. Where is she? Tied up behind a curtain somewhere? Good work." Arthur slapped Percival on his back, so he tottered somewhat on his leg. Arthur stretched out his arm to better Percival's balance. "Er . . . Sorry."

Percival's eyes narrowed, and he placed his hands on his hips. He fixed his eyes on his brother and spoke very slowly. "Tell them not to worry."

"But—"

"Now."

Arthur sighed and turned to the other guests. "Apparently the criminal has already been apprehended. You may all dance freely. And . . . er . . . rise."

Slowly some of the people stood, their eyes still wide, their gazes still fixed on Percival and his brother.

Arthur reached over and grabbed Percival's drink, noisily slurping the mulled wine. "You don't appear to be in such dire straits, brother."

"You shouldn't be here," Percival growled. "What on earth are you doing?"

"Me?" Arthur scowled and swung his gaze around the crowded ballroom. "Right now I'm limited to admiring the outstanding decor. Who knew a place could have so many red ribbons?"

Percival scowled.

"And those chits in their white satin dresses. Lovely!" Arthur continued, his voice carrying over the violins. "But you know we have pretty women in London too."

A few ladies glanced in their direction and covered their smiles with their French fans. At least Percival hoped it was smiles they were covering.

Percival searched for Fiona. He should be rescuing her. He gripped hold of his cane and headed toward her, brushing through the swarm of finely attired people.

"You would think a wooden leg would slow you down," his brother grumbled beside him.

"What brought you here?"

Arthur shrugged. "I got your note and like the dutiful brother I am, I dropped all of London's pleasures, galloping over the countryside in true familial fashion."

Percival sucked in a deep breath of air. "Thank you."

"You're welcome. And of course the mail coach also sent notification."

"Indeed?"

"You shouldn't have insisted on the coach going without the guard." Arthur shook his head. "Your forceful capture was a big to do. Would have been in all the newspapers, I'm sure, if they hadn't been so incredibly embarrassed that they'd lost hold of the mail for a few hours. Not good for their reputation."

"Right." Percival bit his lip.

"I spoke with the driver on his way over here as well. The man seemed rather light on his gun if you ask me," Arthur said. "The thing's not there for bloody decoration. I told the magistrate and army to look out for a woman called the Scarlet Demon."

"Look. About that letter—"

"In which you told the dowager that a highwaywoman had kidnapped you?"

"Er . . . Yes." Percival swallowed hard. "Turns out the situation was not so calamitous."

Arthur rolled his eyes. "Well. Obviously."

Percival raised his eyebrows.

Arthur banged down the empty mulled wine goblet. Or not so empty. The baroness's white lace tablecloth now had distinct crimson splotches on it, not that that was the sort of thing his brother would care about. Instead his brother picked up a glass of negus. The citric smell wafted over Percival, and his tongue prickled.

"The dowager is furious," Arthur said.

"Oh."

"I don't think I've ever seen her eyebrows draw quite so closely together."

Percival shivered. He'd imagined their aunt being worried, and he'd struggled to word the letter gently.

"You mean—"

"You were supposed to be in London to propose to Lady Cordelia. The dowager wants the perpetrator to be punished."

This time Percival grabbed a drink. He sloshed down the liquid, but the mixture of spices failed to soothe anything, and he hobbled toward the wall.

"Percival." His brother's voice was low. The man ambled beside him. "It's not your fault you were kidnapped. These things happen."

"It was just a case of mistaken identity."

"Ah? Wrong victim. Suppose a duke's not quite fine enough for these Yorkshire folk? More into wealthy American heiresses, hmm?"

"Er . . . More like she wasn't really a highwaywoman."

Arthur laughed. Loudly. "You got captured *by accident*? You mean she wasn't even really trying?"

A few finely dressed women craned their necks toward them. The turban of one middle-aged mama tilted to such an extent that Percival marveled it didn't topple off.

He clenched his teeth together and focused on his younger brother. "Please lower your voice."

Arthur stared at him hard, and Percival almost wavered under the man's assessing gaze.

"Just—" Percival inhaled. "I'm sorry I sent you all this way. I'm not ready to go."

"You don't have a choice."

Percival scowled and scanned the room. But he didn't see any red hair, and though there were other red dresses, none of them were hers.

It was too late.

The ballroom was too large, too crowded. The generous draping of greenery, the sparkling ornaments, and the vast amounts of red ribbons, tied with large bows to anything that had a handle, now only served to hide Fiona from him. "You can go now. I'm safe. And I need to speak with Fiona."

"Great Zeus on Olympus!" Arthur's voice boomed. His eyes broadened, and Arthur was the type of man to retain a cool demeanor. "You've found yourself a little harlot."

Percival stiffened.

Arthur's gaze leaped from the silver platters of appetizers to the glass pitchers of punch to the glossy dresses of the gentry, and he smirked. "You're not a hostage. You're enjoying yourself."

"It's true, isn't it?" Arthur stepped nearer him. "I knew you couldn't change your ways. All that noble talk about serving as a replacement for Bernard. All nonsense."

The knot on Percival's collar seemed too tight, and the rows of flickering scarlet candles in golden candelabras resembled Hades more than the supposedly cheery atmosphere of a winter ball.

"You don't need to concoct a flimsy excuse to avoid going to London. Though maybe you should do something about Lady Cordelia."

"I haven't technically proposed."

Arthur waved his hand in irritation. "She's confident enough to think you're not gallivanting about with some madwoman."

"She's not a madwoman. Not a harlot. She's—" His voice dropped off, and his gaze must have clouded as he considered Fiona. The woman was everything wonderful. She was brave and caring, intelligent, and oh so beautiful.

"Magnificent?" Arthur raised his eyebrows, and sarcasm filled his tone.

Percival's chest constricted.

A commotion clattered on the other side of the room, and Percival quickened his path, forcing his way through the throng.

Chapter Twenty

MADELINE AND HER HUSBAND continued to be intrigued by Fiona's findings, and though Madeline threw her hands up in the air a few times and declared her ignorance of archaeology, even she contributed to the discussion.

Fiona had gone to the ball, and the world had not ended. Everything seemed *nice.*

"So . . ." Fiona sucked in a deep breath of air and peered at Lord Mulbourne. "Might you perhaps be able to speak with Uncle Seymour? Tell him of the find's significance? I've spoken to him, but a word from you would be so beneficial."

Lord Mulbourne glanced at his wife, who nodded.

He smiled. "Certainly."

Fiona's heart swelled, and she strove to steady her voice, unused to the gratefulness surging through her body. "Wonderful."

Just then a tall man clothed in austere attire and wearing a somber expression approached Madeline. Fiona smiled, recognizing the local magistrate.

"Hello Mr. Barnaby." She waved at him, and he blinked.

Likely he wasn't accustomed to her being so talkative. But ever since this weekend, everything had changed.

"Miss Amberly." He inclined his back slightly and then pulled up in a jerky movement as if he'd reconsidered bowing to her.

Fiona shifted her feet. The man's solemnity was conspicuous. Come to think of it, there'd seemed to be a skirmish earlier too. Something hollowed inside her.

"That's the lass!" A Scottish-accented man's voice barreled through the ballroom. "That's the Scarlet Demon."

Dread, pure, bitter dread, soared through her, and she swung around.

It was Graeme. Dear Lord, it was the mail coach driver himself.

"Seize her!" The man pointed a stout finger at her, and his bushy eyebrows scrunched together. "See that she's hanged!"

Barnaby squared his shoulders. "Miss Fiona Amberly, I am placing you under arrest."

Fiona froze, and all her happiness, all her festivity, drained from her. She shook her head, as if testing whether the man might be some mirage, manifested from her guilt.

"Mr. Barnaby, I do not appreciate you disrupting our festivities in this outrageous manner." Madeline rested her hands on her waist, as if she were the governess she'd always been afraid she might become, and Barnaby were her debauched charge.

"Lady, the magistrate is trying to do his job," Graeme unhelpfully offered. "She's all done up now, like some fancy woman, but I know who she really is. No fooling me."

Madeline's blue eyes widened, and for the first time her face reddened to such a shade that the result was not pleasing. "This is absurd. Who are you?"

Graeme jutted his thumb at himself. "I'm the man who's helping keep the crime off the highways."

Madeline blinked.

Graeme strutted toward her. "They call me witness number two."

"And just where is witness number one?" Lord Mulbourne asked, his silky voice remaining reasonable.

"We're trying to locate him," the magistrate said. "You haven't seen the Duke of Alfriston about?"

Fiona's heartbeat quickened.

Madeline and her husband swiveled their heads toward each other. Madeline shook her head.

"We haven't got a duke here..."

"Obviously this is some poor semblance of a joke, my dear. There's bound to be a simple explanation." The baron's voice was calm and reassuring, and Fiona's chest tightened, because there was no mistake: Graeme was not teasing her, and the magistrate, a man she'd known all her life, had not inadvertently arrested the wrong Fiona Amberly.

The fault was all Fiona's.

Except it was more than a simple fault, and it was more than the mistake of leaving her season early and regretting it. This was a mistake that had brought the magistrate, clasping a pair of handcuffs. This was a mistake that would bring her to prison, to the courts, and—Lord, forever mark her.

Nice women didn't go around talking to strange men, much less kidnapping them. She'd frightened a driver, she'd taken a mail coach . . .

She sucked in a deep breath of air and attempted to conjure up thoughts of Percival. At least he knew her now; she didn't want to consider what might have happened were he a stranger.

Barnaby's features always tended toward solemnity, but now his eyes hardened.

She'd disappointed him. She'd disappointed everyone.

"Young lady," Barnaby said. "I don't know what sort of hijinks you get up to at Cloudbridge Castle, but I assure you that we try to maintain a peaceful community here. Come with me."

"What on earth are you speaking about, magistrate?" Madeline frowned. "My cousin will *not* accompany you."

"My lady." The magistrate sighed. "Miss Amberly is accused of—"

"It's fine," Fiona hastened to say. "I'll follow him. I'll—"

"What's this I hear about you holding up my niece?" Uncle Seymour's voice barreled through the ballroom. "You were accosting her in that corner."

"Please go!" Fiona cried, and the conversation stilled around her.

"Go when this idiot tarnishes my family's good name?" Uncle Seymour's jutted his finger at the magistrate, and his face purpled. "Not bloody likely."

"Ah," the magistrate nodded. "I now understand where this young lady fell wrong."

"What's that supposed to mean?" Uncle Seymour's voice soared through the room.

"Uncle Seymour!" Fiona begged. "It's fine. I'm fine."

"Highwaymen—and women—are illegal. Fiona Amberly has been terrorizing the neighborhood, masquerading under the name of the Scarlet Demon," Barnaby said. "We have a plea from the Duke of Alfriston himself, a man so mighty we must take attention, to halt this woman's devious acts. He is even now being held hostage—"

Percival was involved in her arrest? Fiona's heart rate galloped, but there was no escape.

"That's absurd," Madeline said. "Fiona? Mousy Fiona is a highwaywoman?"

Fiona flinched.

"Indeed," Barnaby said. "It pains me that her gentle soul would have seen fit to take on a lifestyle adopted by the basest of society, abandoning all feminine values..."

"B-but," Madeline stuttered.

The magistrate stepped nearer to Uncle Seymour. "Your niece is a menace to us all. Not only did she steal a mail coach—a horrendous crime, she also kidnapped one of Britain's most prominent aristocrats. I am arresting her."

"It's not true," Madeline said. "Fiona—tell them it's not true."

Fiona was silent and averted her gaze.

Madeline shook her head. "Is that why you've never been to one of these events before? You were too busy engaging in criminal activity? Stealing *mail?*"

Fiona searched the crowd, but no one was there. "It wasn't like that."

"Do you deny the alleged events? Did you or did you not kidnap a nobleman in a mail coach? Did you or did you not then proceed to steal priceless family heirlooms from that same nobleman?" The magistrate's eyes narrowed, and she stepped back. "Please consider your words. I wouldn't want to find out that you had lied to evade justice."

"I—"

"Answer him!" Uncle Seymour urged. "It's a simple question. Yes, or no."

"Y—yes," Fiona stuttered. "It's true. I-I drove off with him."

The crowd murmured behind her. Even the magistrate's face looked shaken, as if he truly hadn't expected her to actually confess.

Her shoulders slumped. This was a mistake. If she had only been able to stay home, just as she had desired, this would never have happened.

"Oh my goodness," Madeline said. "You wanted to use my husband's good name too. Was that a scheme as well?"

"What?" Uncle Seymour swirled around. This time he fixed the force of his personality on Fiona. His bushy eyebrows moved down as he narrowed his eyes, as if they were cannons directed on the enemy.

Fiona's stomach writhed under his steely gaze. "Just the apple orchard."

"Idiot!" Uncle Seymour sneered. "Stop embarrassing the family. Lead her away, Barnaby."

"Embarrassing you?"

Uncle Seymour frowned. "A baronet has certain expectations to fill. Mad nieces do not generally improve their status. I certainly will not be known as a fool here."

The crowd that had gathered murmured, and Fiona's chest clenched. She glanced at the dance floor, but the couples had thinned, and now only a few young debutantes danced with some soldiers. Everyone who knew her was near her, and quite a few people who did not know her were also there.

The only person who wasn't there was Percival.

It was her fault. It was all her fault. She never should have kidnapped him, but there wasn't a way to make things right.

Fiona stepped toward the magistrate. Her legs wobbled, and she shivered. The crowd parted slowly, in equal shock that she was being dragged away.

Lord, what would happen when Grandmother found out? Shame ratcheted through her. She pulled at her red gown. The scarlet color branded her, and she followed the magistrate through the ballroom.

Percival was nowhere to be seen. The magistrate had mentioned the jewels. Only Percival knew about that. Not the driver.

He must have arranged for this to happen. He'd been so encouraging of her to go to the ball. She'd confided in him, sharing her discomfit of these events, and he'd—he'd asked the magistrate to arrest her, dragging her from this event before everyone.

That's why he'd encouraged her to seek out Madeline and the baron. He hadn't wanted to stand beside her when the arrest happened.

Her eyes stung, and she willed herself to not cry. Not here. Not before everyone.

This morning... Her heart wrenched, and she wrapped her arms together. Percival had seduced her.

Not that she'd put up much of a fight. He'd had her in her very own bedroom.

Her cheeks flamed. She'd trusted Percival. He'd whispered a few sweet words to her, expounding on some beauty that no one else seemed to see. He'd undressed her and touched her most intimate parts, all while intending to have her arrested later on. Had he simply been bored? Was she simply the only female of a certain age in a very snowy radius?

Lord—he'd acted like the very worst rake in the world, like the most unabashed rogue, and she hadn't seen it.

Her fingers clenched together as she strode through the ballroom. The butler swept open the door for her, refraining from making eye contact.

Cold air slammed against her, and the magistrate ushered her into his coach. Highway robbery was likely a capital crime, and her relatives had not seemed eager to defend her. She sat on the seat, every muscle rigid, her body already aching as her heart hammered frantically.

All her happiness had been an illusion; Percival despised her, and the archaeological finds would forever remain in the ground. And Grandmother—lord, she would disappoint her. Even Rosamund would struggle to hold her head up high when the *ton* discovered her sister's criminal deeds. The satin dress provided little protection against the cold, and she shivered, waiting for the magistrate to whisk her to her punishment.

Chapter Twenty-one

PERCIVAL STRODE IN the direction of the crowd, but the cluster of people was thick. His leg ached. He'd stood on it for so long already, and the wood pressed awkwardly into his remaining flesh.

He swallowed a deep breath of air, gulping down the scents of heavy perfumes and cigar-smoke from the thick cluster of the *ton*.

"Percival," Arthur said. "You don't need to see her. You know what she did. I spoke with the driver."

"You don't understand."

"Blast." His brother swore behind him. "So maybe she's not a professional criminal. Maybe you're right. But you're still a duke and you don't need to fall for some silly chit who pretended to be a highwaywoman. Didn't you mention she'd stolen the jewels as well? If you ask me, there seems to be scant difference between her and an actual highwaywoman."

"I didn't ask you." Percival's jaw tightened in a straight line and he pressed against the thick crowd of people. He clutched his cane, but maneuvering was a challenge. Balance was always an issue, and none more when there were actually people pushing against him.

He swerved toward a middle-aged woman wearing too much rouge. She glared at him when he collided against her pearl necklace. "You're not stealing that."

He muttered his apologies, and his brother called from behind him. "It's my brother's leg."

The lady directed her pince-nez downward. "Then he shouldn't be at a ball!"

A hard knot tightened and grew in his stomach. Murmurs sounded from the surrounding crowd. Someone was being arrested. Fiona. It could only be her.

"I always knew she was a ne'er-do-well," someone said. "Keeps to herself. Always thought it right suspicious."

Fiona was being hauled from the ballroom. He was going to be too late.

He quickened his pace.

"She abandoned her season," someone said, "after two mere weeks, and hasn't shown herself in society since then."

"Redheads. Not to be trusted," a third said.

Percival wanted to explain to each one of these people that they didn't understand. He didn't have time though. He needed to get to her.

He inclined his gaze toward Arthur, but his brother seemed all too interested in the surrounding conversations.

"You should listen," his brother said.

He stifled a laugh. "I thought you prided yourself on not heeding gossip."

"I pride myself on being a rogue," Arthur said. "Not on abandoning all sense and reason."

"Right." Percival forced himself to push farther into the crowd, even though that was a desire that everyone else seemed to be sharing now.

He was supposed to be here to protect her. He'd encouraged her to go to the ball, and now he was the reason she was being swept away, arrested before all of Yorkshire's finest society. Zeus, he'd ruined her life.

If only the magistrate had spoken to him. If only the driver's testimony hadn't been so damning. If only he hadn't allowed himself to separate from her.

"There she goes," someone said. "Arrested."

He peered over the neatly swept hair of the people, tamed into a plethora of familiar shapes. Jewelry glinted from some of the women. He could see her. His Fiona. Being dragged away by some elderly fellow who didn't deserve to be in her presence, much less take her away to whatever prison he had before the courts decided what to do with her.

"Fiona!" He hollered her name, forcing his voice to rise over the chit-chatter of the crowd. Never mind that it wasn't proper to address her by her first name. This was the woman he loved.

And for a moment he thought she wavered. But her gaze didn't meet his, and her eyes were rounder, more frightened than he'd ever seen them.

"Stop that woman!" He shouted. "I'm the one she kidnapped. Speak with me."

But if the magistrate heard him, he didn't stop. No one stopped. Fiona vanished, and he was left with nothing except the amused attention of the surrounding people.

"You!" Fiona's uncle spotted him. He wound his way through the crowd, his rotund figure not hampering his speed. He waved his finger at Percival, as if he were a mischievous boy. "You got her arrested."

"I—" Percival shook his head.

"That would be me," Arthur said from behind him. "Percival isn't responsible for this turn of events."

Air blew from Sir Seymour's mouth, and his beady eyes narrowed to thin slits. Finally, he shrugged.

"You're Arthur Carmichael, aren't you? His Grace's brother?"

His brother nodded. "That would be me, Sir."

"Sir Seymour," the man corrected. "Not just any sir. I'm like you. A member of the aristocracy. Titled."

"How nice," Arthur said.

"Yes." Sir Seymour's face brightened, before he flung his gaze to the large wooden doors from which his niece had just exited. "Miss Amberly is not titled."

"Indeed," Arthur said.

"Seems she had a desire to be titled." Sir Seymour eyed Percival, and he stiffened. "I thought it highly strange when she introduced me to you. Until I saw your leg of course. Then it all made sense." He laughed, though Percival did not join him.

"You needn't apologize for her." Percival tightened his grip on his cane.

Sir Seymour's eyes rounded. "I wouldn't dream of that. That woman deserves no apology. From anyone. I hope her erratic behavior won't hamper our relations, should we meet in London. I must apologize for not recognizing you. A man of your position, it's most embarrassing. And me a baronet! I will apologize for that. Though I see that you were off fighting in France."

"A war you didn't choose to join." Percival's voice was frosty.

"Me?" Sir Seymour chortled. "And end up without a leg?"

Percival tightened his lips.

"Or dead like your cousin?" Sir Seymour continued to guffaw.

"You place sole importance on yourself." Percival strove to make his tone as icy as possible.

"Exactly!" Sir Seymour chirruped. He shifted his legs. "I don't mean that as a failing."

"I know. But I find your demeanor insulting to the greatest degree."

Sir Seymour's hand moved to his fancily tied cravat. "I . . . er—"

"And you do your niece the utmost disservice as well," Percival added. "You should not stand here before me and disparage her. I will not tolerate it."

Sir Seymour narrowed his eyes. "Look. The law is the law. Her behavior to you was reprehensible, and I am most sorry that she was your introduction to the family. All Amberlys are not like her. I am not like her."

"Well, we are in agreement on that."

"Good!" Sir Seymour spread his hands on his waist, and it occurred to Percival that perhaps the baron would not have been as poorly suited to His Majesty's Army as he claimed. Drill sergeants might have things to learn from the man's ability to carry his voice.

The surrounding people were silent, everyone focused on the baronet.

"Please take this conversation to another location," Percival said. "I imagine that we would not want everyone to hear."

Sir Seymour narrowed his eyes. "I must divulge the poor character of my niece. I cannot wait. My conscience will not permit it!"

"Let's go," Percival murmured to his brother.

"And miss this?" Arthur chuckled. "This is far more fascinating than the carriage ride would be, even if that leaves us more at risk of highwaymen, or of women pretending to be highwaywomen."

"We must depart," Percival said, but the crowd thronged in a thick circle around them.

"She tricked you," Sir Seymour said.

Percival sighed. "It was unplanned. She didn't know I was in the carriage. She was attempting to warn my driver about a fallen tree, and unfortunately my driver was mistaken and believed that she had put the tree on the road deliberately."

"Oh she would never have *put* it there." Sir Seymour shook his head, and Percival nodded, assuaged that her uncle at least believed this about her.

"But what would she do?"

"Did Fiona's sister, Lady Rosamund, ever have a chance to share with you her theories on catching a husband?"

"No . . . I did not have the pleasure of speaking with your other niece much."

"Such a shame. My other niece is most intelligent."

"As is Fiona," Percival said stiffly, though he wondered at the purpose of this gallantry, given Sir Seymour's disinclination to listen to any favorable word about his very own niece.

"Lady Rosamund managed to marry off many people. She's a romantic." Sir Seymour smiled. "Such a feminine attribute, would you not agree? But we men should not fall for such female manipulations."

Percival's leg throbbed, and he tried to shift his position discretely. Sir Seymour's eyes narrowed.

"Though perhaps you are claiming to have fallen for Miss Amberly? Because I can tell you—she planned everything. I have proof."

Chapter Twenty-two

FIONA PLANNED THIS?

Percival raised his chin defiantly, and his voice was every bit as steady as when he bellowed orders in the battlefield. "Impossible."

"You didn't tell her before?" Sir Seymour smirked.

"Miss Amberly did not know I was a duke until I was at Cloudbridge Castle."

"Are you certain, Your Grace?" Sir Seymour leaned toward him, and his features arranged themselves into a condescending expression usually reserved for tutors who'd noticed a foolish error in a wayward pupil's arithmetic problem.

"I may have announced it before, but she seemed most unimpressed." He chuckled. "She did not believe me."

Sir Seymour raised his eyebrows. "Didn't believe you, or already knew? Because if she already knew—she would also appear unimpressed."

Percival tilted his head. He hadn't expected Sir Seymour to talk about that.

The man pressed on. "You didn't wonder why she chose to spend so much time with you? Despite your deformities?"

"Injury," Arthur said behind him. "Heroic injury."

Sir Seymour waved his hand. "Injury, deformity. I'm not favorable to all these niceties. The problem with the *ton* is that they are all too willing to feign politeness. It's a waste of effort on everyone's part. We would all save time if—"

"My dear," Sir Seymour's wife broke in. "Perhaps it is not reasonable for you to speak to His Grace in this manner?"

"He understands. He was a warrior, for goodness' sake." Sir Seymour gave him a huge grin. "That's why I'm not afraid to speak my opinion freely to him. It's wonderful to celebrate our ability to speak freely to one another here. Quite different from France and its Reign of Terror."

"That was some time ago," Arthur said.

Sir Seymour shrugged. "I'm not prone to visiting the frogs myself. Bloody horrible if you ask me. All too willing to attack Englishmen. As your cousin so clearly discovered."

Pain seared Percival's leg, and he shifted it.

"But I'm warning you about my niece! The chit was clearly in desperate need of a husband. Still is, to be frank, so perhaps I shouldn't say anything." He closed his mouth, and then opened it, as if in desperate desire of speaking.

"You should tell us," Arthur said, his voice firm.

"But—" Percival turned, but Arthur rested a hand on his shoulder.

"You're the duke; she doesn't even have a title," Arthur whispered. "She's already shown an inclination to violence."

"But—" Percival protested.

"Or madness," Arthur said. "I don't want you to get hurt."

His gaze shifted to Percival's leg again, and Percival's chest constricted. He abhorred that even his younger brother, a man completely without any sense of reason or responsibility, felt capable of ordering Percival about.

Even though Percival's leg had been cut off many months prior, and even though he'd recovered from his confinement long ago, his status of invalid was assured. It didn't matter how reasonable Percival acted; he would now always be worried about.

This fact would not be lessened if he continued to insist that Fiona was not as appalling as everyone else deemed her to be. Many of these people insisted she possessed horrible qualities and claimed she verged on insanity.

"Rosamund said it was easy to convince any man to marry someone. One had five paths to do it. The first path was dazzling them, by being pretty and feminine and everything wonderful." Sir Seymour turned and kissed his wife's hand. "Just like my lovely, beautiful bride."

Percival nodded, and a cold chill spread through him. By Zeus, it was bloody difficult to see Sir Seymour as completely lacking in morals. Not when he treated his own wife with such consideration. His shoulders sank, and he wondered if just perhaps Sir Seymour might be saying something of importance after all.

"And the second cause is by befriending them—feigning delight in the things that interested them." Sir Seymour paused. "I take it that my niece did not do that?"

"No." Percival shook his head, but Sir Seymour merely chuckled. The baronet curled his lips upward, revealing teeth tainted by likely frequent consumption of sweets.

"The other method is by ignoring them. Clearly she didn't do that. Otherwise she would have let you be in the coach." Sir Seymour chuckled.

Percival stilled. The horde of elegantly attired people seemed to arch toward him, and he was conscious of the faint fluttering of ladies' fans. The decorative items' proclivity toward feathers and dramatic colors did not mask their owners' open interest in the conversation.

Sir Seymour turned to his wife. "Now what were the other tricks? It was all most clever. Most clever indeed. Ah ha!" He steepled his fingers. "The other trick was mystifying them—well, there may have been a bit of that. But you know what I truly think she did, the clever minx?"

Sir Seymour's wife tugged the man's arm. "Do you truly think you should be telling him all that?"

Sir Seymour grinned. "My niece is married. She won't mind if I reveal all her insights."

"But His Grace might not appreciate—"

"His Grace will appreciate not being married to a calculating madwoman. I think His Grace should be ever so thankful to me."

"I highly doubt that," Percival said.

Sir Seymour tilted his head. "And still you stand here before me, even though your leg must hurt ever so much."

Percival stiffened. The throbbing intensified under the baronet's fixed stare.

"The last rule is simple. Capture them! Keep them alone." Sir Seymour chuckled. "I thought it was a joke myself. I thought surely no one would do that. But didn't Rosamund give the list to her sister? And didn't Fiona capture you? And force you to be in her company? Taking you in that tiny sleigh to Harrogate? Only to turn around? The magistrate said she even insisted on spending the night with you."

"You shouldn't speak about your niece like that." Percival whitened and leaned forward. "I am afraid we are of great risk of being overheard."

People tittered behind him. Percival didn't recognize the people, but he knew they were important gentry in Yorkshire. It wouldn't be long before word would spread to London, haunting him, haunting Fiona.

"She's not here to defend herself," Percival said. "Don't speak of family in that way."

"Oh, I wouldn't call her family." Sir Seymour shook his head. "Relation perhaps, but I'm going to hope that the relationship remains ever so distant."

"I am sure she feels similarly toward you," Percival said, though he did not put much force in his words. Perhaps Fiona had calculated everything, learned of his trip by some deceitful method, and waylaid the course. Perhaps all the emotion he felt toward her was completely false.

"It's a foolish man who does not heed warnings."

"She doesn't desire marriage. She's not some fresh debutante eager to connect herself with a titled man. She's content with her work. She's amazing." Percival smiled now, eager to distract himself with thoughts of Fiona. Pondering her easily led to smiling.

"On the contrary, she's in desperate need of a husband. Once her grandmother dies, she might not have the opportunity to live at Cloudbridge Castle anymore."

"Surely you would not force her out! She adores the castle."

Sir Seymour sighed. "And yet she is not my daughter, merely my niece, and one who thinks I do not notice when she rolls her eyes at me. I adore my wife. Very much. I've no desire to taint the time we have together by having a niece whom neither of us are fond of live with us so she might tear up the beautiful apple orchard."

"I am quite fond of apples," Sir Seymour's wife added.

"You see?" Sir Seymour asked. "My hands are tied."

"Thank you for informing us. We are most appreciative," Arthur said. "You can be assured that my brother will have nothing else to do with her."

Sir Seymour nodded. "You are quite welcome." He paused. "My wife is quite fond of Sussex, should you ever see fit to invite—"

"I doubt we will see you again," Percival said. "Unless we are at a ball, in which case I would hope that we can put sufficient space between us."

"Ah . . . This is most unpleasant business," Sir Seymour said.

"Indeed." Arthur gave a curt bow and dragged Percival toward the exit. Bows had become a more difficult thing in recent months, and Percival did not deign to attempt one before the baron.

Lead seemed to have replaced his heart, and he strained against the pressing weight constricting his chest. He attempted to force Sir Seymour's words from his mind, but they kept on returning. The baronet believed them. That much was evident. He believed Percival had been woefully manipulated and that it was his aristocratic duty to warn him about her. And perhaps the man was indeed correct.

Percival's shoulders sagged. Perhaps Percival had been too eager to be flattered, too eager to believe a woman existed who might admire him for his own merits, even when that included a leg count that ended in one, and even when that consisted of a woman not knowing, or not believing he was truly a duke.

He shook his head. He'd been warned there were women everywhere who would be eager to join themselves to his money.

Perhaps Percival was simply naïve, unsuited for the role of duke. Perhaps it would be unwise for Percival to completely ignore their opinions.

Even if Sir Seymour lacked gallantry toward his niece, the man was likely held with more than a modicum of respect in his own circles. His own wife seemed pleased with him, which was more than Percival could say for many aristocratic marriages. More than he'd hoped for in his own marriage with Lady Cordelia.

His brother turned to him. "Let's go."

Percival followed him through the crowd of men and women, their satins and silks gleaming in the flickering light of the eight-hour candles. His wooden leg clicked against the unfamiliar black and white marble floor, and his leg ached as he pushed through the swarm of guests. The faces ranged from sympathetic to curious, but he didn't want either emotion from these people.

His hands tightened around his cane. This wasn't supposed to be his role. He wasn't supposed to become a duke. He was supposed to live a simpler life, and perhaps the dowager was correct in her ill-masked worry about the fate of the dukedom under his surveillance.

He'd been so close to giving the ring to Fiona. So close to divulging that he wanted nothing more than to join their lives together, to have her spark and her empathy always by his side.

His shoulders sagged. He'd been a fool. He should have learned at Waterloo that it was wrong to hope for anything more. He should have learned then that his life should only be focused on fulfilling the dreams of his cousin. Bernard had sacrificed himself for him, and he should not repay that sacrifice a mere six months later by tying himself to a chit who had found herself hauled off to the magistrate's prison.

Arthur held the door open for him, and they exited the ballroom. They pulled on their great coats and top hats in silence. The servants eyed them, curiosity visible. He wondered what story they would spread to the downstairs workers.

Fiona was right to be frightened of the *ton*. Unless she wasn't frightened and only wanted to isolate him . . .

He shook his head. He needed to speak with her. Even now, that's all he wanted to do.

"Soon you'll be with Lady Cordelia, and this will all be in the past. It's a good thing you wrote," Arthur said. "Seems like you got yourself embroiled in something quite nasty."

"I—"

Arthur sighed. "Look. You're my brother. Of course I'm bound to worry about you. But I don't like the manner in which your eyes soften whenever anyone mentions the woman's name. And I don't like how argumentative you were with the baronet."

"Is that what you took from the encounter? That *I* was argumentative?"

"Weren't you?"

"But he was insulting his own niece."

"And you defended her like she really was your lover."

Percival stiffened, and Arthur groaned. "By Hades, I was right. She's your harlot."

"Not harlot. I told you."

"Only because for some absurd reason you still manage to claim all sorts of respect for the woman, even when she blatantly kidnapped you and proved herself utterly unworthy of any trust."

Perhaps Arthur and Sir Seymour were right. Perhaps Fiona was simply a woman who displayed criminal behavior that he was too eager to excuse because something in her appearance appealed to his baser instincts.

But perhaps again she was more. Perhaps she was everything he longed for, the companion he dreamed that she could be.

Either way, he was going after her. He was not going to leave her in Yorkshire all alone while he gallivanted off to London to propose to another woman. He knew her too well, and she did not deserve that. He did not deserve that.

He wouldn't spend the rest of his life pondering her. The fresh breeze brushed against him. It was chilly, but he didn't mind.

A minuet streamed from the manor house. The party-goers were probably once again merrily bouncing up and down to music, as if his life and Fiona's had never been shattered.

A horse and rider thundered toward the house.

"Perhaps the rider is sorry to have missed all the gossip!" Arthur joked.

"He's certainly a late arriver."

The man leaped from his horse and hastily tied it.

"Ah, Captain Knightley." The man waved.

"Have you got yourself a new name?" Arthur murmured.

"He must be from Cloudbridge Castle," Percival said. "What is it?"

"Is Miss Amberly with you?" the man said.

"No." Percival didn't want to explain that Fiona was at the magistrate's. He was more eager than ever to get to her. What would her poor grandmother think?

"Inside?" The man dashed up the stairs.

"No," Percival called, and a chill descended on him. "Can I be of assistance?"

The man halted. "It's Mrs. Amberly. She's taken a turn for the worse."

Percival's shoulders fell. He liked Fiona's grandmother. "Miss Amberly is in the magistrate's coach. Can you recognize it?"

Shock flickered over the man's face, but he refrained from questioning Percival on the reason for Fiona's unusual location. "I passed it on the way up here..."

Percival nodded. "Then see if you can catch up with it again. Explain things to him. And . . . er . . . tell him that the Duke of Alfriston absolutely does not press charges."

The man blinked, and Percival shifted. His leg throbbed, and he longed to sit down again. Instead he said, "I'll come with you."

"But—" Arthur was quick to protest, but Percival shook his head solemnly.

"Do you think she'll make it?" Percival asked.

The servant's face tightened, and Percival did not press the man further.

Chapter Twenty-three

SHE WAS DEAD.

Grandmother wasn't supposed to die. It was impossible. Grandmother had been there Fiona's whole life, and it wasn't supposed to end. Not like this. Not without Fiona being there. Not without the doctors giving plenty of warning.

The magistrate had hauled her from the coach. She'd hoped for a reason to avoid prison, but it hadn't been this.

Her back was rigid and her jaw was steady as steel, for she thought if for one second she considered what had happened, that Grandmother would never ever wake up, then she'd collapse completely.

They'd told her Grandmother was sick, but when she returned to the castle, the servants were sober-faced. They directed her to the drawing room to wait for the doctor, as if she were a guest.

She'd known then.

Grandmother lay on her bed, her sheet pulled to her chin, as if she were simply sleeping.

Fiona plodded her boots over the hardwood floor, and she slowed as she neared the bed, as if the noise might wake her. But that was another thing she need never worry about again.

Grandmother looked just as she always did.

This *must* be a mistake. She turned to a maid. "Are you sure?"

The maid nodded, and her voice trembled. "Yes, m'lady."

Any last hope that had ridiculously hovered in Fiona's chest was extinguished.

This wasn't like the time when Grandmother had declared the silverware lost, and Fiona had found it, right where it had always been. This was final, forever.

I should have been here.

She hastened over to the bed. But it didn't matter how swiftly she was by Grandmother's side now. When it had counted, when Grandmother had swallowed her last breaths, she hadn't been there. Rosamund was with her husband's family, and Fiona, who was supposed to be taking care of Grandmother, had attended the ball of a cousin she didn't even like, when she didn't even like balls.

She'd paraded her supposed fiancé before all the highest society of the region, but for nothing. What did it matter if a few approving glances were cast in Percival's direction? Her engagement with him was false. She'd been so consumed with trying to impress people that she hadn't been there for her grandmother's last moments.

The only reason she wasn't in prison now was because her grandmother had died. Any hope of social credibility had vanished, and her name would now be linked with more disparaging laughter and remarks than it ever had been before.

She stared at Grandmother. Grandmother's *body*, she reminded herself. Or even—*corpse*. The tears that she'd managed to restrain over the long, jostling coach ride finally flooded.

Even though they'd talked about Grandmother's impending death, joked about it even, nothing had prepared Fiona for this.

Grandmother wasn't supposed to die. She was supposed to live on, sitting in her favorite chair, worrying about Fiona and her sister, and not fussing about herself at all.

Footsteps sounded from the hallway outside. The door handle turned, and Sir Seymour stepped into the room. He cast a glance at the pale body in the bed, and his face whitened.

"My poor mother," he murmured, and the wrench in Fiona's heart tightened. The man had lost his parent. He'd known she was dying, and Fiona had not made his time visiting pleasant.

"I'm sorry."

He gave her a curt nod. No kindness was in his gaze, and the memory of the evening engulfed her again.

"We'll have to talk about your future," he said, and she stiffened. "I think after tonight it's clear you can't live with us."

She blinked.

"You understand?" He scowled.

"Grandmother isn't even in the ground..."

An expression flitted over his face, but he soon firmed his features. "I would like to be alone with her."

Sir Seymour's mother had just died, and Fiona wasn't permitting him to grieve in peace. Her pain was incomparable to his. "N-naturally."

She pushed open the thick door, and this time hot tears stung her eyes. She blinked furiously. Some servants scurried from the hallway when she exited the room, and their thick black frocks disappeared behind a corner.

She sighed. She didn't know what she would say to herself either.

For it wouldn't be alright. Grandmother was dead, and nothing would return her to her peaceful life. Percival had betrayed her, for a reason which indicated more her lack of morals than his, and her dream of wiling away the rest of her life doing archaeology on the estate was exposed as the fantasy it was.

Fiona's throat had evidently malfunctioned, for all attempts to frantically swallow, to dislodge the clay that seemed to have stuck there, failed.

She glanced around the hallway. Now every object was familiar: the cast-iron doorknobs adorned with stiff, black, molded grapes that seemed poor replicas of the actual fruit, the caramel-colored paneling, and the black sconces from which candles perched, dripping wax onto the floor, the color depending on the season.

Soon it would all be a dream, the vividness fading. She'd struggle to remember the shape of the stiff grapes, if she remembered them at all, and her onetime home would be demoted to vague recollections. She might visit, were she ever to return to Sir Seymour's good graces, but Aunt Lavinia, who had never lived in the castle before, would be free to make all the changes she desired.

And Grandmother—dear, sweet Grandmother, was dead. Her chest constricted further, and her legs wobbled as she attempted to walk. She sucked in a deep breath, but the air was thick and stale. The doctor had ordered the curtains shut, and the maids had kept the sooty fireplace going.

Voices murmured from downstairs. Someone was calling on them. She longed for bed, on the off chance that she might wake from her nightmare.

Footsteps padded below, and she recognized the characteristic thump of Percival's wooden leg. She straightened her shoulders and tossed her hair, but that couldn't halt the sobs surging from her.

She didn't want to see him. The man had gotten her arrested and dragged from the Christmas Ball before everyone. Soon word of her misdeeds would spread throughout the *ton*. Because of him, she would never live at Cloudbridge Castle again. Because of him, she would never be able to pursue her beloved archaeological project again.

The very worst of everything was that he'd made her adore him—love him, and nothing could subdue the burning surge of pain.

Percival's grim face peeked from the stairs, and rage racketed through her. The man didn't have the right to act mournful. Not after he'd ruined Fiona's world. She hurried away.

Her dress swished against the furniture, and startled servants rushed from her path. She tightened her fingers into sharp fists and strode down the corridor. Once in her room she pulled her arms around herself and begged her body to calm.

PERCIVAL'S LEG ACHED. The ball had been tiring, and he'd spent the past hour on horseback in the frigid winter air, chasing the magistrate, and then finally convincing the man to release Fiona.

"Ah, it's you again." Sir Seymour's voice boomed. "I thought it might be another doctor. Not that anyone was able to save my mother."

"My condolences. She was a kind woman."

Sir Sidney's face tightened. "Indeed. Too kind at times."

"I wanted to see your niece."

"Gentleman callers at this hour? I shouldn't allow it."

"Please."

Sir Seymour sighed. "You don't believe me. You don't believe anything bad about her."

"Why do you want to demean her? She's your relative."

Sir Seymour shrugged. "I take pride in telling the truth. Perhaps we'd never met before tonight, but my wife did tell me that she'd heard from Her Grace, the Duchess of Belmonte, that their daughter Cordelia was going to marry you."

Percival stiffened.

"I hope my niece knows."

"She does."

Sir Seymour fixed steely eyes on him. "Hmph. And you wonder why I berate her for her lack of morals."

"It's not like that—"

Sir Seymour arched his eyebrows up. Finally, he shrugged and picked up a cloak. It was the dark one Fiona had worn when she first met him. "She didn't want to wear it to the ball. I found a pamphlet in this. The very one I told you about."

"You shouldn't search through her things."

"Don't you want to read it?" Sir Seymour flicked through the pages. "It's all about capturing men. Isn't that what you were—captured?"

"I—"

"And look, it even has a handy list of the most eligible rakes and rogues. And you're at the top. Because—shall I read to you?"

"You mustn't—"

Sir Seymour cleared his throat. "No space exists between the body and spirit. If you find an injured man, you find a vulnerable one. No man was more handsome than Percival Carmichael, and now no man is more flawed. He struggles to make it from one end of the ballroom to the other. He's now a duke, and the prize for his affections cannot be higher, nor can his affections be easier to obtain. Wallflowers, bluestockings, even you can capture him."

Percival's heart stopped. "That was—"

"Educational?" Sir Seymour smirked. "You probably didn't realize why your aunt was so eager to marry you off. She's probably terrified you'll marry the first woman who pays you attention. Even one who masquerades as a highwaywoman."

"I—"

"Tell me. When did you first find my niece attractive? Because I can assure you, no other man did. Was it after you found out that she had respectable blood coursing through her? Or was it before? When you thought her a common criminal?"

Percival's chest constricted, and he rubbed his hand over it. He'd never felt more powerless, not even when the blood had rushed from his leg on the battlefield.

Everything had been an illusion.

Fiona, his sweet Fiona, had expertly used him. And why not? The woman was clever. He didn't know how she'd found out that he'd been traveling near her estate, but clearly she had.

And the whole *ton*—did they all see him as this vulnerable? As destroyed? He fought to keep his breath steady. Sir Seymour continued to sneer.

"I don't like being contradicted before a vast crowd. You should respect the consideration I've shown you." Sir Seymour tossed the pamphlet to him, and Percival grasped the pages with the automatic reflex of an athlete.

Percival gazed at the pamphlet, wondering if the well-worn quality derived from careful perusing or could be ascribed to a poorer quality paper. "I need to speak with Fiona."

"Truly?" Sir Seymour shook his head. "Clearly you're as weak as the pamphlet claimed. My niece is in her room. She's already a ruined woman. You may see her there. I imagine you don't need directions."

Percival flinched and headed toward the steps.

"I trust even you will not be susceptible enough to fall for her trifling charms again."

The pain in his leg had never been more piercing, more searing, yet all he could think about was Fiona.

A SOUND RAPPED ON THE door, and Fiona sprinted up. She ran her hands over her skin. It felt puffy beneath her touch, and her eyes stung from crying.

It was Percival.

Or some semblance of the man.

His face was stern, and his lips were pressed into a tight, unwavering line. His eyes, usually so vibrant and lively, were replaced with a piercing stare, and she shivered.

He brushed past her. "My condolences about your grandmother."

The words could have belonged to any of her neighbors, any of her servants, any of the local gentry, and she wrapped her arms around the chest.

"You captured me on purpose."

"I—"

"I'm furious. Or are you going to tell me you've never seen this before in your life?" He tossed her a pamphlet.

She took the pages from his hand. The pamphlet was somewhat crumpled, but she recognized the cheerful prints. "It's mine."

"I see." His face seemed to crumple. He shook his head, and any emotion that had been there was replaced with the rigid expression of a stranger.

"My sister gave it to me."

"She's in on it as well?" Percival's eyes widened and flickered back into a dull glare. "You have a horrid family."

"Excuse me?"

"I'm leaving."

"Wait! What?"

He grasped the doorknob. "I don't think there's anything more for me to tell you. You don't even attempt to hide your contemptibility."

"Me? You had me arrested."

She glanced toward Grandmother's room, considering the cold, still body that lay inside. She couldn't bring herself to think about the ball. She'd been ridiculous, attiring herself in splendid clothes, smiling and chatting with everyone whom she knew she couldn't trust.

She clenched her fingers together into fists and forced her eyelashes down. She hadn't changed her dress yet, had headed straight to Grandmother's room, and the scarlet color was at odds with the sobriety of the moment. The ruffles, wrinkled from the long coach ride with the magistrate, hung limply from her. "Why are you here?"

His features hardened, and she laughed. The sound was ugly, but now was not the time for any pleasantry. "You shouldn't be here."

"I know."

She stiffened. Against all reason a sliver of her had imagined his presence would ease things, and he could explain away the pains of the night. He would tell her that he hadn't really seduced her this morning only to call the magistrate to have her arrested before everyone. He would tell her that this morning had meant something.

Instead he was a stranger. Worse even, for he despised her.

"You wanted to rake your gaze over my misery?" Her voice was haughty, but she couldn't bring herself to care. "You? The person who told the magistrate that I'm a highwaywoman? The person who made me the talk of the ball, in the most horrible way imaginable?"

"I—"

"It's not your fault. I know. It's mine."

Percival fixed her with a regal glare. "It is."

She blinked.

He strode toward her, as if he had no idea how much he affected her. As if he didn't know that she longed to bury her face in his wide chest, as if he didn't know she wanted his arms to pull her close, protecting her from everything in the world. As if he didn't know how much she adored him—still—even now that he was horrible.

Her chest tightened. "You're imaginary."

"I am not."

"No, but—" She swallowed hard. She didn't know what had happened to the Percival she once knew. He was gone. Maybe he always had been. "I concocted up a fiancé to please Grandmother. And now she's dead and I need to prepare things. I need to speak to the doctor and to the staff. I'll need to move. I don't have time to talk to you."

He continued to approach her.

Her heart pommeled her ribs, and she lifted her chin. He still appeared to resemble something—more. But she couldn't trust him. "You had me arrested."

"No!"

"You were the only person who knew I'd taken the jewels. And what is so upsetting about that pamphlet?"

"You knew about me."

"What are you talking about?" She glared at him.

"You said you'd never heard of me."

"I hadn't."

He stared at her.

She sucked in a deep breath of air. "Look... You come here right after my grandmother dies to insult me?"

"I—"

"Because I don't have time for that," she interrupted. "Go back to London."

"You really didn't know?"

She blinked again.

"Did you read the pamphlet?"

"Some of it. Those things are too silly to take seriously."

"Forgive me," his voice was hoarse, but she shook her head.

"It doesn't matter." She tried to laugh. "You were never real. Not to me."

"You're upset." Percival swallowed hard. "Let me be a comfort you."

She steeled herself from his charm. "We both know just what that ring in your parcel is for, and it has nothing to do with me. Do your duty, be a dutiful duke. I'll do my duty here."

She glanced down at her red ball gown. The silky fabric was garish, and she pressed her arms together, aware of Grandmother's unending sleep. Fiona lifted her chin. "Please leave."

He swiveled, his steps echoing through the hallway, and she stood silent, listening as the steps grew fainter and fainter, listening as she heard him murmur to Evans downstairs, and listening finally at the sound of horses trotting away.

He was gone, now just as much a dream as when she first described Captain Knightley to Grandmother.

Chapter Twenty-four

THE HORSES SLOWED, and the sounds of the city pervaded the carriage. Post horns blared, their honks mingling with the crunch of carriages grinding against cobblestones, and men and women shouted and jabbered outside.

Only one thought careened through Percival's mind, usurping the clamor and clatter of the city: he'd lost her. His stomach tightened, and he fought to square his shoulders and relax his face, lest his brother comment again on his misery. He clenched his fingers together and forced his breath to remain calm, for heaven help him, it was all he could do to keep his breaths steady.

By Zeus, he'd been an absolute fool. He didn't deserve her. What sort of man stumbled into the room of a woman whose grandmother has just died to accuse her of misdeeds? When he'd only just had her arrested?

He'd been too willing to believe society's gossip. He'd been too prideful, on guard of anyone taking advantage of his supposed vulnerabilities. She wasn't desperate for his money or lifestyle.

She wasn't the type of woman to care about dukedoms. Fancy balls meant nothing to her, and long dinners were dismissed as unpleasant. All the things which might have made women chase after him were disadvantages to her.

He should have been begging her to make her his. Instead he'd only hurt her more.

She was right. He shouldn't be anywhere near her.

His leg throbbed, pain pulsating through it. He shifted in his seat, but no position could ease the straining of his heart.

Ten years of being a rake, yet he'd lost his composure with this woman. She'd shattered all his pre-conceptions. She'd been braver, more intelligent, and more passionate than the ladies of the *ton* with whom he'd been familiar, and he'd claimed her for his own.

He closed his eyes as the memory rose of the day before, of soft curves pressed against him, of a woman unperturbed by his wooden leg. He directed his gaze at the offending appendage.

Maybe it wasn't his injury that had made her oust him from her side. Maybe she'd simply despised London, despised the *ton*, or found his company tiresome. Clearly it didn't matter—she was gone from his life. She'd made it clear that this was a time for real family and real friends, and not the ones caught along the way.

Percival sighed and thrust open the curtains. Tall white buildings flanked both sides of the carriage, and men rode on horses. Top hats perched on their heads, and their great coats spilled over both sides of the horses' rears.

It would be difficult to rejoin the *ton*. The woman had showed him what it was like to truly live, and he wasn't ready to live the dull, staid, responsible life he should.

He massaged his fingers over his aching leg. The long drive had done little to ease the pain. Sleep had been a rarity on the journey. They'd spent the night at another tavern, another blasted reminder of Fiona and all the wonder he'd thought he'd gained in his life, only to lose it.

A bird squawked outside, and Arthur rubbed his eyes. "Good grief, Percival, this is the absolute last time I'll rescue you. You look appalling."

"I feel appalling."

"At least you're honest with yourself. That's the first step to recovery."

Percival scowled, and Arthur heaved a heavy sigh. "Don't worry, old sport. You'll be back to your old dastardly self soon enough."

He laughed, but Percival did not join in.

Yesterday at this time he'd had Fiona on his lap, had gazed into the liveliest eyes in the world and dreamed of their lives entwined together.

Now he sat rigid in an uncomfortable carriage meant to take him to the finest neighborhood in the finest country in the world, and he couldn't feel more miserable.

He wrapped his arms together. Fiona's grandmother had died. Even though war had tried to teach him that the fact a person was there one moment was no guarantee he'd last until the next one, the news still shocked him. Death always did.

Percival sighed. His brother appeared bleary-eyed; it had been decent of the man to come after him. "I'm sorry for dragging you away from London."

Arthur stretched his arms over his head and eased his legs into a new position. "Gives a chance for the chits to miss me."

"Anyone in particular?"

Arthur tilted his head at him. The two weren't prone to discussing much beyond gambling halls and horses. "I prefer widows. They don't get their hearts broken as easily." He grinned. "Though married women are even better. They never confess to getting their hearts broken at all."

"You're enjoying being a rake."

"It's the perfect life." Arthur smiled, but something in his face flickered, and the words lacked his characteristic enthusiasm.

Percival tilted his head. He was older than Arthur, and by the time his younger brother had mastered talking, and playing without toppling over, Percival had been ushered off to Harrow.

"What's Lady Cordelia like?"

"Feeling romantic?" Arthur winked.

"Hardly," Percival growled.

Arthur shrugged. "Impeccable. She's a Belmonte after all."

"Hmm . . ."

"She's fluent in French, just perfect when you want to take your European tour. And quite knowledgeable about horses, if her brother's passion for them is any indication."

"Splendid," Percival said, though the thought of dragging his leg around Napoleon's former empire or buying horses failed to conjure an immediate rush of pleasure.

"And her watercolors are divine," Arthur continued. "The dowager was quite raving about them."

Percival narrowed his eyes. "Have you even met her?"

Arthur shrugged. "I met her last season. She's too proper to have spent time in London when parliament wasn't in session."

Percival considered Lady Cordelia. Everyone assumed he would propose, and it would be easy to do so. He clutched the package that held the jewels and traced the sharp edges through the velvet bag.

The coach halted. By Zeus, it would be grand if it were some highwayman. He could use a distraction now. But of course they were in the middle of Mayfair, and the coach had halted at the dowager's London residence.

He clambered from the coach, his legs stiff and his heart nowhere prepared for what was to come.

He only had to climb a few steps before the butler swung the door open.

"Dearest Percy." The dowager stretched out her arms to him in an uncharacteristic display of affection, assigning him a nickname he'd never used. Thick ebony taffeta crushed against him, and the dowager peered at him from famed, icy-blue eyes that her generation had lauded as beautiful, but which now appeared simply cold.

"Aunt Georgiana," he murmured to his late uncle's wife, bestowing a similar affection.

A woman, slightly younger than the dowager and clothed in a tangerine orange dress embellished with frills, regarded them. Her pale blonde hair was tied in a dainty chignon, and she'd pasted a bland smile on her face. She must be the Duchess of Belmonte, his new mother-in-law.

The dowager fixed a piercing gaze on him, and he sighed.

"You're late," she whispered.

"Yes."

"My nephew would never have been late for an event of such importance." The dowager stepped away from him and laughed, even though neither of them had said anything in the least bit amusing. She raised her voice. "My delightful nephew managed to get on the wrong mail coach. He slept almost all the way to Edinburgh, before he realized. And then he was held up by all the bad weather."

"Indeed," the duchess said.

"Quite amusing," the dowager said. "Clearly he requires a wife."

The Duchess of Belmonte's shoulders relaxed a fraction. "All men do."

"Indeed." The dowager arranged her features into something resembling a smile.

She was gifted at knowing what worked best for appearances. Usually the Duchess of Alfriston excelled at selecting the correct Staffordshire china to match somewhat, but not overly, with the other decor. She flaunted her knowledge of whether it was more appropriate to have the chef cook roast goose or stuffed pig, serve brandy or port. She invited the finest scientists and artists to her soir*é*es and knew just when they'd fallen from favor.

"You're just in time to prepare yourself for the winter ball," the dowager said. "Higgins is upstairs."

Right. He rubbed his hand through mussed locks. "How thoughtful of him."

"You're to look your best," she said sternly.

“Fortunately the man looks handsome,” the duchess interjected.

Percival strove to garner enthusiasm. Instead he sighed. “Forgive me. I'm tired. The long coach journey. Perhaps it is best if I do not come tonight.”

His aunt chuckled, though the sound seemed strained. “Ah, my darling nephew is amusing. The things he says. Of course you will attend, my dear. You mustn't think you can fool me.” She turned to the other duchess. “The man does like to jest. As if he wasn't able to sleep in the coach. Why, my nephew cannot wait to meet your daughter!”

“Yes,” Percival said finally. “My aunt knows me too well.”

A tightness in the duchess's jaw eased. “Good.”

“It will be a pleasure.” Percival bowed and headed up the stairs, grateful for the banister as he pulled himself up the marble staircase, as pain still shot through his leg and heart.

Higgins, his valet, waited for him at the top of the steps, and he succumbed to the man's ministrations.

Chapter Twenty-five

THE BALL RESEMBLED all the other London balls, and Percival steeled his jaw as he wound his way through sumptuously attired people, their faces enhanced by the soft candlelight and the previous toil of their valets and ladies' maids.

Laughter from the dance floor wafted toward him. Men and women swirled, and their fingers touched as they formed intricate patterns to the sound of the up-tempo violins. This time he did not regret the loss of his leg. He'd never had less of a desire to dance.

"You haven't forgotten the jewels?" The dowager lowered her voice to a whisper.

"No."

She'd asked him when they'd entered the coach, and when they'd departed. He still hadn't left the gems anywhere.

"You must propose at once," she declared. "No time for contemplation."

He raised his eyebrows.

"And then you'll be able to devote the whole evening to celebration. Quite in the Christmas spirit."

"I should speak with Lady Cordelia." He would grant his aunt that much. It was ridiculous to find themselves on the verge of marrying without actually having met.

The dowager's shoulders relaxed, and he scoured the ballroom, searching for some doe-eyed beauty.

Balls in London were a rarity at this time of year. Most of the *ton* had escaped to sprawling country estates they deemed cozy, and anyone left seemed to be at this one. Christmas Day had passed, but garlands dangled from every ceiling, and the aroma of mulled wine still wafted through the room. No one would stop celebrating the season until Twelfth Night.

A few people directed curious looks at him, and their gazes lingered on his cane and wooden leg. He glowered and did his best impression of a haughty duke, satisfied only when the cheeks of the nosiest guests pinkened in what he hoped was a result of guilt and not just from the culmination of copious imbibing of alcohol.

He felt someone's gaze on him, and he turned his head. Likely the elusive Lady Cordelia. Instead his heart tumbled.

Lord Somerville scowled. Beside him stood a couple gentlemen whom Percival did not recognize, though they seemed to have decided that abhorrence was the favored emotion to direct at him. Their dark coloring and lanky figures resembled Somerville's. These must be the man's brothers.

Percival tightened his grip on his cane, conscious of his deformity under the scrutiny of the Worthings. "One moment."

"You desire to speak with them?" The dowager sniffed. "At least they're titled. But you mustn't forget—"

"I won't." The ring burned in his pocket.

Percival wound his way through the clusters of finely attired guests, wondering at the swiftness at which the gossip must have traveled, until he stood before the man who'd once called him a brother.

Somerville's frown had not lessened, and the earl lowered his torso in an exaggerated bow. "Your Grace."

Percival flinched at the man's obvious sarcasm.

"May I present my brothers, Your Grace?" He turned to the swarthiest man. "This is the Marquess of Highgate."

"I have heard much about you, Your Grace."

Percival gave the marquess a tight, unreturned smile.

"And this," Somerville continued, "Is our youngest brother, Sir Miles."

"Pleased to meet you," Percival said.

Somerville nodded. "You might find it extraordinary, but those are actually their true names. Quite unusual."

Percival sighed. "I am sorry—"

Somerville raised his hand. "No need to apologize. I'm a mere earl, after all. Not prone to understanding the ways of the greater aristocrats. I'll only say that you gave no indication of being under duress. Instead you seemed content in the company of my wife's sister."

"I was happy," Percival croaked. "Believe me."

"You smeared her reputation."

Percival's shoulders slumped. The man was right. Percival had only hurt Fiona. He swallowed hard. "I don't see the countess."

Somerville frowned. "She's supervising the packing. We're departing for Yorkshire in the morning. I'm only here now to socialize with my brothers."

"Right." Percival stiffened. He knew when he'd been dismissed. "If you see Miss Amberly, please assure her of my utmost condolences."

"How polite," Somerville said. "To be frank though, she needs rather more than that. And Your Grace, you're not the person to bestow it."

Percival steeled his jaw. He wanted to smooth things over, not worsen them. But clearly the thought was ridiculous. He couldn't help Fiona. He'd only harmed her.

He scanned the ballroom.

"Are you searching for Lady Cordelia?" The marquess tilted his head.

"Perhaps."

"That's all her mother has spoken about."

"Right." Percival tightened his grasp on his cane, conscious of three pairs of glaring eyes on him.

"She's over there." The marquess extended his hand. "The woman in the gold dress. Not that you would have any difficulty finding her, since she considers herself the most desirable woman in England."

"You disagree." Percival raised his eyebrows, for a moment puzzled by the vehemence of the man's dislike of her.

The marquess shrugged. "From what my brother has told me, you will be well suited."

"Indeed." Percival didn't want to hear any more sarcasm, no matter how much he deserved it. He gave a curt bow and headed in the direction of his fate.

He observed with a bizarre impartiality that Lady Cordelia was beautiful. No one had exaggerated this woman's appearance. Her face was as symmetrical as any statue's, and her eyes appeared as cool.

"Allow me to introduce you." The marquess strode to the woman, who gave him a stiff bow from her shoulders. The marquess winked at Percival, and his heart ratcheted as he made his way to them.

"Lady Cordelia, this is His Grace, the Duke of Alfriston. You might find him most entertaining. He's in the habit of adopting new names at a whim."

"I am sure I will find him enchanting," Lady Cordelia murmured. Her voice was low, almost sultry, and irritation flashed over the marquess's face.

"Splendid," the marquess said, before disappearing into the throng of finely clad guests.

"Your Grace." Lady Cordelia glided toward Percival, every bit the goddess, and when she reached him she curtsied deeply. A diamond necklace sparkled on her chest, and he wondered at the necessity of fetching the jewels for a woman who clearly already possessed priceless ones.

Her voice was perfect. Calm and contained, and it didn't shake. Her cheeks were no pinker in his presence. Her gait was poised, her expression serene. She was unperturbed at meeting the man who would become her future husband. She couldn't be more different from Fiona.

Good. All the better to forget her.

He bowed. "I am no longer one for dancing, but perhaps we might find a quiet alcove."

Her eyes gleamed, and she nodded her head. His heart heavied as she steered him to a corner of the ballroom. Some wallflowers sat nearby, their gazes focused on the eligible men who ignored them. Lady Cordelia did not acknowledge them.

"So." She sat down and smoothed the folds of her elaborate, silky dress. "I heard you had some adventures these past few days. You must regale me."

His smile tightened.

From across the ballroom the dowager gestured to him. She pointed her peacock-feathered fan in a manner she probably considered discreet, even though the green and purple feathers could not be more ostentatious.

The gold ring burned in his pocket, and he moved his hand there. Lady Cordelia's lengthy black eyelashes swooped up, and a smile flickered on her perfect rosebud lips.

The chit likely thought he was about to propose. His heart dropped, an unpleasant sensation, since his stomach also seemed to want to rise. He stiffened his fingers and forced his breath to keep a steady beat.

Lady Cordelia ran her fingers over a sapphire bracelet. The stones seemed cold, despite their beauty.

He searched for something, anything to say.

"I've always wondered what a London garden looks like," Lady Cordelia chirped.

"Indeed?" He pressed his handkerchief to his lips. The woman might be from Hampshire, but he considered it highly unlikely that Lady Cordelia had never seen a garden in London before.

She peered at the French windows near them. It would be easy to stroll there, despite the cold. He tilted his head. Did Lady Cordelia think him *shy?*

His aunt glanced in his direction with frequency, and he shifted his position on the bench and tried to ignore meeting the gaze of the dowager.

"Have you had a pleasant time in London?"

She laughed. "It was dreadful waiting for you to arrive for so long. No one is in London during Christmas. The Serpentine is frozen, Hyde Park is muddy, and even the horses seem unwilling to venture far."

"Indeed."

"But surely you must know that."

"I am familiar."

"But there are many wonderful house parties at this time. If one can't go outside, one wants to at least have an enormous manor house in which to wander." She hesitated. "My mother mentioned to you that you are welcome in Hampshire."

"Ah, yes. That is very gracious of your family."

Lady Cordelia beamed. "Splendid."

"But I'm afraid I won't be able to join."

"Your Grace?" Lady Cordelia's voice squeaked.

"Please forgive me. But I have many duties—"

Her shoulders relaxed. "I understand. Completely. I am the daughter of a duke."

He nodded, and the ring prickled his tightly clutched fist.

He was supposed to invite Lady Cordelia to stroll around the garden with him, not that his injury would permit him to do anything that conventional. He was supposed to offer her flattery. He was supposed to confess to having promptly fallen in love with her, even though they'd only just met, and he was supposed to slide his family's ancestral ring over her finger, as if he just happened to carry it with him.

Except—even though Fiona's rejection had been adamant, even though he didn't deserve her anyway, the thought of dropping to one knee before Lady Cordelia and joining their lives forever seemed like betrayal.

He sighed.

"Most men are quicker to shower me with compliments," Lady Cordelia said, her expression rueful.

"Then you are a fortunate woman."

"Yes." She lifted her nose, and he had the distinct impression she thought him unfamiliar with the practice of conversing.

Bernard would have proposed to her by now. Even if Fiona had captured him, he would have found a way to escape, whether in Harrogate or even sooner.

Were he alive, Bernard would be showering her with compliments with the force of a March storm. He would have understood that she would make the perfect duchess. She was the daughter of a duke, and would be the perfect mother for future ones. Her family's pedigree was even older than the Carmichaels. Her aptitude in French, watercolor and singing already made her ideal.

"Lady Cordelia..."

She fixed him with a serene smile, and his heart hammered.

He was about to say the words which would change everything. Nothing could be the same after this. He sucked in a deep breath of air. "I am afraid I must tell you that I am in no position to marry you."

She blinked, and her gaze fell to his wooden leg. "Your wealth and pedigree show you are in the perfect position to marry."

He cleared his throat, clear he'd broken all protocol. "Not that you would marry me, if I . . . er . . . asked."

"But you're not going to ask." Lady Cordelia frowned, but her voice remained unflappable, and her fingers did not tremble.

"No." He heaved a sigh. "Please know that I hold you in the highest esteem. You are a beautiful and accomplished woman."

The room seemed silent as she appraised him. Her gaze scrutinized his features as if she thought she might uncover some secret about him from the slope of his jaw. She tilted her head. "Is this about your leg?"

"I fear I would not be able to devote my attentions to you with the consideration you deserve."

"I would find it odd if you were to sit here beside me and proclaim your love to me, given that we have only just met."

Percival's shoulders slumped a fraction.

"I might be able to assist you through society," Lady Cordelia continued. "The Duchess of Alfriston practically begged my parents for the match to take place. She said you were quite in love with me."

"Without ever having met you?" A bitter taste burned Percival's throat. He thought of the *Matchmaking for Wallflowers* pamphlet Sir Seymour had shown him.

"I hope this does not come from some misguided sense of honor." She frowned. "I'm rather accustomed to looking the other way."

He tilted his head. "What exactly do you mean?"

"Simply that I know that men are hard-working beings. It is understandable and perhaps even to be encouraged if they decide to indulge themselves from time to time."

Percival stiffened. The woman was practically his sister's age. She shouldn't be speaking such.

Lady Cordelia smiled, perhaps taking his silence as approval. "I am also an accomplished pianist."

"So you can pound keys while I pound whores?"

"Your Grace!" Lady Cordelia widened the distance between them. Her tranquility was finally ruffled, and she glanced around the room.

"Forgive me," he murmured.

After a pause she shrugged. "I suppose you conform to your roguish reputation. You needn't apologize for that."

"No?"

She laughed. "Virility is an admirable trait. Everyone says so. They also say that with your looks and mine, our children would not lack in beauty."

"Ah, yes. I suppose it's too much exertion to have a child with unsymmetrical features."

"You tease me. Just know that that there were rumors you were at a ball with the daughter of some dead country squire." She sniffed, as if the fact that Fiona's father was dead heightened Fiona's negative reputation.

"I am sorry you had to hear from someone else." He sipped his hot drink, and the faint hints of clove and nutmeg reminded him of Fiona. "The rumors are true."

"Your behavior indicated that."

They were silent, and the cheery sounds of the violin quartet sounded jarring, an improper background to the stilted conversation between Lady Cordelia and himself.

"I heard you were kidnapped."

"That was a misunderstanding. Why, the woman's family even lives in a castle."

"Indeed? How terribly quaint. I suppose the north is filled with all sorts of curiosities." Lady Cordelia laughed, though Percival didn't bother to join her this time.

Feigning joy was difficult in any situation, but his chest had never felt so hollow. He shut his eyes, but when he opened them, nothing had changed. He didn't love her, he didn't think he ever could, and he wouldn't settle for anything else. Not after he'd met Fiona.

Percival was not going to propose. Hades himself couldn't force him to. Not after spending the past few days with the most fascinating woman he'd ever met. It didn't matter if that same woman had sent him away, and it didn't matter that he didn't deserve to beg for her forgiveness.

He had a conscience, and by Zeus, he was going to listen to it.

"THE DUCHESS OF BELMONTE told me that you did not propose to her daughter." The dowager's voice was firm.

"Sternness doesn't suit you, Aunt Georgiana. You should try being happy for a change."

"Simply being happy?" The dowager sucked in a deep breath of air and then exhaled loudly. She waved her hand in a frantic motion before her chest and was about to repeat the process when he sighed.

"Let's sit down."

"So you can rest?" Her gaze swung to the void where his leg should be, and he stiffened. "No. You don't get to rest. I chose the perfect woman for you, one willing to overlook your flaws."

"I don't want a woman who will overlook my flaws."

"Then you don't want any woman at all."

His fists tightened. "I want a woman who will embrace my strengths."

She sighed. "My son would never have—"

Percival's chest constricted. The wrong Carmichael had died. He knew that. Not that he could do anything about it.

He raised his eyebrows, and his aunt's voice wobbled. "On a purely theoretical level though, your cousin was more trained to take on the responsibilities of the dukedom. That's all I mean."

"You're correct."

"Then you will marry Lady Cordelia?"

He turned his head toward the ballroom and then shook his head. "No."

The dowager stiffened. "This is a simple task, Percival. If you can't do even this, how are you supposed to accomplish any of the tasks of the dukedom? Running an estate is not something you should abandon to your estate manager. The incomes of many people depend on you. And with your leg—" She pointed her fan toward it, flashing the item with as much derision as any schoolmaster. "You'll be under more scrutiny than ever before. It won't be easy to find another woman for you. You've already proved yourself untrustworthy, breaking the understanding—"

He swiveled, and his heart pattered an unsteady rhythm in his chest. He tightened his grip on his cane. The dainty silver head was more suitable for show than for practicality, and his fingers slid over the rounded dome.

Losing a leg meant more stress on the other portions of his body, and even standing seemed a challenge now. The candles continued their relentless gleam, dazzling his eyes, and the fire leaped and lurched in the stone fireplace. The heat continued to brush against him, and sweat continued to prickle his clothes.

The dowager glanced at his cane. "Perhaps you should sit."

"I'm fine."

She shrugged. "Just as long as you resist any urge to fall. You've rather disgraced us enough already, and I'm sure Her Grace's footmen are sufficiently occupied managing this marvelous ball without having to haul you from the floor."

In the past he would have suggested they continue their conversation in the courtyard, and in a few moments they might be enjoying the crisp air and remarking on the winter garden and the beauty of the bare branches. He had no desire now to hobble before everyone, and he would endure the heat and the curious glances from the other party-goers.

Exhaustion struck him. The journey to London had been rough, the coach jostling as it sped over poorly maintained roads. He longed to close his eyes. "There was no understanding."

"You were fetching the family jewels. Why you wouldn't just let a servant do it..." She shook her head. "It's not like you could be any help to protect them. As evidenced by what happened."

He stiffened. Perhaps he had used the jewels as an excuse to escape London. He was tired of the false sympathy from the other members of the *ton*. Their condolences seemed often mixed with the glee of seeing the man who had soared to a position of prominence so suddenly with so few qualifications to redeem him.

"You're tired," the dowager said, her voice lowered to a mollifying note. "You mustn't worry. I'll go to Her Grace and explain the misunderstanding. I'm sure you really meant to propose, but you were simply overwhelmed by Lady Cordelia's undeniable beauty and charm and overly conscious of your lack of a second leg."

"I—"

The dowager's lips spread into a smile, one he recognized from his childhood. "It will be fine. You can go home and rest. Perhaps it was a mistake to bring you here in your position."

"You mustn't speak with her. My mind is determined. Let us depart."

"But—"

This time he smiled. "The Duchess of Belmonte might find our presence unwelcome."

The dowager slammed her fan shut, and her hand tightened around the grandiose material. "Very well. But do not believe me to be the least bit content."

"No." He sighed. "You're right. I will depart now, and if you choose to remain here, you may naturally do so. But I am not going to marry Lady Cordelia, and you need not arrange any other wife."

"Are you saying you have someone else in mind?" The dowager narrowed her eyes. "Because a wife is of the utmost importance if you desire to be a good duke, as you claim. I'm sure I needn't explain the usefulness of a wife in procuring legitimate children. Your cousin did not die in order to see the estate divided or given to a person even less lacking in merits than you."

The image of Fiona flitted before his mind. The woman was warm and amusing and of more intelligence than even the much-lauded Lady Cordelia.

But she'd never sought to be a wife. She'd stated the fact to him, and well, he had to believe that. Fiona struggled to attend one provincial ball. She wouldn't have any desire to manage a household and host her own balls. She'd pretended to be a highwaywoman, for goodness' sake. She was suited for a life that consisted of digging up old ruins and avoiding high society.

He bowed his head. "I have no one in mind."

Chapter Twenty-six

FIONA HAD PUSHED HER colored dresses further into her wardrobe and shifted her attire to black. The servants removed the Christmas adornments, and bare walls surrounded her. The period reminded of her when her parents had died, except now Grandmother could not console her.

Grandmother's body was buried. Fiona hadn't been permitted to attend the funeral, but she'd heard servants muse of the blessing that Grandmother's death had preceded any possibility of her learning of Fiona's disgrace.

Perhaps the gossips were justified, though Fiona would have gladly accepted any discomfit or embarrassment, were Grandmother only to have lived a little while longer.

The magistrate never imprisoned her. She'd received a stern warning instead.

She deserved to be punished. Had her family not had a reasonably good name, she would have experienced a harsher penalty.

Graeme did appear, telling her it was a crime she was allowed to roam the countryside still. He did return Ned to her though he didn't explain what had compelled him to return the animal.

Fiona did not press him.

She reminded herself that Percival was a distant memory, an aberration in her life. Yet even though five months had passed since Grandmother's death, even though more snow had fallen, only to now melt, she could not forget him in the least. The crisp white snow of winter, followed by the pummeling of rain and hail in spring, had finally lulled. Bluebells pushed from the ground and cheerfully spread their vibrant blossoms.

In vain she reminded herself those three days in his company should not feel longer and more real than anything else in her lifetime.

Percival had been a fantasy. She'd told him, and he'd left, and that was that.

She stared at her rows of trunks. Uncle Seymour and Aunt Lavinia were moving in tomorrow. Their current manor house was pleasant, but not a castle, and Uncle Seymour had said he'd postponed his inheritance long enough.

"I'll send a footman to help you with your cases, Miss Amberly," Evans said. "It will be strange without you."

She gave the butler a tight smile.

She'd miss him. She'd miss everyone. Soon she would move in with Rosamund. She pressed her lips together. Living in the midst of her sister's marital bliss was not Fiona's vision of happiness. Not when a similar happiness would always be denied her.

"Everyone's dying," Evans said, uncharacteristically talkative, perhaps moved by the fact they would rarely see each other again. "So tragic."

"Someone else died?"

Instantly she thought of Percival, and she struggled to remind herself that it would be highly unlikely for her butler to be musing about a man he hadn't seen in months. Her heart hammered.

"Lord Mulbourne is dead. I would have thought you would have—" He paused and shifted his feet, and his cheeks darkened. "Forgive me. I don't believe there's been a formal announcement yet. Word spread through the servants."

The man didn't need to say that he thought Madeline would have informed Fiona herself. Her shoulders shrank together. She hated this conflict between her and her cousin. "How horrible. He wasn't even *that* old."

"Ah, yes. There was something sordid about the whole business. Rumors are swirling about. But who's to say? He wasn't young either." Evans shook his head in a somber motion suited to his profession. "His wife is so pretty and never had a child."

A hollow pit formed in her stomach. Madeline was a widow. They hadn't always gotten along, but Madeline didn't deserve to have her husband snatched from her. No one deserved that.

Fiona couldn't imagine the anguish she'd feel if Percival died. And he wasn't even... She drew in a sharp breath. "Thank you. You were right to tell me."

She'd been a fool these past few years. An absolute fool.

She headed outside and trudged through the thick grass that swayed under the slight breeze. She lifted her skirts and proceeded into the ever denser area. Lambs leaped and played in the adjoining field, and birds chirped from trees. The sun shone in full force, and she slid her head up to bask in the warmth.

Madeline's manor house adjoined the property. She'd avoided seeing her for months, too humiliated after the ball. Madeline had called on her after Grandmother's death, but their exchange had been limited to platitudes.

Now she needed to speak to her cousin. Fiona had spent so long decrying the *ton*. But she'd been as narrow-minded and quick to judge as everyone else. Fiona was tired of keeping to herself and assuming the worst of people.

The Dales were at their finest now. The once-white, once-brown hills were green, and lavender and blue flowers dotted the steep slopes. A blue sky spread over the arching hills and smatterings of trees; no clouds marred the horizon, though athletic birds dipped and swirled above.

It was late afternoon, and some children shouted with glee, apparently amused by the prospect of rolling down the hill, something which they were already putting into practice. Fiona hesitated for a moment, and then pushed further over the trail, until, five miles later, she reached the elaborate manor house.

She sucked in a deep breath. The last time she'd approached these steps, Percival had been at her side. She could almost feel the coarse wool of his great coat beneath her fingers. Her chest tightened, but she continued up the steps.

Madeline's butler widened his eyes when he saw her, and he led her to the drawing room.

The manor house was impeccable. More paintings than ever lined the rich garnet walls, their gold frames sparkling.

Elegance soared through the manor house. Roses arched from opulent vases. At one time Fiona might have been intimidated, but instead she waited for Madeline to arrive.

Her cousin's face was tight, and Madeline's golden hair was arranged in a rigid knot. The vibrant frocks her cousin favored, oft-embellished with lace and satin ruffles, were replaced with a dull ebony dress that drained her face of color.

"I came as soon as I heard," Fiona said. "I'm so sorry."

Madeline nodded. "Thank you."

The words were trite, and Fiona flickered her gaze to Madeline's strained face.

A maid arrived with tea, and Madeline's shoulders remained rigid as the maid placed the gleaming silver cake stand on the lace table cloth.

"I only just learned," Fiona said.

Madeline shrugged. "He died two days ago. The paper hasn't printed anything yet."

"How did it happen?"

Madeline tensed, but her voice was calm when she spoke. "He was in London."

Had they possessed more semblance of a family relationship, Fiona would have learned right away. Yet Madeline hadn't sought Fiona for comfort, and for the first time, Fiona despised this. They were cousins and neighbors. They should share more.

Perhaps she might never see Percival again, but he'd taught her not to make quick judgments. Just because a man was handsome did not mean that he took advantage of it, nor that he'd always lived a comfortable life.

Madeline should not be seen as less worthy because she interested herself in fashion. Perhaps some of her snide comments might be excused. Fiona had been so willing to see signs of Madeline's untrustworthiness, she should not be surprised when that was what she'd found.

Madeline had never truly harmed her, only contributed to the gossip of the other girls during their season, leaving her betrayed when Madeline laughed with others about Fiona's failure to grasp whether something was fashionable or not or when she spoke too long about the Romans.

Perhaps in her own way Fiona had acted as childishly as her cousin. She was determined to apologize. She inhaled. "I haven't been a good cousin."

Madeline fixed her perfect blue eyes on her. Fiona stiffened, the motion automatic, but her cousin simply shook her head.

"I fear I haven't been either."

"I lied about Captain Knightley," Fiona said. "He didn't exist."

"I never thought he did."

Fiona tensed.

"Until you arrived at the ball," Madeline said. "Then he seemed rather alive. Not quite a figment of your imagination."

"I'm sorry for ruining your ball."

"Oh, I think you made it quite memorable for people." Madeline smiled. "That's a good thing, you know."

"Oh."

Madeline tilted her head. "So I've been so curious—how did you manage to find a duke willing to masquerade as your fiancé?"

Fiona shrugged. "He was scared of my knife."

Madeline giggled, and Fiona joined in.

"So all that time he was saying nice things, he was forced to say them." Madeline's eyes were round.

"But he seemed so genuinely caring," Fiona said. "After a while. I mean after he stopped escaping. I even offered to release him at one point, and he didn't go."

Madeline laughed. "Definitely a foundation for love."

Fiona smoothed her fingers over the folds of her dress, hoping her cousin would neglect to notice the tremble of her fingers. "You mean because he pretended to be my fiancé?"

"Because of how he looked at you. I could tell. All the way on the other side of the ballroom, it was obvious."

Fiona shifted her legs. Her heart pattered uncomfortably in her chest. "He was acting."

"I don't think so," Madeline said. "And he was so desperate, so devastated when you were hauled away."

"But he didn't stop them." Fiona picked up her cup.

"He tried to. And if he hadn't argued so passionately for you . . . Well, Barnaby would like an excuse to prosecute a member of the *ton*. It would give him the illusion of fairness when he is overly vigilant with all the peasants."

Fiona's hand shook, and she set the cup back on the table.

"Didn't you wonder why you never went to prison?"

"Grandmother died..."

"If a death in the family was all it took to be released from prison, the cells would be much less full. You're fortunate the magistrate had a sufficient appreciation for aristocratic order to not contradict the duke's wishes."

"Oh." She flickered her eyes down.

"He seemed quite devoted," Madeline said. "What did he say after?"

"Many things. But at the end—that he wanted to be there for me. To comfort me."

"And what did you say?"

"That I never wanted to see him again." Fiona's voice was miserable.

Madeline's eyelashes flickered up. "And that's what you wanted?"

"No." Fiona wrapped her arms around her chest.

"Then why—"

"I thought he was being polite." Anguish racketed through her, and the words resembled a howl.

Madeline leapt to her side and wrapped her arms around her. The contact was strange, but not entirely unwelcome. Even if they'd stopped being close, they were still cousins.

"And now he's married." Fiona sniffed and tears spilled from her eyes.

"He's not married."

"He is! He had the ring. I saw it. He was going to propose to Lady Cordelia."

"I very much doubt that," Madeline said. "No engagement has been announced."

"Oh." Fiona ceased her sniffling. She stared at her cousin. Finally, she shook her head. "It doesn't matter. I ruined things for us."

Madeline scrutinized her. "Then you need to stop thinking of him."

Fiona nodded, even though the advice was absurd. She'd long ago realized that her thoughts would always include Percival.

"So I heard that Rosamund is taking you in.," Madeline said.

Fiona nodded. "But I want more from life."

Madeline tilted her head. "Indeed?"

"Yes." The word tumbled out.

"And what does this more consist of?"

"I don't want to spend the rest of my life reading books on how a great civilization lived, when I could be exploring how great my own civilization is. I want to still do archaeology."

"Hmph." Madeline took a long sip of tea. "My dream is to visit Italy."

"Truly?" Fiona leaned forward. "I love that dream."

"You wish you could still speak with the baron?" Madeline's smile wobbled.

Fiona hesitated, but she shook her head. She remembered her cousin's interest in her project during the ball. "I have an idea."

UNCLE SEYMOUR SQUINTED at Fiona as the footmen hauled in trunks, and Aunt Lavinia fluttered her arms around, directing the servants where to place everything. "I expect you are going to beg to stay here."

"I'm not."

Uncle Seymour's eyebrows rose, but he then shook his head. "I expect you are going to beg to still dig up the apple orchard."

Fiona sighed. This part was more difficult, and she fought to resist her natural inclination. "I'm not."

"Oh." The baronet's face darkened, as if she'd halted a speech he'd practiced giving. "It doesn't matter. You still won't be in our good graces. Not after the way you behaved at the Christmas Ball. You're mad if you think my dear wife and I will ever forget."

"You've made that fact clear on other occasions."

"Always good to repeat things, that's what I say," her uncle mused. "Doesn't do any harm and always drives the point through. You don't use a hammer and nail without banging the nail multiple times, no matter how thick and obvious the hammer should be."

"Most enlightening. I had no idea how gifted you were at carpentry."

"I'm a man of many strengths." Her uncle's skin finally returned to a shade of red more normal for him, even if for no one else. "That was an . . . er . . . metaphor. Never touched a hammer in my life. Never wanted to and never will."

Fiona smiled. "I wanted to thank you."

"Ah, yes," the baronet said. "What . . . er . . . for?"

Fiona tilted her head, and her uncle rubbed a beefy hand against his brow. "It's hard to keep track of all the good I'm doing in this world."

She lifted her chin. "I'm going to grow up."

"Thought you came of age when you were thirteen," her uncle grumbled.

"I'm not going to stay at home anymore, reading about all the interesting things people did ages ago."

"I never thought the Romans were that interesting," her uncle said.

"I know."

He sniffed. "I suppose you can't follow all my words of wisdom."

"That's most understanding of you."

"So you're moving in with your sister? Good thing she's got her life sorted, even though she's younger than you."

Fiona smiled. "It's wonderful she's happy, but—no, I won't be doing that."

"You'll be homeless?" Her uncle's eyes bulged. "You won't—you won't really take on the life of crime? Be that—what was it—Scarlet Devil?"

"Scarlet Demon," Fiona corrected. "I'll overcome that temptation. I'm going to become an archaeologist."

Uncle Seymour blinked. “I don’t think that’s a real occupation.”

“It will be. One day,” Fiona said. “Grandmother gave me a small inheritance.”

“I think she intended that so you didn’t have to debase yourself.”

“I’m not debasing myself.” Fiona lifted her head. “I have an outside supporter too and a plan to excavate some promising sites throughout England.”

Uncle Seymour sputtered, and Fiona laughed.

“You needn’t worry, uncle. I won’t make you wish me luck. I have a feeling I won’t need it.”

Chapter Twenty-seven

HOME. He was home.

The season had ended, and here he was.

Percival made his way expertly from the coach, knowing just where to place his cane to best support him.

A long row of servants waited to greet him. Their postures were stiff, though he didn't miss the curious glimpses they fixed on his foot.

He shrugged. He would do the same if he were them. The wooden leg was bloody well unusual. He strode toward them, limping somewhat on the uneven terrain.

He'd been to Wentworth Place before, but as a child. The long mansion had been the home of his crotchety grandfather and demanding grandmother, and he'd only seen it as a somewhat frustrating experience. What good were long acres of a green lawn if one wasn't allowed to play on it?

His lips turned up. He wouldn't be doing any sort of playing in this place either. Places like this didn't manage themselves, as the dowager frequently reminded him, and the war hadn't helped matters. The former Duke had indulged his belligerent side through frequent and large donations to the war effort. His generosity had secured him invitations to the finest wartime balls and allowed him the opportunity to wear his finest regalia from battles decades before.

Now the estate was suffering, and nobody could quite be certain if the former Duke had needed to be quite so extravagant in his funding of cannons and other arms for Bonaparte to have never attempted to invade England again. It didn't help that the weather rarely co-operated, and crops everywhere were failing this year.

"Ah, your prison," Arthur's voice boomed behind him.

"Remind me why you've come?" Percival asked.

Arthur straightened his cravat. "Because you wanted someone to distract you from your bloody misery."

They strolled toward the entrance and paused to meet the servants, who issued them their deepest bows and curtsies.

"This place is enormous," Arthur remarked.

"And expensive." Percival flickered his gaze back to the legion of servants who manned the place.

"Right." Arthur shifted his legs. "Let's see the library, shall we? Perhaps your predecessor left us some brandy."

Percival followed Arthur in his search for liquid delights.

The butler had already arranged for brandy and he'd also ironed a newspaper. Percival picked it up curiously, skimming the headlines. They'd traveled at a more leisurely pace, stopping at various taverns to indulge Arthur's curiosity in the local ales and ciders.

"You need a wife," Arthur announced.

Percival's eyebrows jolted up, and he set the newspaper aside. "I'm not accustomed to you being the advocate for marital bliss."

"Hah. What marital bliss?" Arthur shrugged. "Mere practicality. You're going to be stuck in this God-forsaken place half the year, and it's good to have some female company."

"I could have a house party."

"Female company that will permit you to do your work. Who will give you greater peace than a wife? You just need to add some nocturnal duties to your list of other responsibilities, and you'll give her a brood of yowling Carmichaels in no time."

"I don't know..." Percival rubbed his hand over his leg.

"Lady Cordelia is still available."

"I thought the Duke of Carlisle was courting her."

Arthur shrugged. "Apparently he died."

"Dreadful."

"I imagine he was grateful he lasted so long, what with all his indulgence for vices."

Percival nodded, though his jaw was decidedly more tightened than it had been earlier in the conversation. "I'm not marrying Lady Cordelia for anyone."

"Naturally." His brother leaned forward. "But are you sure you shouldn't marry her for you?"

"I—" He tilted his head and blinked.

His brother gave a cocky grin and poured some more brandy into his tumbler. "I must say the very best brandy comes from France. Don't you agree?"

"Why would I want to marry Lady Cordelia?"

"Because despite all your protestations against the match, she remains very suitable."

"She cares about balls."

"And you claim you don't anymore." His brother smiled. "You complement each other perfectly."

"We should have somewhat more in common."

"You would have your future wife, the mother of your children, take an interest in gaming halls and racquetball?" Arthur tsked. "Hauling that wooden leg around does seem frightfully cumbersome. Might be nice not to have to go from house party to house party to court someone."

Percival nodded. The leg was a blasted pain. Sometimes he still felt it, still woke up and felt it aching. But more often he felt his thigh, and the way his wooden stump pressed against the remainder of his leg. He didn't like to complain about the pain and the irritating necessity to clean it. After all, he was lucky.

"Your jaunts about Europe are behind you. You know that. What you need is a nice, sweet woman who will manage your household and your friends, so you won't need to."

"You make it sound so simple."

"Or I could compile a list of other suitable matches?"

Percival shook his head. He was tired of all of it. "Wouldn't want to delay the process of living happily ever after."

Arthur laughed. "You sound like you've been reading fairy-tales. But I don't like seeing you unhappy. A pretty woman will ease your troubles, and a marriage will ease your conscience."

Arthur was right, and Percival slumped his shoulders.

Perhaps he'd protested Lady Cordelia's qualities, but he'd never attempted to truly get to know her. He'd been too quick to see in her all the qualities of the *ton* he despised, but he'd also not taken the time to appreciate her good qualities.

He certainly hadn't fallen for any debutantes that season. When he lay in bed, his mind dwelled on soft, rosy cheeks, curly red hair and emerald eyes. He reached for a curved figure beside him who was not there. Would never be there.

His face tightened. "I need to prepare for tonight."

"I'll join you," Arthur said. "It's always amusing observing your struggle with Higgins."

Percival made his way upstairs, clasping the banister firmly. He swept his gaze around, taking in the high ceilings and the view of the estate.

Arthur was right. This place was too large for just him. It needed a family.

His valet cleared his throat. "Shall we commence?"

"You may torture me."

His valet's eyes glinted, and he chose a starchy cravat.

Percival shuddered. "Perhaps you needn't torture me to such an extent."

"It's very fashionable, Your Grace. Clean, crisp lines." Higgins fixed him with an expression of bemusement.

"The man's right," Arthur said cheerfully, passing him some brandy.

At least his brother had had the foresight to carry the crystal tumblers upstairs. Arthur stretched out on Percival's armchair, swung his legs onto a velvet ottoman, and read the butler's carefully ironed paper.

Percival narrowed his eyes as Higgins approached with the cravat. "I wore that bloody concoction last Friday."

"For the Dowager Duchess's ball. That was very good of Your Grace. But the locals might expect a similar degree of formality." Higgins leaned closer. "I've heard the Prince Regent is rumored to make an appearance."

"Well if he is," Percival replied, "I can guarantee he'll be looking at the bloody food, and not my cravat."

"Your Grace! I'm not sure one can speak of the future king in such a manner." Flustered, the man fumbled for a silver tray and handed him an envelope. "I believe, Your Grace, that this is an invitation to Brighton."

"My word." Percival grabbed hold of the stiff envelope and he glided his fingers over the embossed gold letters and the red seal depicting the Royal Pavilion. "Already getting mail here? I suppose I really am a duke now."

"Indeed, Your Grace." Higgins' smile faltered somewhat.

Percival nodded, not for the first time wondering how easy it had been for Higgins to switch from calling him My Lord. Percival hadn't found the transition nearly as easy. He sighed. "Bernard would have been so much better at this."

"Your cousin was gifted."

Percival removed the seal and scanned the invitation. A summer at the Brighton Pavilion with the Regent himself. *What could be more pleasant?*

He attempted to draw up some of the joy that he was sure Bernard would have been feeling at such an invitation. But the only thing he could think about was that Brighton was bloody far removed from Yorkshire. Which was ridiculous, because he had no need to be in Yorkshire again. Being a duke did not come naturally to him, and his estate would hardly be helped were he to be coupled to an anti-social wife who was open in her dislike of the *ton* and modern society.

Fiona had agreed it was for the best that the two never saw each other again. And since Fiona displayed a definite dislike of London that seemed like a very firm possibility.

"But perhaps you would like to be more adventurous during the summer." Higgins buttoned Percival's waistcoat. "Now that the war has ended, people are returning to Europe."

"Yes, must be filled with lots of middle-aged men reliving their Grand Tour." Percival sniffed, though in truth the idea didn't sound half bad.

"Perhaps, Your Grace, they are congregating there because they have already visited and possess familiarity with its charms." Higgins picked up a white linen.

"My generation's experience there was imperfect." Percival said, envisioning the sprawling battlefield in Waterloo. Normally he would shut his eyes tight or demand a glass of brandy, but instead he attempted to control his breaths. One day perhaps the images of carnage, the pangs of killing, and the guilt for surviving when abler men than he had fallen would fade. He bit his bottom lip. "I suppose Europe has its charms."

"I've heard quite good things about Paris, Your Grace."

Percival shrugged. "That blasted Corsican's former capital? Not for me."

"But the architecture—"

"By Zeus, this isn't something my younger sister has put you up to, is it?"

"No, no," Higgins sputtered.

Percival relaxed his shoulders. His sister had a habit of over-idealizing Paris.

"I'd adore the chance to go to Italy," Arthur mused. "Venezia. Firenze. Roma."

Percival swung his head over to Arthur. The man's accent was surprisingly good. Sometimes he underestimated his brother.

"Why just today I was reading in the newspaper about two ladies who were planning to travel," Higgins said. "If ladies can do it, you can consider it. Even with your foot."

Percival smiled. "I am pleased at your confidence in me."

"Yes, one of the ladies was a bit of an archaeologist. That's what she called it. Sounded most interesting. She's been finding all sorts of interesting things in the ground over here."

"A female archaeologist?"

Percival's heart lurched. *Fiona.*

"What female archaeologist?" He said hoarsely, taking another swig of brandy.

"Some chit's been digging near Chichester."

"Oh." Percival slumped back into his armchair. He closed his eyes. Clearly archaeology was simply spreading at a more rapid pace than he'd expected. Fiona wouldn't have found herself on the south coast. She was a Northerner to the core. She'd told him even going to Harrogate was an unusual event.

He sighed. He'd hoped that she'd been able to secure her uncle's permission to dig up the apple orchard. He wanted her to receive the renown she deserved.

"Yes. She's going up north next. Should be there now. A Miss Fiona Amberly..."

"Fiona?" Percival dropped the crystal tumbler, and brandy splattered on the floor.

"I say!" Arthur rubbed a hand though his hair. "Just because you've inherited *everything* doesn't mean you need to go around smashing it all."

Percival snatched the newspaper from his brother and scanned it furiously until he saw Fiona's name. His heart lurched in his chest. It was her. His Fiona. She'd been in Sussex.

The woman who abhorred leaving the confines of her family's estate was digging up a site, just like she'd always dreamed of. It wasn't Cloudbridge Castle, not the place she always dreamed of excavating, but it was amazing.

He perused the newspaper. She'd discovered things. And what's more, she'd been developing a system of measuring where the items were found and labeling them to help future researchers. She wasn't just interested in getting her hands on a pretty Roman vase to display. She was interested in the cultural history of the objects, and her research was developing a new way to look at the Romans in Britain.

She'd gone out and changed her life even though he couldn't imagine how difficult it must have been for her to do so. No one dug up ruins, least of all women.

He sighed. He still missed her. He'd miss her every day of his life. He squeezed his eyes shut and tried to remind himself that it wasn't to be.

"Ah . . . I see you're interested, Your Grace. Apparently they're both going to Italy soon."

Percival dropped the newspaper, and the cream-colored pages fluttered downward. Higgins dove to catch it.

"They're not planning to visit *alone?*"

Surely they possessed a modicum of sense. Fiona was content willing away her days digging in the dirt behind Cloudbridge Castle. She couldn't even stand London. She had told him that.

And Italy—Italy was far away. Why, one had to first cross the channel, and then make one's way over France—an experience probably filled with scowling peasants glaring over battered vineyards, and then one had to traipse over the Alps in whatever ridiculous contraption the Europeans called a carriage, staying at horrid inns. And after doing all of that, one's reward was being in Italy, which had just survived a war.

If she went, would she ever want to face the journey back?

"I believe they will travel on their own, Your Grace."

"Right."

Higgins placed the cravat round Percival's neck. "I'm sure they'll take care of each other, Your Grace."

"Let's hope!" Percival released another strangled yelp when Higgins tightened the knot that earned him a raised eyebrow from his valet. "But—"

His valet's carefully groomed eyebrow arched higher, and he narrowed his eyes, holding each end of the snowy-white monstrosity.

She would be in Italy, right in the home of the Romans. He couldn't offer her that. Any travel was painful for him, and he was tied to this blasted estate. Unlike Cloudbridge Castle, he hadn't heard any rumors of ancient ruins in this vicinity.

"Here's the mirror, Your Grace. You're all set for this evening."

Percival picked up the carved handle gingerly. The gold sheet glimmered in a manner he couldn't strictly describe as masculine, but he obediently peered into the looking glass.

The knot was splendid. Elaborate and tied with a real flourish.

"You'll have all the ladies eye you at the ball, Your Grace." Higgins' voice was filled with pride.

"It's a shame that the other men's valets won't be there to admire your good work."

"Thank you, Your Grace." Higgins bowed his head.

Percival brushed his fingers against the knot, running his finger over the crisp edges. It was perfect. It always was.

"You look like a proper duke," Higgins said.

Percival sighed. "I rather fancy that you're correct."

He could act the part of duke. He could marry Lady Cordelia, just like his aunt wanted, and receive more and more praise for conforming to the expectations of his role.

Soon people might forget about Bernard and think Percival had always been duke, and he'd never been the hastily installed cousin, criticized for spending too much time outside the *ton*.

He tore off his cravat, observing as Higgins' face transformed from bemusement to horror. Percival flung the now-wrinkled linen on the bed.

"But your Grace!"

"Please inform the groom to prepare the carriage."

Percival pressed his lips together, and Higgins nodded. "Ah, yes. You needn't worry. It's being prepared for the ball."

"No." Percival gripped his cane with vigor. "I rather fear I have another destination in my mind. A place somewhat farther removed."

"You're going after Lady Cordelia after all?" Arthur beamed. "Such a romantic."

Percival was on the verge of something. He was sure of it. If Fiona could go traipsing around Italy, looking at art with a person Percival remembered her despising, Percival could make some changes too.

He considered Fiona. *Lord, she'd been brave.*

"I will not attend the ball tonight."

"But, the Prince Regent!"

"He can be there without me. Please pack my things. I am going to settle my life."

Chapter Twenty-eight

HE LOVED HER.

And he'd never told her. She didn't know, and now she was off to the southern-most tip of all of Europe.

He clenched his fingers together. But there was no one he could fight. Only himself.

The whole thing was absurd. It would be easy to go to the local ball, meet all of Sussex's most prominent men and women, and chat with the Prince Regent. That's what he was supposed to do.

He certainly wasn't supposed to direct his driver to head hundreds of miles in the opposite direction. Traveling from London had been sufficiently painful.

But if there was a single chance Fiona might return his affection—by Zeus, he'd be the largest fool on earth if he didn't try to plead for her. His chest clenched, but he ordered a servant to put his still unpacked valise in the carriage.

"Should I come with you to see the fair Lady Cordelia?" Arthur asked.

"No."

"You're not much of a host," Arthur complained.

Percival tried to chuckle. He was doing the most exciting thing he'd ever done. Possibly also the most foolish, but it was far too easy to imagine Fiona beside him. *For the rest of their lives.* He blinked. He wanted to brace himself for the pain of her likely dismissal, but he'd been doing that in London the entire winter and most of the spring. He couldn't do it anymore. He couldn't live in a world where he hadn't attempted everything to see if they could be together.

Likely he'd need to live in a world where she'd tossed him aside. Later he would deal with that.

He scrambled outside, dragging his bad leg over the uneven cobblestones.

The groom scurried to swing open the door to the carriage.

"You got it ready quickly," Percival said, noting the new horses. "Thank you."

The groom nodded. "Where would you like to go, Your Grace?"

"Yorkshire."

The word was ridiculous. They'd just traveled practically all the way to the south coast, but he'd have to leave gazing at the ocean for another day. There was only one being, one wonderful, wonderful person he wanted to gaze at now.

The groom's facial muscles flickered, but he retained a stoic expression. "Then we'd better get moving."

OF COURSE THEY HADN'T been able to drive the whole night. The horses required rest, and even with switching horses, the trip lengthened to a multi-day journey. Percival had never felt more that he lacked control. He attempted to tell himself that Fiona would be accepting of him, but all he remembered was her hardened face the last time he'd seen her.

He'd been a fool then.

Perhaps Fiona would think Percival not worth the inconvenience of being chained to a man who was required to make frequent appearances in society, who needed to spend significant time in Sussex, and who suffered from a deformity.

He gritted his teeth. Fiona was wise, and if she thought those things, she would be right to.

Percival might be strong now, but he didn't want to consider the future. Most men clung to canes in their old age; he did it now.

He pushed the velvet curtain aside. The Dales loomed outside, their dark green peaks reminding him of places he couldn't venture anymore. He scrunched his fists together.

He'd told the driver to go to Fiona's cousin's home, and he struggled to smooth the wrinkles from his clothes. He brushed his hand over his cheeks and met rough stubble. He hadn't dared to take the time to shave at the last coaching inn they'd stopped at.

I may have already lost her.

He pressed his lips together in a firm line. Some things were too horrible to contemplate, and he exhaled when the carriage pulled into the baroness's estate. The wheels rolled over the meticulously kept lane.

He inhaled and checked that his cravat was in a decent state. He was a duke. The baroness would tell him where Fiona was. The coach stopped before the elaborate portico, and Percival grabbed his cane and climbed down the carriage steps.

One of the gardeners gave him a surprised glance, but he continued on. Probably the man's reaction could be attributed to not seeing dukes often.

A curtain flickered in a window, and then the main door swung open. He hurried his pace to greet the butler.

Except it wasn't the butler.

A round woman wearing an apron greeted him. Her sleeves were rolled up, and her arms were grubby. "No one is here. Most of the staff are setting up a residence in Italy."

"When did she leave?"

"This morning."

He had the curious sensation that someone had just hit him.

"Though they were stopping at one of Miss Amberly's new archaeological sites on the way."

He squared his shoulders and hope spread through him, despite his best intentions to protect himself from further disappointment. "Where is it?"

"Ah . . . Just four miles north of here. Near the old mill. You can't miss it."

I hope not. He smiled, thanked her, and sped back to the coach as quickly as his foot would allow.

"Carry on," he shouted, repeating the housekeeper's instructions. He tapped his foot inside the coach, willing the driver to move more swiftly past the baroness's manicured lawns, faux-Greek temples, and elaborate rose garden.

The driver urged the horses on, and the coach dipped and swerved in an uncomfortable fashion over the dirt lane. Thick hedges lined the road, reminding Percival of the night he'd first met Fiona.

The coach barreled through a village and passed the *Old Goblet Lodge.*

And then finally the coach slowed. Percival craned his neck from the window, but no aristocratic carriage, flourished with a golden crest, blocked the drive.

The coach halted, and he scrambled out, cane in hand. He swept his gaze over the field.

She's not there.

A group of men was digging, and he headed toward them. They might know where Fiona was. *Zeus, they were his only hope.*

Something about them seemed familiar. The ground was squishy, and his steps were more uneven than normal.

"Hullo there!" He waved both hands above his head.

Some of the men turned to him, including a man with white whiskers. A man he recognized.

"Mr. Nicholas!" Percival's eyes widened, and the older man smiled.

"Ah . . . Mr. Percival." He turned around and shouted, "Mr. Potter!"

Percival tensed and gripped his cane more tightly. A burly man whom he'd vowed to never see again turned his head. He might have been a dozen feet away, but Percival could still see contempt flicker across the man's face. He strode toward them.

What on earth was Fiona doing with these men?

A younger man nudged Mr. Nicholas and whispered in his ear.

Mr. Nicholas raised his not-insignificant brows. "Apparently you're actually a duke."

"I am."

Mr. Potter wiped dirty hands on his buckskin breeches. "If I was a duke, I wouldn't pretend to be a man who'd abandoned his expecting wife."

Percival flashed a tight smile. He needed their help. "Do you happen to know where she is?"

"Who?"

"Mrs. Percival?"

Mr. Nicholas chuckled. "She don't go by that name anymore, Your Grace. I would think you would know that."

"Seems you don't have to be very smart to be a duke," Mr. Potter chided him. "I could be a duke. I would be good at being a duke."

The other men murmured assent, and Percival sighed. His eyes flickered around the field. Poppies swayed in the wind, and a bright sun shone from the blue sky above. A large pit sat in the middle, and some of the men pored over it.

"What are you doing here?"

Mr. Nicholas grinned. "Archaeology!"

"Better than hangin' round the tavern." Mr. Potter flexed his forearm. "I'm getting me muscles back!"

Percival eyed him. He wasn't convinced the man was in any need of more muscles. The man rather epitomized brawniness. That said, the men did appear content. He'd regarded them poorly before, scoffing that they seemed to spend their entire lives in a public house. But work was likely hard to come by. The torrent of returned soldiers clamoring for work hadn't helped anyone, and crops were failing all over Europe because of an onslaught of frigid temperatures.

Mr. Potter jutted his thumb out at Mr. Nicholas. "We dig, and this man labels and records everything."

"Then that makes you all very important," Percival said gravely, and the men beamed.

"Miss Amberly's talking about putting all our work in a Museum of Yorkshire."

Percival blinked. "That sounds wonderful."

"We're making history," Mr. Nicholas declared. "This 'ere soil is filled with Roman and Medieval treasures. It will all look right nice in a museum. Makes one right proud of being a Yorkshire man. Sorry, Duke—I know you're not one."

Percival smiled. "You must be a great help to Miss Amberly."

"Now what brings you here?" Mr. Nicholas asked.

Mr. Potter laughed. "It sure ain't to dig things up, not with your foot there."

Percival lifted his chin. "My arms have never lacked for strength. And I believe that arms are the chief appendage used when digging."

Mr. Potter's face reddened.

"Anyway," Percival said, "Where is Miss Amberly?"

They were sure to tell him that the housekeeper had been wrong, and that she hadn't even visited the site. Or if she had visited the site, it had been hours ago. He tensed.

"Ah . . . She's on her way to Italy." Mr. Nicholas nodded sagely.

"Never seen a woman so excited," Mr. Potter declared, and some of the men guffawed behind him.

"Is she far away?" Percival's heartbeat quickened, and time seemed to still as he waited for the answer.

"Ah . . . Quite far away by now."

"Oh."

So it was over. He tightened his grip on his cane.

Mr. Nicholas tilted his head and offered a benevolent smile. "But I reckon we could take you to her. That contraption you've arrived in won't make it, but I know a shortcut."

"That would be wonderful," Percival stammered.

"I rather am wonderful," Mr. Nicholas mused. He flickered his gaze to Percival's wooden leg. "Can you ride a horse?"

Percival broadened his chest. "I can indeed."

"Good." Mr. Nicholas pointed to some horses tied to a wooden fence. "Let's go."

Percival smiled and scanned the field. Shovels and axes flickered in the bright light, and the rest of the men returned to work.

Chapter Twenty-nine

THE COACH JERKED TO a halt.

"Oh for goodness' sake!" Madeline tapped her boot against the carriage floor. "The driver knows we're going a long way. We can't start taking our time now."

Murmurings sounded outside. An image of a tall, chestnut-haired man with striking, chiseled features and bright blue eyes pervaded Fiona's mind. She pulled the velvet curtains of the carriage aside and stared into a thick cluster of trees.

Some things were best not pondered.

Percival was in the past. Firmly in the past. He'd be in London or Sussex or perhaps at a house party at some grand estate. He wouldn't be here.

Lord, the man refused to be forgotten. The man was braver than any she'd ever met. He'd been kind to Grandmother, kind to her. He'd been handsome and brave, smart and funny, just like Captain Knightley. He'd been everything she'd ever desired, and far more than she'd ever hoped for.

It would be impossible to forget his noble figure, and the pleasing composition of firm, straight lines that composed his face. It would be difficult to forget arguing with him, but more impossible still to forget his kindness, and the way they'd laughed over things together. Even when he'd been most exasperated with her, she'd always sensed he'd understood the ridiculousness of the situation and had never entirely dismissed her. And that morning in her workroom—goodness, it would be impossible to forget that.

Sometimes she even imagined she heard his voice. Sometimes it seemed to ring in her ears. Deep and rich and velvety, like the sound of everything reassuring.

Something rustled in the bushes. "Fiona!"

She bit her lip. *Lord, it sounded just like him.*

The voice called again, and she told herself that it wasn't him. Perhaps the driver had an assistant or friend or acquaintance she didn't know about. Not that that would explain why he was calling her name. Perhaps—perhaps she should have had a second cup of tea after all, and was simply exhausted after yet another night of poor sleep.

That didn't mean she was crazy. Just that she was a bit sleepy.

Slightly delirious.

Really, completely normal.

Almost.

"Fiona!" the voice echoed again, and her heart sped up, even as she tried to tell it that there was no need to because it absolutely couldn't be—

Him.

She leaned back in her seat. She would not look. She refused to look. She would not deign to see if her imagination had concocted him.

There was no earthly reason in the world why the Duke of Alfriston would be outside.

"Most irritating," Fiona found herself saying. Madeline raised her eyebrows, and she hastened to add, "The carriage stop, I mean. It's taking a while."

"Probably a loose cow. Or little lambs. As if they don't know they're there for eating and not for prancing around the middle of the lane."

"Madeline!"

"I'm jesting!" Her cousin settled back into her seat. "Somewhat."

Fiona sighed and poked her head from the window. The fresh air brushed against her, and the scent of spring flowers and grass caused her nostrils to flare. In fact—it almost seemed like she could smell cotton and pine needles, though that was ridiculous. Madeline and herself were firmly clothed in linen, and deciduous trees dominated the scenery: no pine needles were about. "Driver! What seems to be the trouble?"

Something that sounded like a muffled cry answered, and she shivered. She raised her voice. "Excuse—"

"I wouldn't do that if I were you." A deep voice wafted into the coach. The voice was wonderful, and the deep notes reminded her of all things splendid. "You are being attacked."

"Attacked?" Fiona squeaked.

She swung her gaze toward him, but the man, whoever he was, wore a black mask.

"By the very worst highwayman." The strange man whispered, and for some absurd reason, her skin prickled.

"Are you very terrible?"

The man laughed, and Lord, it sounded like *his* laugh. Rich and melodious like velvet. "I hang out with the likes of the Scarlet Demon."

"Truly?" Her heartbeat fired, beating wildly.

"Truly!" he said, lowering his voice, "And I have plans to spend increased time with her."

A sound rustled behind her, but all she concentrated on was him. The man was tall, and his dark great coat hung from broad shoulders. She wondered what would happen if she were to trace her fingers over his mask, whether she might find the well-formed nose, the sturdy jaw, the high cheekbones of *him.*

She extended her hand from the carriage, as if she were in a trance.

A footstep creaked behind her.

Thump. The man toppled down from the side rail.

"I did it!" Madeline's triumphant voice soared behind Fiona.

"You didn't—you didn't shoot him?" Fiona's eyes stung with tears that didn't have time to fall. She jiggled with the door handle, exhaling when it swung open.

"I'm not some violent creature." Her cousin called after her, in a voice that almost seemed affronted. "I simply threw my valise at him."

Fiona scurried toward the highwayman.

"I'll check the driver," Madeline chirped, and Fiona nodded weakly.

She stared at the lumpy heap before her. At least no blood was visible, though she knew that didn't eliminate the possibility of the most advanced injuries. The man's great coat sprawled out, the edges rippling over the muddy ground. The mask still sat firmly on the man's face, and she knelt down beside him. Her eyes roamed to his legs. The man just had one.

It's him.

Though maybe he's dead.

She grasped hold of the edge of the mask, and jerked the fabric upward, trying to prepare herself for pimpled-skin, a full beard, or anything else that could signify that this was not, in fact, *him.*

A regal brow, firm nose, and even firmer chin appeared before her. She resisted the urge to trace the planes of his face. The man was most definitely, most assuredly him.

Her heart thumped against her ribs, as if trying to pound the sounds of Handel's Messiah for all the world to hear.

Percival's dark eyelashes were fixed downward, and his skin was pale.

"Please, please be fine." She grabbed hold of his cold hand.

He'd been in her thoughts every hour of every day, and yet she'd done nothing. And now it was too late. She pushed her hand toward his mouth. Warm air puffed against her fingers, and she exhaled.

He was alive.

She peered at him again.

Barely alive.

She loved him. She truly, completely loved him.

"The driver's fine! Some highwaymen waylaid the coach," Madeline called, and footsteps squished over the mud. And then a gasp sounded.

"It's His Grace!" Madeline exclaimed.

"Whom you took out." Fiona pressed her lips together.

"Not permanently I hope." Her cousin bent down. "Oh my goodness."

The man's eyes—Percival's eyes, darling Percival's eyes—fluttered open. "You needn't fret on my behalf."

His voice was hoarse, and Fiona wanted to kiss his cheeks. She settled on stroking them and running her fingers through the soft curls of his hair.

Percival turned his head toward her, and his eyes expanded and softened all at once. "Am I in heaven?"

"Oh don't tell me it feels like you've died!" Madeline exclaimed. "Forgive me, Your Grace. How do you feel?"

"Like I'm looking at the most beautiful angel." Percival's tone was reverent, and his gaze didn't depart from Fiona's.

"I assure you you're not!" Madeline said.

And then she paused. And coughed. "Oh."

"Baroness, please give me some privacy."

"I'm not sure that's proper, Your Grace."

"Now."

Madeline scampered back up the steps of the carriage, and Fiona stifled a giggle when the door slammed shut.

"Are you quite sure you're fine?" Fiona asked.

Percival nodded. "It's dangerous spending time with the Scarlet Demon."

"Mm-hmm." Fiona swallowed hard. "What were you saying?"

"Before I got cobbled with your cousin's valise?"

Fiona nodded, her throat dry.

It was too much to hope that this was anything more than a moment's spontaneity. Likely he saw their coach and wanted to amuse himself. *That's all.*

Except—she hadn't been traveling in her own coach. She'd been in her cousin's.

Except—his family estate was in Sussex now. He shouldn't be huddled behind trees, waiting to have a laugh.

Except—he was looking at her with something that looked very much like adoration, very much like something more than adoration.

Her heartbeat escalated, as if it were galloping through the lanes like a very real highwaywoman.

Though it needn't look for treasure, for she'd already found it.

It was him.

"What on earth is going on?" Mr. Potter's voice boomed.

She swung her head toward some trees. "I—"

Mr. Potter brushed through a thicket. Mr. Nicholas stomped through some bushes after him. Both men glared at her.

"We heard the commotion," Mr. Nicholas said. "Came straight back."

"We were tree-cutting," Mr. Potter boasted. "Not quite as intellectual as archaeology, but it's good to be well-rounded. Good for the ladies."

"The gentlemen were careful to only cut down a tree which would be highly visible to coaches," Percival said.

"Aye. We pride ourselves on being very safety-conscious highwaymen. When we pretend to be." Mr. Potter darted a nervous glance.

Fiona smiled. "I think you'd better move the tree."

"Right, right." Mr. Potter scowled, and he and Mr. Nicholas scampered away.

"We're in a hurry," the coach driver called out.

Percival's jaw tightened, and Fiona tensed.

Madeline shook her head. "We can delay our journey. We cannot fail to help this man. It's my fault that he's injured. He requires a doctor."

"I'm not sure how I'm supposed to find one," grumbled the driver.

"I'll come with you." Madeline turned to Fiona. "Will you be able to remain with His Grace? It's best not to move him."

Fiona nodded, and her cousin scrambled back into the coach. The glossy black coach grew fainter as it rolled toward the horizon, leaving Fiona alone with Percival.

Chapter Thirty

EVERYTHING ACHED, AND Percival shifted. Long strands of grass blew in the wind, prickling his skin, and fluttering his tousled attire.

Fiona's soft hand brushed against his forehead and sent a joyful jolt through his body. He wanted her hand to remain there forever.

Instead she glanced at the sky, darker than before, and that sweet brow furrowed. "Hopefully the doctor will be here soon."

Percival smiled at her sudden primness. That said, a doctor sounded bloody good.

Raindrops fell, and Fiona peered up. "Oh, no."

"Help me rise," he said. "Let's follow the direction the carriage went in. At least we'll be able to meet it more quickly and hopefully we can find shelter en route."

She blinked. "You're supposed to be ill."

He shrugged. "I'm not unaccustomed to pain."

In truth he hadn't felt this good in a long time. Fiona was here. Beside him. Perhaps he could have reassured Fiona's cousin. But then again—now he was alone with Fiona.

She hesitated, but lightning fissured the sky.

"Springtime in Yorkshire," she muttered.

"Time to go?" He grinned.

Fiona nodded and pulled him up. He couldn't ignore the blissful warm sensation that spread through him at her touch. He wanted nothing more than to pull her into his arms.

Her expression was once again reserved. She handed him his cane. "You dropped this."

"Thank you." He despised the strange formality. Not that he didn't deserve it. "Forgive me. My behavior the last time we saw each other was despicable."

"How did you find me?"

"I went to the baroness's home. One of the maids told me."

Fiona nodded. "And the mask?"

"An improvisation. A stocking." His shoulders shrank. "It's been so long. Forgive me. I thought—I had this crazy sensation I was being romantic, but I see now, that . . ."

The raindrops toppled at a quicker pace, and the gray sky darkened. Rain flooded the now muddy lane, bending the green stems of wild flowers.

Fiona bit her lip and craned the horizon. Finally, her shoulders relaxed a fraction. "I see a cottage."

"Good."

Ambling on slippery leaves and grass was even worse than braving the mud, but he forced himself forward. Fiona slipped her hand around the arm not wielding the cane, and he smiled.

It was bloody good to have her in his life.

He just hoped she might remain in it.

The next minutes were a blur of slimy branches and squishy leaves. Finally, they halted their muddied slide.

"Edmund Grove." Fiona read the name on the outside of the cozy, red brick cottage. "Oh, no."

"Sweetheart." His reply was instant, and her face flushed.

A lump in his throat thickened. She wasn't his sweetheart. Not yet. Maybe not ever.

"No one's home," Fiona said, averting her eyes. "The cottage belongs to Madeline's butler... But he went ahead with some of the other staff to Italy."

A forlorn expression appeared on Fiona's face. Her lovely auburn locks were swept into an elegant chignon; she had changed.

"Let me have one of your pins."

Fiona's eyebrows darted up, and she moved her head toward him. He shivered as the familiar scent of vanilla wafted over him. He'd missed this. So much.

He delved his fingers into her silky locks and slid a long pin from her hair.

She frowned at him, and some curls fell forward.

"You can take them all out." He placed her hairpin in the keyhole, fiddling with it until it sprang open.

"Oh," she gave a startled cry of approval, and his lips twitched.

"His Majesty's Army has trained me for just such a moment."

She swept by him and grabbed the hairpin, tucking it expertly back into her hair. "I'm sure we shouldn't be here."

"I don't fancy huddling outside the cottage in this rain."

She smiled. "Neither do I."

For a moment his eyes flared. The woman was an angel. Every bit as beautiful as he remembered, though she now moved with an increased confidence, and her attire was elegant.

"I should have come back to you earlier."

"But you didn't want to," Fiona said.

His eyes widened. "No. That's not it."

"You didn't want to see what Lady Cordelia was like?" There was a bitter tone to her voice, and she immediately shook her head. "Forgive me. And—thank you for getting Graeme to send me back Ned. And for everything else as well."

"I don't deserve you. Though I should say I definitely did not leave out of curiosity for Lady Cordelia."

She stilled. "Why are you here?"

"Because—I couldn't stand the thought that I might never see you again. I acted so horribly to you when your grandmother died. I'm afraid I can't offer very much."

She smiled. "You have a dukedom."

"With responsibilities to see to in Sussex and festivities to attend to the rest of the year. You were wonderful at the ball, but I wouldn't want to make you uncomfortable."

Fiona settled onto the sofa and smoothed her bronze traveling dress. He settled beside her, stretched out his arm, and rested it on her shoulders. She tossed him a startled glance, and he did his best to smile at her.

Perhaps nothing had changed. She was going to Italy. He couldn't offer her that. But he needed her to know everything.

"So what do you think about Yorkshire in the spring? Rainy, isn't it?" Her voice rose an octave higher than her customary tone, and a jolt of happiness lurched through him.

Against all odds, she was here, beside him.

And from her wide eyed expression, she was every bit as amazed.

FIONA NEVER LEARNED his musings over the county's climate, for he swooped her into an embrace. Firm arms encircled her and pressed her against the hard ridges of his chest. Her breath quickened and caught in her throat, and her heartbeat, usually so unobtrusive and steady, careened wildly. The thought of any normality when he was near her seemed impossible for her body to comprehend.

Life only consisted of his steady gaze and the angular arcs of the chiseled features of his face.

"Fiona," his voice roughened, and he clutched her more tightly against him. The gesture made her heart hammer, but there was nothing wrong, only everything good and wonderful with what was happening.

Everything had changed. Everything was perfect.

His gaze remained tender, and she had the feeling he understood her completely. "No other woman makes me laugh quite as much."

"Oh?" She croaked.

"And you're intelligent, skilled in something apart from water colors."

He smiled, and she was transfixed by the tantalizing proximity of his alluring mouth.

The space between them narrowed, and her heart galloped. "Water colors is a good skill," she said, conscious she was rambling. "And I'm dreadful at it."

Percival shook his head solemnly. "I don't care. You're curious and amusing and—"

She pressed a finger to his lips. "Stop."

He stared at her, and she fought to resist the temptation of succumbing to his deep blue gaze.

"Are you simply here to apologize?" Her voice trembled, and he shook his head solemnly.

The strained line of his sculpted mouth quivered, and he inhaled. "I love you."

She couldn't answer him. The words were too much what she'd always dreamed of someone saying, and the fact that that someone was him . . . Her heart pounded with greater vigor, and she had the mad thought that if she said anything she might break the spell, flinging her back to her old world.

"I don't want us to be apart," he continued, as if answering her fear, and he leaned forward.

This time his lips angled, and her eyelashes flickered shut. The whole world vanished, and all she concentrated on was the blissful sensation of his lips caressing her own, and the deep sweeping strokes of the velvety warmth of his wicked tongue.

He explored her body, and the tender motion of his firm hands gliding to her arms, and settling on her waist, gave life to a swarm of butterflies fluttering in her stomach.

She shivered, and he drew back, his eyes still on her. She grabbed hold of his coat, conscious of her forwardness. But she pulled him toward her anyway. Right now she didn't want to think about all the reasons they might not be together. She didn't want to think about his dukedom. She didn't want to think about how he was charming and sociable while she was most comfortable poring over tomes and pottery.

He kissed her again. He devoured her. "I've missed you so much."

She closed her eyes. Maybe if she opened them, she might find this had all been a dream, for certainly there could be no possibility in which Percival was simply stating all the deepest desires of her heart.

His hands fumbled on the buttons of her dress. "The rain was not ideal. I'm worried you might get cold."

"And you once wanted to be a physician." She chuckled.

Amusement flickered through his eyes. "You know me well, sweetheart."

Blood surged through Fiona, and Percival reverently removed her hairpins.

His pupils darkened, and he slid her dress and various undergarments off.

"I love you," he repeated, and she longed to answer him.

She loved him, she was sure, but she'd never said that to anyone before. And the last time they were together like this, he'd left in the night.

He brushed a loose strand of hair behind her ear. "I'm sorry for everything. Truly."

Percival leaned down, exposing the wide breadth of his back, and removed his boot and stocking. He then winked at her, as if he were fully aware of how her heart was fluttering in his presence, and unbuttoned his waistcoat.

Her throat dried. "I'm not sure that's proper."

Percival stripped off his shirt, revealing his broad and powerful chest. "There's plenty of time to be proper. Though I have to say, I dream of a lifetime of being just this sort of improper with you."

Fiona blinked. His words blazed through her, even as the lantern's rays jostled over the planes of Percival's body. She ran her fingers over his chest, brushing against the hair that curled over the hard surface.

"My darling." His voice thickened, and he swooped her toward him. "The things I desire to do to you."

He trailed kisses over her bare flesh, seeming to revel over every inch, and her skin tingled beneath the warm attention of his delicious mouth. He circled her bosom with his hands, sending pleasurable jolts through her body, and tightening the mound between her legs.

He brushed his fingers over her rosy peaks and swallowed hard as they pebbled beneath his touch. "I know I've seen these before, but Zeus, I swear I haven't seen anything more perfect in all the world. Fiona. Darling. I cannot wait to make you my wife."

"Your wife?"

Percival flushed. "I'm sorry. That wasn't the proposal I had in my mind. I had imagined something with rather more flowers. And perhaps even champagne and a splendid view. Forget I ever said anything."

Joy cascaded through her, and her lips twitched. "I can't forget."

Percival kneeled before her, his voice solemn. "Then, Fiona Amberly, sometimes known as the Scarlet Demon, will you do me the tremendous honor of making me the happiest man in the world by becoming my wife?"

Fiona's heart raced, and warmth leaped and lurched through her. This was everything she'd ever dreamed of.

She stared at him, almost to ascertain he was not in fact a mirage.

But it was him. It was her Percival, and he was saying the most brilliant things in the world to her.

"You think I'll be a suitable wife?" Her voice trembled.

"The very best, my dear."

"But I haven't been in society much, and my season was, well, rather less than mediocre. People will wonder why you chose me. They might gossip. You're a new duke, you don't need cause to make anyone think less of you." Saying each word slashed her heart, but he had to know, simply had to know how unsuitable she was. She wouldn't want to do anything that might harm him, even if that would mean giving up the one thing that would bring her the most joy in the whole world.

"And you, my darling, are quite incredible for telling me all that."

"I mean it—"

He kissed her hand. "I know you do. I also know that you're sweet, and mostly honest, when you're not trying to pretend to be a highwaywoman, and that you would do anything for your family."

Her fingers shook, as if unsure this was really happening, that everything actually would be just fine.

"Fiona..." His voice trembled, and she realized she hadn't responded to his proposal.

"Yes! Naturally, yes, I—" She stammered on her words, and drew him into an embrace. Speaking was too difficult an action right now, but he had to know, that she wanted nothing more than to have him beside her.

Forever.

Her heart pounded against his chest, and his hands moved over her.

"Darling," he murmured.

There was something she needed to say. Something she'd never said before, even if it was the truest thing in her heart. "I love you, Percival. I love you so much."

His eyes misted, and he held her more tightly in his arms. "I love you too, sweetheart."

His murmurings turned to warm, wet kisses. His lips caressed her, and his arms held her close. She'd never felt this safe before. And this was just the beginning of the rest of their lives.

He lay her down on the cottage floor. The thick wooden boards roughened her back, and her hair tangled against the rigid floor. She only pulled him toward her, satisfied only when his body pressed against her own.

Everything had changed. She wasn't the same bluestocking, the same wallflower she'd once been. Percival's charm, his consistent sense of humor in the face of all manner of ills, made her adore him. Life was fuller than she'd ever imagined.

"We needn't do anything, Fiona. I'm quite willing to postpone any delights until after the wedding. Whatever you want."

She shook her head firmly. She'd thought for so long she might never even see the man again. She wanted this moment. Her whole body craved him.

She raised her chin. "I choose you over any tradition."

"Thank God." He pulled her downward, so that the space between her legs touched his manhood. He rocked her over the tip over it. "Just like that, my dear. Just become used to it. You needn't do anything more."

The contact with something hard and firm was spectacular, and he slid her gently over him. "It will hurt less if you're in control."

She smiled down at him. His hands rubbed along her thighs, reminding her that he was here, with her, for this moment. She arched down over him, placing her hands on either side of him.

He was inside her. They were joined, and everything in the world was marvelous. Sweat beaded over his muscular chest, and pink tinged his cheeks. Some of his hair clung to his forehead, and she squeezed her hands over the wooden floorboards.

Perhaps she was acting disgracefully, but she'd never been happier in her life.

And then the bliss grew larger, for Percival thrust inside her. She joined him in this new, exciting rhythm. Percival urged her lower still, and he returned his attention to her, capturing her tight peaks in his mouth.

Percival's eyes glistened. "Fiona. Darling."

Any coldness she'd experienced had long since disappeared, and she moaned as his hand traveled over her thigh.

The tempo quickened, and their breaths joined. Fire swept through her, and her body shook and quaked. Percival grasped hold of her. And then he was shaking beneath her, filling her with his seed. She rested her head on his broad width and rubbed her fingers over the smattering of chestnut curls and his own tawny peaks.

This was happiness.

Chapter Thirty-one

FIONA'S BREATH STEADIED as she nestled in Percival's arms. He stroked the arch of her back, seeming to find fascination in its simple curve.

Light streamed through the thin curtains with more force, and rain no longer thundered against the walls of the cottage.

Percival brushed his lips against the corner of her eyes, and his lips moved to her cheeks. "Fiona, my sweetheart."

When he pulled her toward him, warmth whirled through her, as if his mere presence was enough to send joy sauntering through every part of her body. She squeezed his hand, tracing the way in which the hairs on his wrist glistened under the light.

"We should leave," Fiona said regretfully.

"Very well." He appeared equally reluctant, and Fiona smiled.

They dressed and made their way down the path.

After a short wait, carriage wheels rolled toward them. Fiona forced herself to at least give the appearance of calm, though her heart still seemed to beat a jubilant melody.

"You seem better." Madeline poked her head from the coach. "Mrs. Rogers is having a baby, and I was going to take you to another doctor. But perhaps you're fine?"

"Never better," Percival said.

"Mm-hmm." Madeline assessed them. "So I'm chaperoning you two?"

Fiona smiled, and Percival linked hands with hers.

"Because I'm not sure I'm doing a good job." She narrowed her eyes at them. "I like doing a good job."

"I'm not removing my hand," Percival said testily.

"Hmph." Madeline sniffed. "So are you joining us in Italy as well?"

Percival stiffened. His hand was, as promised, still around hers, but it was more rigid than before.

"How long will you be gone?" Percival turned to Fiona. "This doesn't change anything."

"As long as we can," Madeline chirped.

"I don't want to keep you from your dreams, Fiona," Percival said, his tone softer than she had ever heard it. "You have brilliant dreams, and I—I have duties."

"Well, you should probably decide, unless you want to wait until we reach Hull to make your decision," Madeline said.

Fiona shot her cousin her most confrontational look.

"I'll wait for you," Percival said. "Go to Italy. Enjoy yourself."

Fiona hesitated. She'd spent her life dreaming about the Romans. She'd never expected to go to Italy, and her cousin's sudden enthusiasm for the trip had spurred her on.

Italy was the very loveliest of dreams.

"My stepfather adores the country," Percival said, and his voice trembled.

She peered up at him. She knew Percival's stepfather used to be a sea captain, but he hadn't spoken much about his family.

"You would have a good time with your cousin," Percival said.

"I'm not as horrible as people make me out to be," Madeline added cheerfully.

"Good." Percival bit his lip. "My leg—it makes traveling more painful. Not that I won't do it. I just—probably couldn't do it with as much enthusiasm. Wandering cobble-stoned streets in the rain no longer sounds appealing."

Fiona squeezed his hand. "I'm not going anywhere."

Percival's eyes shone, and he pulled her toward him.

For a moment her cousin's face seemed to crumble, but then her lips arched upward with a swiftness suited to a gifted hostess. "I'm happy for you, Fiona."

"I'm sorry, Madeline. Perhaps one day—"

Her cousin nodded. "Perhaps. You'll have a large estate to manage," Madeline said. "You'll be meeting many people."

Fiona tilted her head. She'd never allowed herself to ponder a life so conventional in its form of happiness. She'd always assumed that that life wouldn't be available to her. She considered her cousin's warnings. It would be difficult. Yes, she knew that. She hadn't lived her whole life as a bluestocking and wallflower to not know that finding her way into society would not come naturally.

Worry flickered through his eyes, and his chin jutted out, as if bracing himself to hear the worst.

She looked at Percival and smiled. "I'm not going anywhere," she repeated. "Except to be at your side."

He beamed and drew her close, and this time their lips met again. His firm, hot lips pressed against hers, sending a jolt of happiness racketing through her body.

Her cousin cleared her throat noisily. "Let me speak to the driver."

Fiona laughed softly as Madeline scurried away.

FIONA WAS FIRMLY PART of Percival's life at Wentworth Place. They'd darted up to Gretna Greene before traveling down to Sussex. He beamed as he contemplated her and turned to Higgins. "It's odd, isn't it, how one's whole life can change because of a fallen tree?"

"Terribly," Higgins muttered. "Now let me finish here, because I can assure you your visitor will expect you to look your very best."

Percival's beam faltered. "Just who is here, Higgins?"

"The dowager duchess herself."

"She should have sent word of her arrival."

"I believe she was aspiring for the element of surprise."

"Well that's the only thing she will succeed at getting." Percival grabbed his cane and headed out the door.

"I haven't finished your hair," Higgins called after him.

Percival shook his head as he strode down the corridor. "She'll just have to put up with it."

He clutched hold of the banister and gingerly made his way down the marble steps to greet the formidable woman pacing the entry.

"Your Grace!" The dowager exclaimed, her gaze flickering to his unwaxed hair.

"How surprising to see you," he said in his frostiest voice, swooping his torso into a bow.

The dowager curtsied. "I wanted to warn you that I have heard the most horrific rumor."

"Indeed?"

"But you needn't worry. I told everyone it was incorrect."

"And what was the rumor?"

"People are saying that you are married. To a former highwaywoman. The daughter of a county squire."

"That's correct."

The dowager blinked. "Indeed?"

Percival nodded solemnly. "Most definitely."

"Then you must annul the marriage!"

"Impossible."

The dowager's gaze drifted to his leg. "I think in your position, you might be able to convince people of the need. Perhaps if you reference your injury—"

"No."

"Your masculinity need not suffer. People will understand that you are injured."

"I love her," Percival said. "With all my heart."

"Oh." The dowager's gaze flickered down.

Percival sighed. "You have been so helpful to me over these past few months. I'm afraid I haven't told you how grateful I am. But please, do not worry. I may have never planned to be a duke, but I am committed to being a good one. Your son would have been an excellent one, and it is unjust that he is not here now instead of me."

The dowager bit her lip.

"I cannot bring him back," Percival continued. "But I cannot either lead my life imagining what he would have done in my position. You will get to know my wife more, and you will also see her many charms."

The duchess rubbed a hand though her hair. "Thank you. Perhaps I was foolish to barge in like this."

Percival shook his head. "You cared. As someone who also now cares about this estate, I can understand and appreciate that."

The dowager flickered her eyes to the door. "I suppose I should go."

Percival shook his head. "Nonsense. Not after your long journey. Let me introduce you to my wife. I have a feeling the two of you might get along. She was very fond of her grandmother."

Epilogue

DECEMBER 1816

Yorkshire

Fiona hadn't prepared herself for such joy.

Her life wasn't supposed to be like this. Any joy was supposed to be reserved for the heroines in Loretta Van Lochen's romances.

She wasn't supposed to have married a duke. She was supposed to while away her time in Yorkshire, helping her sister with her child, and reading up on the Romans when she could.

And she might have eventually found contentment doing that. But this—this was more.

Branches of holly spread from vases throughout the bedroom. The scarlet berries countered the silky azurean blankets, gold-framed mirrors, and sumptuous oriental carpets. A large bay window dominated the room, revealing views of the towering Dales, their slopes whitened, glistening under the outside lanterns. The servants had scraped away the snow in preparation for the guests' arrival.

Most of the year needed to be spent at Wentworth Place, but they were spending Christmas in Yorkshire, at one of Percival's smaller estates.

Her husband strode into the room. The man was growing increasingly at ease with his cane, and his blue eyes brightened when his gaze found hers. Higgins had clearly managed to convince Percival to allow him to tie one of his more elaborate cravat knots, and her husband was a vision. His black trousers tightened around his muscular thighs, and his chestnut hair glimmered against his black coat.

Warmth never failed to rush through her at the sight of him. "You look like a complete Corinthian, my dear."

"I'm going to take that as a compliment, given your obsession with everything Classical."

"I'm afraid I must bore you dreadfully."

"Not bore. Not for one second. You enchant me." Percival grasped her hands in his, and warmth soared through her. He nodded and lifted his chin, and in that moment he looked every bit as grand as the most impressive statues in the new British Museum. He winked. "Appropriate for the Scarlet Demon."

She chuckled, but she knew the fact was true. Despite Percival's once easy dismissal of art, the man enjoyed discussing her finds and the historical significance.

Carriage wheels ground against the frozen cobblestones, and Percival squeezed her hands. "They're arriving."

Fiona inhaled. There'd been a time when she'd hidden from the world, seeing each social occasion as an unwanted intrusion and scrutiny into her life.

"Come, sweetheart." Percival offered her his arm. "We have a ball to attend."

Fiona slid her fingers against his velvet tailcoat. She tilted up her face, and he brushed his lips against hers. He uttered a moan, or maybe she did.

Percival withdrew and he flickered his gaze to the bed. "I would be quite happy if Evans told the guests we'd both gotten sick and that they should enjoy the festivities without us."

"That would be most inappropriate."

"If you insist, sweetheart." Percival opened the bedroom door, and they exited. "I'm forever being captured by you."

Fiona giggled. "Our children are going to roll their eyes at you."

"Children?" Percival swallowed hard.

"Well, the plural might be premature."

The noise of the ball was louder, and the scent of Christmas grew stronger as they proceeded down the hallway. The servants had draped garlands of greenery over every arch and looped the luscious leaves from the ceiling.

Fiona had spent so many years dreading large celebrations like this, but now she was hosting her own.

She smiled at all the people gathered there. She wanted them all to feel welcome, even the shyer wallflowers, and more awkward blue-stockings.

They greeted Arthur, Rosamund and her husband, and a swarm of new people she was enjoying becoming acquainted with.

"Are you perhaps—" Percival ran his hand through his hair. The man's tongue did not seem to function as well as it normally did, and his gaze lingered again on her stomach.

Fiona laughed. A footman offered Percival and her some appetizers. She sniffed and waved the platter away with a smile.

"Darling." Percival inhaled. "Can you be—"

"Ah, Fiona." Uncle Seymour's voice boomed in her ear. "So . . . er . . . delightful to see you."

"Uncle." She smiled and allowed him to kiss her cheek.

Percival still looked somewhat stunned, but he managed to raise his eyebrows.

"My niece, the duchess," Uncle Seymour continued, his voice maintaining its consistent fortissimo.

"Her uncle, the baronet." Percival bowed.

"How is Cloudbridge Castle?" Fiona asked.

"Ah, yes!" Uncle Seymour said. "Very nice. You should consider visiting some time."

"And sleep in the tiny guestroom?" Percival asked.

Uncle Seymour shifted his legs. "No, ah, that won't be necessary. We—well I could offer my room to you. It would only be proper. It would be an . . . er . . . great honor to see you again."

Percival's mouth twitched, and Fiona murmured gratitude for the invitation.

Uncle Seymour took a deep sip of negus. "And . . . er . . . if you happen to still be interested in the apple orchard . . ."

"Oh?" Fiona swiveled her head to him.

Uncle Seymour shifted from side to side, and he rubbed his cravat, rumpling the flourishes. "Well—my wife was reading about your latest discoveries in Chester. It seems lots of people are actually interested in stones that come up from the ground."

"Ah, yes," Percival said. "The general population is rather more intelligent than they are often given credit for."

"Well." Uncle Seymour coughed. "My wife was curious if you were right and if there might indeed be treasures of some sort in the orchard. And since you're so famous, it didn't seem right to bring just anyone to dig through the garden."

Fiona had missed Cloudbridge Castle, but she was glad the world now extended beyond the manor house's constraints. She smiled at her uncle's hopeful gaze. "I would be honored to work on the project. Though I won't be doing much digging either."

"Ah . . . I gather you'll be bringing in your own crew again," Uncle Seymour said. "Quite good. We've been able to give some of them jobs."

Fiona nodded. "So I heard."

"I reckon you'll be busy with your museum," Uncle Seymour said.

"Oh, indeed," Fiona responded. "I have no plans to give that up."

Italy might be postponed, but one day, certainly, she would make her way there. In the meantime, there was still much to be discovered here.

"Suppose even becoming a duchess couldn't change you much," Uncle Seymour sniffed.

Fiona raised her eyebrow, and her uncle's face reddened. He made his excuses and hastened in the direction of the punch table.

"My dear . . ." Percival didn't mask the tremble in his voice. "Just what is keeping you from digging around in the ground as well?"

A jolt of happiness surged through her. "Next Christmas, there will be another person here."

"Sweetheart." Percival beamed.

She smiled and entwined her hand with his, enjoying the warmth of his palm and the knowledge her life with him was merely beginning.

THE END

About the Author

BORN IN TEXAS, BIANCA Blythe spent four years in England. She worked in a fifteenth century castle, though sadly that didn't actually involve spotting dukes and earls strutting about in Hessians.

She credits British weather for forcing her into a library, where she discovered her first Julia Quinn novel. Thank goodness for blustery downpours.

Bianca now lives in California with her husband.

Connect with Bianca:
www.biancablythe.com[1]
Wonderful Wallflowers - Facebook Group[2]

1. http://www.biancablythe.com
2. https://www.facebook.com/groups/229610907371529/

Join Bianca's list to be notified of new releases and special deals[3]

Bianca's Instagram[4]

Matchmaking for Wallflowers

How to Capture a Duke[5]

A Rogue to Avoid[6]

Runaway Wallflower[7]

Mad About the Baron [8]

A Marquess for Convenience[9]

The Wrong Heiress for Christmas[10]

Wedding Trouble

Don't Tie the Knot[11]

Dukes Prefer Bluestockings – *Coming soon!*

The Sleuthing Starlet

Murder at the Manor House[12]

Danger on the Downs – *Coming soon!*

---

3. http://biancablythe.com/newsletter
4. https://www.instagram.com/biancablytheauthor/
5. http://biancablythe.com/capture
6. http://biancablythe.com/rogue
7. http://biancablythe.com/runaway
8. http://biancablythe.com/baron
9. http://biancablythe.com/marquess
10. http://biancablythe.com/heiress
11. http://biancablythe.com/knot
12. http://biancablythe.com/manor

Excerpt from a Rogue to Avoid

LADY CORDELIA FLUTTERED her fan though the ballroom hardly qualified as warm.

Or perhaps she'd simply never spent a ball sitting down.

Thick Yorkshire accents rumbled around her and merged with the notes of poorly tuned violins. Guests clomped their slippers over the stone floor, and women swirled in murky blue and brown dresses. Most gowns seemed hastily modified from several seasons' past, though some seemed as if no one had even attempted to rectify their unfashionable lines. The guests' faces were flushed, their eyes sparkled with vivacity normally seen on jeweled tiaras, they changed dance partners with an exuberant frequency—and not a single person had asked Cordelia to dance.

Cordelia kept her torso at the ninety-degree angle her governesses had advocated. Unfortunately, the gesture did not compel any of the plethora of gentlemen to ask her to dance despite the adamant assurances of her numerous etiquette books that men found rigid postures desirable.

She resisted the urge to tap her foot as the music switched to a popular melody. The joyful notes might be crescendoing, but she couldn't permit anyone to think her unhappy. She desired no one's sympathy.

Perhaps the gentlemen simply were unaware of her status. Or perhaps they found her beauty intimidating. Blonde hair, blue eyes, and rosebud lips might overawe some people. Especially when the locks in question were glossy, the eyes large and wide, and the lips exquisitely shaped. More than one ardent suitor had compared her eyes to azure skies seen in the art of Renaissance masterpieces.

But that had been—before.

The guests continued to prance over the floor, and the men continued to ignore her.

It was almost as if—

The thought was impossible, and she took a lengthy sip of her orgeat, despite her lack of affection for the cloyingly sweet taste and the unlikely pairing of almonds and oranges.

She couldn't be a wallflower.

She simply couldn't be.

That was a fate for other women, ones with smaller dowries, and educations at less vigorous finishing schools.

Cordelia scanned the ballroom again. But unlike in her favorite Loretta Van Lochen novels, no charming prince weaved his way through the crowded assembly rooms.

Which, come to think of it, was utterly fine. Dancing meant being on display, and despite her mother's habit of dragging her to the finest dressmakers, Cordelia favored being away from the scrutiny of people she was beholden to impress.

Her mother frowned at her from behind the silver punch bowls and rows of crystal glasses.

Cordelia raised her hand to her locks, prepared to brush away any loose strands, but her hairstyle was immaculate. She smoothed her dress, but the sumptuous fabric was unstained and devoid of wrinkles. Her gown remained impeccable.

People *should* be dancing with her.

Last season the men had begged her for the honor.

She scoured the groups of assorted men again. Most avoided her eye contact. Enraptured in their own conversations, they were likely discussing cricket and cigars.

Purchase A Rogue to Avoid.[1]

1. http://biancablythe.com/rogue

Made in the USA
Columbia, SC
26 March 2019